Chibundu Onuzo was born in Lagos, Nigeria in 1991. Her first novel, *The Spider King's Daughter*, won a Betty Trask Award, was shortlisted for the Dylan Thomas Prize and the Commonwealth Book Prize, and was longlisted for the Desmond Elliott Prize and the Etisalat Prize for Literature. She is completing a PhD on the West African Students' Union at King's College London.

Further praise for *Welcome to Lagos*:

'Fantastic . . . peels back the beating heart of a complex and richly beautiful country.' *Irish Examiner*

'An immersive novel . . . Onuzo's characters come together and trade fortunes in surprising ways.' *New Statesman*

'An effervescent novel.' *Daily Telegraph*

'A fine novel . . . worlds – rich and poor, urban and rural, privileged and powerless, Muslim and Christian, Igbo and Yoruba – collide to spectacular effect as their paths cross and power shifts hands in surprising and unexpected ways, and then does so again, and again. It is an unlikely plot, but Ms Onuzo pulls it off, revealing the fault lines in her country's society – or indeed those of any half-formed democracy. Though drenched in Lagosian atmosphere, the book wears its Nigerian setting lightly: it is clearly the work of a pan-African and an internationalist – and is all the better for it.' *Economist*

'An entertaining and provocative second novel . . . a dazzling

road trip from the badlands of the Niger Delta to Nigeria's sprawling and chaotic megacity ... Under the global media spotlight, each character faces up to a life-changing choice between morality and truth.' *Reader's Digest*

'A hugely accomplished tragicomic farce about life in Nigeria, written by one of the country's brightest young stars. Nothing evades Onuzo's biting prose and whipsmart humour. From the allegedly corrupt ministers who run the country, to the BBC journalists covering breaking news, and from the idealistic newspaper editor trying in vain to hold the country to account, to the beleaguered army officer who would rather be homeless than follow orders, all show the multifaceted shades of humanity that creates the kaleido-scope of Lagos.' *Herald*

'Lively, shocking, colourful and entirely convincing.' *Age* 'Pick of the Week'

'An engaging, thoughtful look at how society works and how it is viewed by both its people and outsiders.' *Writes of Woman*

'Onuzo brings a series of remote and daunting environments to life with great clarity, with bittersweet observation, and a kind of melancholy for the difficulty of living decently. She has a knack of capturing a personality quickly on the page, and these main characters quickly become individuals with whom we identify.' *Shiny New Books*

---

by the same author

THE SPIDER KING'S DAUGHTER

Welcome to Lagos

Chibundu Onuzo

FABER & FABER

First published in 2017
by Faber & Faber Ltd
Bloomsbury House
74–77 Great Russell Street
London WC1B 3DA
This paperback edition first published in 2017

Typeset by Faber & Faber Ltd
Printed and bound by CPI Group (UK) Ltd, Croydon CR0 4YY

A CIP record for this book
is available from the British Library

ISBN 978-0-571-26895-5

FSC
www.fsc.org
MIX
Paper from
responsible sources
FSC® C020471

8 10 9

To God be the glory

I

Zombie

I

Bayelsa

Evening swept through the Delta: half an hour of mauve before the sky bruised to black. It was Chike Ameobi's twelfth month as an officer in Bayelsa, twelve months on the barren army base. His first sight of the base had been on an evening like this, bumping through miles of bush, leaves pushing through the open window, insects flying up his nostrils and down the dark passages of his ears. They came to a clearing of burnt soil with charred stumps still rooted in it. Out of this desolation had risen the grey walls of his new home. Later, he would note the birds perched on the loops of barbed wire wheeling round the base. He would spot the garganeys and ruffs gliding through the sky, their long migration from Europe almost over.

He had grown quite fond of the canteen he was making his way to now, a low, squat building with thick plastic sheets tacked to the windows, the walls crumbling with damp. Officers and lower ranks sauntered into the building in an assortment of mufti: woollen bobble hats and black T-shirts, wrappers knotted over the arm or tied round the waist, the slovenly slap of slippers flip-flopping their way inside.

Colonel Benatari sat by the door, watching the soldiers file past. Chike's commanding officer was a stocky box of a man, his bulk filling the head of his table. The most senior officers on the base flanked the Colonel. They ate from a private stash of food cooked separately in the kitchen. There was always a struggle to clear the Colonel's table, lower ranks jostling for the remnants of fresh fish and the dregs of wine left over in the bell-shaped crystal glasses.

Chike threaded his way through the hall, edging past square wooden tables and round plastic ones, past benches, stools and armless chairs, no piece of furniture matched to another. His platoon was already seated.

He was in charge of twenty-three men, charged to lead them in battle and inspect their kit, to see to their hygiene and personal grooming. They were all still in uniform, not a single button undone. When he sat down, they stretched their hands, the clenched fists of their salutes blooming like doorknobs on each wrist. The conversation did not stop.

'O boy, you see Tina today? That her bobby.'

'What of her nyash?'

'Like drum.'

'I go beat am.'

'Nah me go beat am first.'

'You think she go 'gree for you?'

'Why she no go 'gree?'

Tina was a new kitchen worker. His men could talk of little else these days. Chike too had opinions on whether Tina was more beautiful than Ọmọtọla but he knew not to add to these conversations. If he spoke, they would listen politely and then continue, a column of ants marching round a boulder.

Still he ate dinner with them instead of joining the junior officers' table. He felt an officer should know the men he was in charge of even though these soldiers under his command would rather not be known. They obeyed his orders but questions about their lives and families were met with a silent hostility. His only friend was Private Yẹmi Ọkẹ, the lowest-ranked man in his platoon, now seated next to him and eating his beans without bothering to pick out the weevils. It was the fourth day in a row they were eating beans and dodo but Yẹmi did not seem to mind.

'Did you shoot today?' Chike whispered to him.

'No.'

'Good. Meet me by the generator hut when you finish.'

There were a few slices of dodo left on Chike's plate, overripe and soggy with oil. Yẹmi would eat them before coming. Chike left the canteen and went outside to wait for his friend.

*

Night had come and with it, the sense that Chike could be anywhere. The sky was wide and open, the stars visible in a way he never grew used to. The militants would be out in the creeks tonight, piercing the pipes that crisscrossed the region, sucking out oil, insects drawing on the lifeblood of the country. The army would be out too, patrolling the waters.

He stood with his back to the generator hut, the tremor of the machine passing through him. It drank over two hundred litres of diesel each day, its belly never satisfied. The land sloped away from him, a scattering of buildings and tents running down the mild incline of their base. Soldiers clustered in groups, their cigarette ends glowing like fireflies. The air was warm and heavy, almost too thick to breathe. It was the flaring that did that, great bonfires of gas burning night and day like stars.

The oil companies worked at all hours, filling and floating barrels of oil to overseas markets that decided what they were worth: fifty dollars today, a hundred tomorrow and the whole of Nigeria's fortunes rose and fell on what foreigners would pay for her sweet crude. Chike had seen the spills, black poison running over the waters, fish gone, fishermen displaced, flora destroyed. Who was to blame? Not for a soldier to answer.

He saw Yẹmi approaching in his slow, loping gait.

'Sah,' Yẹmi said, saluting when he arrived. Chike returned his salute.

'At ease. You were saying.'

'I no shoot. When Colonel order us to kill that boy, I ready my gun, aim, put my finger for trigger but I no fire am.'

'I didn't either,' Chike said. 'When those white journalists came, I should have found a way to talk to them. I should have whispered to them that they should look out for freshly turned soil. Must we destroy a whole village before people start to notice?'

The futility of his and Yẹmi's resistance, the cowardice of it, fingers bent but never pressing down. They would be found out. Someone would notice their limp index fingers or see them slipping their unused ammunition into the

6

creeks. But for their sanity, he and Yẹmi must register their protest in some way.

Chike had not taken much notice of the lowest-ranking member of his platoon until he came upon him one day, crying.

'Nah young girl. E no good,' was all Yẹmi would say. There were others who felt the same about the woman shot for allegedly harbouring militants but the only protest he had heard voiced was from the runt of his platoon. Their friendship had begun then, an unequal one where he gave the orders and Yẹmi obeyed, but a friendship nonetheless, based on their mutual distaste for the Colonel. A treasonous friendship.

The 9 p.m. bell clanged. The generator would go off in half an hour; the water would dry up soon after, the electric pumping machines silent till morning.

'Sah, I wan' wash my cloth,' Yẹmi said.

'Dismissed. Thank you for your report.'

Chike walked to the room he shared with three other junior officers. The space was small for four men, eight foot by twelve with only one window, but they were all disciplined, neat with their possessions and clothing. A single, naked bulb hung from the ceiling, drawing a lampshade of insects to its hot glass surface. His roommates would be in the junior officers' mess, a tent he rarely went to these days. There was a bottle of gin passed round and drunk in thimblefuls, there was a radio with a long spoke of an antenna and there was guilt, evident in how fast the alcohol disappeared.

He sat on his bottom bunk and unbuttoned his shirt before drawing out a slim Bible from his pocket. He read the

Bible often now, flicking to a new passage each day, one evening on the plains of Jericho, the next in the belly of a whale, sunlight streaming through the blowhole and into his underwater cell. He liked the improbable images, flakes of manna falling like dandruff from the sky; the formal language of thees and thous, begetting and betrothing betwixt the Jordan and the Red Sea. There were stories of rebellion in the book, of slaves standing up to their masters and waters parting for their escape. Things were less straightforward in real life.

He lay down and stared at the wooden slats of the bed above him, the Bible unopened by his side. His bunkmate had stuck Nollywood starlets to his portion of wall: actresses Chike did not recognise, clutching handfuls of synthetic hair and thrusting their hips at the camera. Chike's patch of wall was blank. He had put up a picture of himself and his mother, her arm around his waist, her head below his chest and her left hand raised to the camera, asking the photographer to wait. As the months passed, the hand became a warning, an accusation, a signal from beyond the grave. The photograph was face down in his trunk now, stowed away under his bed.

Even to witness Benatari's crimes was to take part in them. There were strict rules of engagement, fixed codes detailing how soldiers should deal with a civilian population and the Colonel had broken every one. Chike could desert, drop his gun and run off into the darkness one night. He could abscond to Port Harcourt, or Benin or perhaps even Lagos, any large city, with back streets and crowded houses he could disappear into.

8

And what would he do when he got there? He was not fit for life outside the army. His four years on military scholarship studying zoology at university had proved that to him. He had held his first gun at twelve: induction week at the Nigerian Military School at Zaria. By fourteen, he could crawl a mile under barbed wire, shoot accurately from a hundred paces, lob a grenade, curving it in a neat arc that landed on its target. He was nothing more and nothing less than a soldier. He closed his eyes and willed himself to sleep, anxious over what new blood the next day would bring.

2

The news that two sentries had been killed was all over the base the next morning. No one in the ranks saw the bodies before they were buried. Breakfast was stale bread with a watery egg stew, eaten with murmuring throughout the dining hall. After breakfast Colonel Benatari assembled the entire base of almost a thousand soldiers on the dirt expanse that served as their parade ground. The Colonel was dressed in full regalia, his hand resting on the hilt of a sword.

'It is with great sadness that I report the loss of the two brave soldiers. We have been gentle with these people because our superiors have told us to promote national unity. They don't know what is on ground. The Niger Delta is not a place for ideas. I am from here and I know. You tell an Ijaw man about nation building, all he wants to know is what's for lunch. These are stomach people and it is time to show them we are muscle people. This evening, we attack!'

The Colonel's wildness seemed barely constrained by his starched uniform. Hair spilled out of his collar and cuffs, climbing down to his knuckles and creeping up his Adam's apple. Chike sensed that if permitted, the Colonel would string the scalps of his enemies into a belt and do away with the leather and steel contraption that encircled his waist.

No work was given that day. No marching in the afternoon. Double lunch rations. A smoggy expectation hung over the base. Tina was not in the canteen today. Was she a spy, Chike wondered?

*

Chike's platoon was chosen. His men were skittish in the back of the van, knees knocking, starting at every sound in the bush. They all wore charms, amulets and talismans strung round their necks to ward off evil. Their battalion had been cursed so many times. After each execution, the victim's mother or sister, or aunt or grandmother or wife, would call on native deities to devour them, half-fish, half-man gods to swallow them up. The land was against them, the water, the air, conspiring to smother and drown and bury them alive.

Any moment they could be ambushed. There was no tarred road, just this narrow path with the bush pressing close, leaves and branches swishing against the bodies of the vans. A hundred men in total snaked quietly to the village, the line of vans rolling forward slowly, headlights dimmed with strips of dark paper. At night, the Delta was as it had been centuries ago, black and seething with spirits.

The moon appeared, a full white disc spilling light on the thatched mud huts and squat concrete bungalows that lined the village entrance. The Colonel was in the first van. He was always first in an attack. Chike's men said bullets bent when they touched Colonel Benatari, that metal bounced off skin made impenetrable by juju. He saw the Colonel now, walking into the village with his indestructible body, a compact black shape with a line of soldiers following him. They flung petrol on every roof they passed, quick and efficient in their movements.

The first hut bloomed into flame, and the next and the next, a garden of orange flowers. Was it the heat that drew the villagers from their huts or the smell of smoke? Village men were dashing into houses and rescuing the bric-a-brac of their lives, boxes, chairs, clothes bundled and dumped by the feet of their families. Women were carrying babies and smacking children that strayed too far from the family group. Chike and his platoon stood by their vans, watching this scene and waiting for their orders.

'When you hear the gunfire on that side, start shooting. Between us, these murderers will be destroyed.'

The voice belonged to Major Waziri, a thin, pallid man with a loud voice.

'And what if we refuse?' Chike asked.

'Who said that? Anyone who refuses will be shot.'

The villagers' panic was giving way to common sense. Some were still blindly surging into their homes and emerging with items that would be useless without a roof over their heads: bedsteads and pots and kerosene stoves. But most were organising themselves into fire-fighting units. Buckets of water appeared, thrown wildly and then with precision on the largest part of the flames. The humid air was on their side. One house was doused and another, then another. The women joined in. Even the children. They were winning when Colonel Benatari opened fire.

Chike had seen it enough times, civilians, at the sound

of gunfire, dispersing like light spreading from a source. Mothers forgot children, husbands left wives, the old were pushed down and trampled.

'Fire!' Major Waziri said.

For a moment, there was silence. Only Colonel Benatari and his contingent were shooting. This is a mutiny, Chike thought. Unplanned and unconcerted, they had all decided to revolt. Then the first gun stuttered into life and the others found their voice.

'Let's go now before we take part in this,' Chike said.

The men of his platoon turned when he spoke, fingers relaxing from triggers. Chike did not know the words that would make them drop their guns. Perhaps if he had led them, really led them instead of only giving orders, they would have followed him.

'Oya make we go,' Yẹmi said, 'I don tire for this their army.'

3

The two soldiers walked through the night with Chike leading. They would make their way to Yenagoa, the closest city, and from there find a bus to Port Harcourt or Benin or perhaps even Lagos. Even now, Benatari might already be searching for them. In theory, they should be given a chance to defend their refusal to carry out the colonel's order. In theory.

They still carried their guns, another crime to add to their desertion but it would have been too dangerous to wander through this bush unarmed. Morning was already starting to show. Without hesitating, any party of militants that came upon them would kill them.

'Remove your shirt,' Chike said to Yẹmi. They could do nothing about their trousers that announced their occupation, camouflaging nothing.

'I wan' rest,' Yẹmi said.

'We stop when we reach the main road.'

'I never drink water. I no fit.'

Chike eyed Yẹmi but his former subordinate did not drop his gaze.

'At ease,' he said, just before Yẹmi flopped to the ground. The semblance of command must remain until they reached

Yenagoa. After that, they could go their separate ways. For now, two were better than one.

Dawn cracked over the forest. The sun rose slowly, an orange yolk floating into an albumen sky. He was hungry. Beside him, Yẹmi was starting to doze when the young man with an AK-47 slung over his shoulder walked into view and began to urinate, his back turned to them. Chike left Yẹmi and crept up to the man, who had squatted to defecate.

'I am officer of the Nigerian army. You are under arrest. Hand over your gun. Do not turn. I said do not turn. Throw your gun on the floor and stand up with your hands behind your head.'

'How do I know you have a gun?'

'I should shoot?'

'My people are close.'

'So are mine.'

'Chike.' The man stiffened at the sound of Yẹmi's voice and dropped his gun on the ground.

'Stand up. Slowly.'

'Can I pull up my trousers?'

There was a foreign tang to his speech, something in his diction striving to be American.

'He fit take us to the road,' Yẹmi said.

'We're trying to get to the main road.'

'I wanna see you first.'

'You can turn. Slowly.'

It was a boy, not a man, just leaving his teenage years. His eyes were deeply planted in his face, giving him a starved look, but the rest of his features were regular. A furrow ran along the middle of his forehead, a crevice that deepened when he looked beyond and saw no signs of a Nigerian army.

'If I refuse?'

'We go shoot you. You think say we be soldier for nothing?'

To the best of Chike's knowledge, Yẹmi had never shot a living thing but his bravura was convincing.

'If you lead us into a trap, we will still kill you before your friends get to us,' Chike said, adding his own threat.

'No, no. I was going to the road myself anyway.'

'Your name,' Chike asked, as the militant led them into the undergrowth, his gun a few inches from the boy's spine.

'Fineboy.'

'Na which kind name be that?'

'Na my mama give me,' Fineboy said, for the first time dropping his accent and sliding into pidgin.

4

Chike had grown accustomed to the back of their hostage's head, his thin neck, the pulpy scar behind his ear, the scattering of razor bumps on his otherwise smooth hairline, clipped within the last few days, in a militant camp no less. Perhaps, as well as a barber's, the militants had cinemas and shopping malls.

The militants said they were fighting for compensation for the millions of gallons of crude that had gushed out of the ground since the 1950s, when a Shell-BP drill struck oil in 'commercial quantities', the magic phrase that would draw the French, the Dutch, the Chinese to this small corner of Nigeria, destroying the land and water from which the Niger Deltans gained their livelihood. The government called the militants criminals, who spent their days hacking into pipelines and causing oil spills, kidnapping petroleum engineers and smoking insensible amounts of weed.

If he were a civilian, Chike would have had sympathies, would have tried to puzzle out the rights and wrongs of each side, but his military training disposed him to neutrality. It was for politicians to decide who they fought and why, which causes were just and which were not. Soldiers dealt in orders alone and it was because the Colonel's orders were illegal that he and Yẹmi were wandering through the bush now, following this young man who might or might not be leading them into an ambush. He was thirsty, almost deliriously so. The sun was now high in the sky and still no sign of the road.

'Halt,' Chike said. 'In which direction is the road? North, south, east.'

'I don't know. I just know how to get there.'

'We'll kill you if you're leading us into a trap. I swear it. Your water. Please.'

He had just noticed the plastic bottle, tucked into the rebel's belt.

'Please? When you're pointing a gun in my face?'

Chike took four sips, letting the water sit in his mouth before swallowing. It was warm with a back taste of petrol. The oil seeped into everything in this place. His first urge was to spit it out. He passed the bottle to Yẹmi.

'Don't finish it. Do you have anything to eat?' Chike asked their hostage. The boy put his hand to his pocket and Chike followed the movement with his gun.

'What the hell? You asked me for food and I'm getting it.'

The boy drew out a black polythene bag and then a newspaper-wrapped bundle from within it.

'Smoked fish. Maybe the last fish in the Niger Delta.'

Chike saw the longing in Yẹmi's face.

'We'll take a short break.'

They sat on the ground and the boy placed the fish between them. They all three stared at the white flesh, charred and blackened on the outside.

'You think it's poisoned.' The boy smiled, showing even

teeth. He took fish in his fingers and shoved it in his mouth. 'More for me.'

The fish was dry but flavoursome. Beside him, he could hear the workings of Yẹmi's jaw as he ate the flesh and then the slivers of silvery bone.

'So what are you two running away from?'

'Na who say we dey run?' Yẹmi asked.

'Soldier man wey lost for bush, no dey find fellow soldier. Dey look road. Looks like desertion to me.'

'We want a change,' Chike said. 'What about you? You're young to be a militant.'

'My juniors are back at camp. Don't look at me as a small boy.'

'Explain something,' Chike said. 'How will kidnapping oil workers bring roads to the Delta?'

'How will soldiers here bring peace? Money from our oil has built every infrastructure you see in Nigeria and yet we, the owner of the oil, don't have hospital, schools, roads. When I was a child, you dip your hand in the water and you pluck out fish. Now everything is destroyed from oil spill. We didn't start with violence but no one wants to hear the way of peace so the people have chosen war.'

They were borrowed words, the manifestos of others delivered with a conviction that would have been catching if Chike had been a journalist or a person passing briefly through the Delta. But he had seen the villagers harassed by militants and soldiers alike, just wanting to be left alone.

'The people have chosen?'

'Of course. We could not keep up the struggle without them. They feed us, their sons join us, they even send their women. You should see how many of these girls want our babies. Just yesterday, one came out of a tree and opened her legs.'

There was a loud rustling above them. It startled the soldiers to their feet and they took aim with their guns.

Whenever Chike described what happened next, he began by saying it was mythical. Not like the silvery European myths of winged men and wood sprites but like the denser African myths of living trees that devoured human sacrifice.

He saw a girl appearing as if from the tree itself, her legs sprouting from the bole, her arms from the branches, her hair a compost of twigs and leaves. He heard Yẹmi release the safety on his rifle.

'Hold fire!'

She was running, upon them and past them, straight into Fineboy, ploughing him to the ground. She struck him, with her elbows, with her hands, straddling him like a wrestler, her trousers fitted to slim legs, too thin surely to keep a man pinned under her weight. Fineboy cried out, in a tangled stream that was rising in pitch. It would not do for them to be discovered.

'Cover me,' he said to Yẹmi.

Chike dropped his rifle by the private. Then he approached and took the girl by the elbow, dragging her halfway to her feet. Fineboy lunged, catching her on the right side of her face, and in a grotesque reversal, she fell to the ground. Chike held him back but it was too late. The strange girl had fainted.

*

'She don wake o,' Yẹmi said. 'Oya make we dey go.'

They had lost time waiting for the girl to come round. Even now she was conscious, she seemed too weak to stand. Chike stood over her, looking down on her face. She was very dark, black as crude. Her lips were dry, whitened strips of skin standing out on them.

'Are you alright? Bring the bottle,' he said to Yẹmi.

'Don't give my water to that bitch.'

She flinched at the rebel's voice.

'That's enough from you.'

The girl took the bottle from Yẹmi and poured the water down her throat without pause for breath, slurping until the empty bottle contracted from the pressure. Chike was standing over her, he realised, in a way that she might find threatening, a gun slung over his shoulder, his hand resting on the stock. He stepped back.

'What's your name?'

'Isoken.'

'Where's your home?'

'I'm lost.'

'But your village. Where are you from?'

'I came from Lagos with my parents. To my mother's village. It's somewhere in this bush.'

'Where are they now?'

'I don't know. There was fighting near our village. We ran

but my mum was too slow. She's ill. That's why she came back home. For the local medicine.'

'Is that how you got separated? When you were running?'

'I left them. My dad said I should go. That he would stay with my mum. My dad is a hairdresser. He does his work in Lagos but none of the women in the village would let him do their hair. They said they can't put their head between a man's laps. He taught me how to do hair. Any style you want.'

'How long ago was—'

'While you're asking twenty-one questions,' the rebel said, 'find out why she attacked me.'

'You,' she gathered saliva in her mouth and spat in a clean arc. 'If I hadn't been wearing jeans.'

'If you hadn't been wearing jeans what?'

'You would have raped me.'

The revelation slipped easily from her mouth.

'Are you crazy? Do I look like somebody that needs to rape girls? Me. Fineboy.'

'Hold him back,' Chike said to Yẹmi.

'I was in a tree yesterday evening,' the girl said, turning to him. 'I had been walking the whole day, trying to get back to the village, but I was tired. I dozed off. When I fell, I hurt my back and I couldn't move. There was a group and he was in the group. They attacked me. They beat me, see my face, but they couldn't get what they wanted because of my trousers. He said I offered myself to them. It's a lie. I'm still a virgin.'

The rebel was stepping forward again despite Yẹmi's gun aimed at his chest.

'Who dash you virgin? See this prostitute.'

'Your mother is a prostitute.'

The boy charged past Yẹmi. Chike fired in the air, a single, clear shot that resounded in the bush.

'You. Stand back and put your hands behind your head. That's how you're walking from now on. Hands behind your head I said. Yẹmi, if he lowers them, shoot him. Isoken,' he said, turning to her last, 'we must go. We just waited to see that you're alright.'

'You have to arrest him. Are you not a soldier?'

'Soldiers don't arrest people. That's for the police. We must be leaving. Anyone could have heard that shot.'

'They'll find me then. Let me come with you. Where are you going?'

'Yenagoa.'

'I have an uncle in Yenagoa.'

'She go slow us down,' Yẹmi said.

Chike gave Isoken his hand and helped her to her feet.

'You'll walk between me and Private Ọkẹ.'

6

'Thank you,' Chike said to Fineboy when they got to the road. It was narrow, barely wide enough for two cars, but it would take them to Yenagoa.

He flagged down the first bus he saw. It listed to one side from the weight of yams strapped to its roof. The other passengers were thin and hard-looking, their clothes threadbare and ill-fitting. There was a smell of toil in the bus, of sweat and labour in fields whose yields had decreased since the oil companies arrived. A woman with withered lips stared at Yẹmi's camouflage trousers. She looked away when she caught Chike's eye.

The four of them squeezed into a back seat designed for two, Fineboy suddenly deciding that he wanted to see his mother in Yenagoa.

'Don't let him sit next to me,' Isoken said when the militant started to climb in after her. Chike placed himself between the two of them. Isoken's body was warm, almost febrile in its heat. Chike could feel her knee against his thigh. Once he shifted in his seat and his hand brushed her arm. She shrank, her elbows contracting onto her stomach, and there they remained until they reached Bayelsa's capital.

Yenagoa was more town than city, a settlement of dwarf

houses, roofs level with the raised road. Billboards were particularly effective in this stunted landscape, malaria drugs, Alomo Bitters, Coca-Cola, Durex, Indomie, Winners School, and churches, plenty of them. Evangelists, pastors, apostles, prophets and bishops beamed down, inviting Chike to Amazing Grace Ministry, Fire Fall Down Tabernacle, Jehovah Always on Time Assembly. The air above Yenagoa must be thick with prayer, petitions flying and colliding on their way to heaven.

At the bus park Isoken stood blinking in the sun. She was just about a woman. It would not have been long since she was asking 'Mother may I?' in a backyard. There was still something of the child about her cheeks and the way she balled her fist into her eyes when Chike asked, 'Can you get to your uncle's house from here?'

'I only know the address. Plot 16, Dongaro Road. We went just once. We stopped there on the way to the village.'

'Please tell her how to get there,' Chike said to Fineboy.

'Or what? You'll shoot me?'

They had abandoned their guns in the bush, taking out the cartridges.

'I can have you arrested for your time spent in the creeks.'

'I'll deny it.'

'The word of a Nigerian officer against yours.'

He expected the boy to see through him. Two soldiers deserting were in no position to threaten arrest. Instead, he kicked his foot in the soil.

'The place is not far,' Fineboy said in words shorn of every trace of an accent.

*

The buildings on Dongaro Road had not seen fresh paint in years. The road was worn in many places, the thin tarmac stripped to the red earth beneath.

'This is the place. His flat is on the ground floor,' Isoken said, in front of a house streaked brown with rain tracks.

'Should we come with you?' Chike asked.

'Please.'

There were chickens in the yard, a mother hen with a troop of grey chicks marching in line behind her. A car stood rotting in the sun, propped on four cement blocks, its tyres, mirrors and bumpers long gone to a younger model. The uncle was sitting outside on a bench, fat with adolescent breasts that showed through his worn singlet, a raffia fan idle in his hand.

'Isoken, is that you?'

'Yes, Uncle.'

'What are you doing with these soldiers? Have you brought trouble to my house?'

'No, Uncle.'

Briefly Isoken told what had happened to her hometown, saying nothing of the attempted rape. Hers could not be the village Colonel Benatari had torched. That had been in the evening.

'Wonders shall never cease,' the uncle kept saying, as if his niece had come from the bush to thrill him with anecdotes.

'Come and sit next to me.'

She sat at the end of the bench but the uncle moved towards her and put an arm round her, his hand resting on her stomach where her shirt stopped and her jeans began.

'Officers, how can I thank you for bringing back my daughter to me?'

Isoken remained rigid in his embrace.

'No thanks are necessary,' Chike said. 'We're just doing our job.'

'At least tell me your names so that I can remember you in my prayers.'

'Chike.'

'Yẹmi.'

'And you?' Isoken's uncle said, looking at the militant. Why had Fineboy come into the compound? He had seen this kind of fatuous curiosity in the lower ranks. Before the boy could give his absurd name, a man appeared in the door of the flat, addressing the uncle in a language Chike did not understand, the words locking into each other without space, like pieces in a jigsaw. Their exchange was short. It seemed heated until the uncle laughed and the man returned into the flat. 'Officers, don't mind my business partner. Will you take something to drink?'

'No, we must be on our way,' Chike said.

'Goodbye, Brother Chike,' Isoken said to him. 'Thank you.'

Chike had never had a sibling and the filial title pleased him. Outside the gate, he noticed the smirk on the rebel's face.

'What are you smiling at?'

'From frying pan to fire.'

'What do you mean?'

'Something her uncle said.'

'What?'

'I'm not sure. He was speaking Kalabari.'

'Tell me what you heard.'

'He said she was ripe.'

'For what?'

'I think sex.'

*

The uncle's hand still rested on Isoken's stomach when they returned to the compound. Chike swung his arms stiffly as he walked towards them, a reminder of his military status. The chickens scattered at their second entrance, darting behind the old car in a streak of clucking feathers.

'Please, sir, will you allow your niece to escort us to the end of the road?'

They could take the girl by force but he preferred to try a ruse first. He did not know how many 'business partners' this uncle might have.

'Officer, my niece is tired.'

'Please, Uncle, my parents would want me to see off these people that helped me.'

'It would only be to the end of the road,' Chike added.

'OK. But don't be too long. You need to rest.'

Isoken glanced at Fineboy, who was still standing outside the compound.

'Pay him no attention. Just walk with me,' Chike said.

They moved in silence, her head drooping on the slim

stalk of her neck. Yẹmi and the militant walked a few paces behind. At the top of the road they stopped.

'How well do you know your uncle?'

'I— When we were going to my mother's village we stayed here overnight from Lagos. That was my first time of meeting him.'

'Fineboy. He heard something your uncle said to his business partner. Something like what happened to you in the bush. Is there any way you can reach your parents?'

'They have one GSM they are using but I don't know the number. It's new. Uncle Festus has it.'

'Is there anyone else who would have the number?' Chike asked.

'They live in Lagos.'

'Don't cry. We'll go there and drop you.'

'Say wetin? Who tell you I wan' go Lagos?' Yẹmi said.

'We can go our separate ways then.'

'Na who tell you I no wan' go?'

'You,' Chike said to Fineboy, 'the drama is over. You can be on your way once you give us directions to a motor park that will get us to Lagos.'

7

Isoken did not speak until they reached Edepie Motor Park. It was a large, trampled field with vehicles of all sizes coming and going, small, dusty minivans, large, sleek luxurious buses, trailers with art twisting all over their bodies, movement and noise and dust rising from the spinning tyres. A market had sprung up for the human traffic, clothes, books, food, toys on display for the discerning traveller.

'Please can I go to a call centre,' Isoken said to Chike when they arrived. 'Maybe I'll remember my parents' number with a phone in my hand.'

The owner of the kiosk stood by Isoken as she dialled wrong number after wrong number. With each try she grew more flustered.

'There are others waiting,' the kiosk owner said after her sixth attempt. She cried out when the phone was taken from her, a harsh, bleating sound.

'Don't worry. I won't charge you,' the owner said, beckoning to the next customer.

Chike would have preferred tears to Isoken's twitchy silence. Her hand rose to her hair, then her collarbone, then her elbow as if she were counting her body parts, checking nothing was missing.

'So we'll have to go to Lagos then,' Chike said to her when her fingers were resting on her ear.

'My mum used to say that if we ever got separated we should meet at home. The first time it happened was when I was a child. I ran off in the market after an orange and when I caught it, she was gone. I clutched so many strangers that looked like her from behind and then I got tired of disappointment and decided to go home. She came home that night with dust in her hair. She was already planning how she would tell my father that she had lost their only child.'

'So you think they'll be in Lagos.'

'I don't know but I can't stay here.'

She stared away from him when she spoke. There was swelling on her cheekbone, the skin puffed and raised, encroaching on her eye. The cut on her temple had formed a deep purple scab, the shade of an onion. He had not asked for this new responsibility. He hoped there would be someone to help her in Lagos.

Yẹmi and Chike bought trousers from a stall and went behind a tree to change. They emerged civilians, their muddy boots the only sign of their former life. Their dinner was a simple meal of beans and stew, eaten on the same bench with Isoken as far from him and Yẹmi as possible.

They found a Lagos-bound bus and waited for it to fill up. It would not depart until all its seats were taken. Chike paid for three spaces and climbed into the front seat. His knees touched the dashboard riddled with stickers preaching platitudes. God's Time Is Best. No Food for Lazy Man. A silver Christ dangled crucified from the rearview mirror.

He and his mother had always sat in the front seats when she accompanied him to his military school in Zaria.

All through the journey from Ibadan to Zaria, his mother would hold his hand and he would look out of the window, Ogbomoso, to Jebba, to Kutiwenji, to Machuchi, breathing in the changing air, and the landscape changing, and the people changing, growing leaner and more dignified, calmer and more reposed. It was years later, reading the memoirs of a colonial officer, that he realised that he had seen the north like a white man, looking for differences: thinner noses, taller grass, different God.

'Don't sit at the back,' he said when he glanced in the rearview mirror and saw again that Isoken was as far from him and Yẹmi as possible. In his last year in Zaria, on his way home for the holidays, there had been an accident. A bus hit them from behind and the whole back row died instantly, spines snapped. He had bled from a few surface wounds but he had made the trip back to Zaria when the holiday was over. He would be an officer and a gentleman before he let the vagaries of an expressway stop him. And now he was an officer and a deserter.

Even at sixteen, he had known it was partly rubbish, the dross of an empire, the dregs of a martial philosophy that had led countless Africans to fight for 'King and Country'. But there had been something seductive about it, something about these military principles, stated like the first principles that governed the world: honour, chivalry, duty.

Evening was falling. The bus was filling. A couple boarded, the man's frayed Bible held to his chest, the woman in a skirt that covered her ankles, her earlobes smooth and unpierced, her neck and wrists bare of jewellery. A man was moving from bus to bus, peering inside and then darting to the next one. He disappeared into one of the luxurious buses, behemoth American imports as large as whales. A moment later, like Jonah spat out, the man came rushing down.

Their trail had been picked up from the guns abandoned in the bush, their movements traced to this motor park. Were they so important? Would the Colonel expend so much energy to find him and Yẹmi? The man was only a few buses away. Chike recognised the brown singlet he had spent the morning walking behind.

'Brother Chike!'

When had Fineboy picked up his name? He was knocking on the side of the bus now.

'You know him?' the driver asked.

'Brother Chike, please, I need to talk to you.'

Brother. Such respect. The boy had put his hand through the window, stopping just short of touching his arm.

'I know him,' he said, opening the bus door.

'Na why you dey answer this boy?'

'Don't let anyone take my seat,' Chike said to Yẹmi.

Chike climbed down and faced him.

'Yes. What do you want?'

'Please can we move away?'

There was a carcass of a lorry stripped to its frame, resting on its side and waiting for the resurrection to rise again. A rubbish heap grew like a shrub beside it, emptying the area of passers-by. Fineboy led him there.

'I need to get out of Yenagoa tonight.'

'Your affairs do not concern me.'

'Please. I take God beg you. Soldier is looking for me. I could not go home. I saw my friend Amos on the way. He said there are people watching my house. I don't have the money to leave.'

'What about your family?'

'They have my picture. They will kill me. They have already killed one of the boys who came home on my street.'

'I should put you and the girl you tried to rape in the same bus?'

'I wasn't even there. It was a story they told me when they came back to camp. Nobody raped her. That's what she said. I got the story wrong. Let thunder strike me if I am lying. Let thunder kill my whole family.'

He touched his index finger to his lip and raised it to the sky.

'You can come with us to Lagos. Stand up. What's that your name again?'

'Fineboy.'

'Fineboy, stand up. It's a loan you'll pay back when you find your feet. Make sure you don't sit next to her.'

He paid Fineboy's fare and the boy climbed into the back. The last space in the bus was next to Chike. Whoever sat there would feel the driver's hand each time he reached down to change gear, his knuckles brushing against legs and knees. Women in particular hated this seat.

'This driver is too greedy,' a passenger said.

'So because of one seat, we will leave Bayelsa so late.'

'Driver, make we dey go o.'

'Look, I can't take this any more. Do you know who I am?

I'm coming down from this bus.'

'Lagos?' a woman asked, running and out of breath.

'Yes.' She paid and he got down for her to enter. She smelled expensive, like the clear alcohol perfumes his mother sprayed for special events, crushed flowers and party stew, the scent of an occasion. The driver started the bus.

'Wait!' the man carrying the large Bible said.

'Mister Man, I have an appointment tomorrow morning. Let's be going.'

'What if you die before then? Can a dead body attend a meeting?'

'God forbid.'

'Then let us pray. Father, in the name of Jesus, we commit this bus journey into your hands. We command that no accident shall befall us.'

'Amen,' the other passengers said.

'We declare that we have not set out on a night when the road is hungry.'

'Amen.'

'I cover each and every one of us with the blood of Jesus.'

'Blood of Jesus,' the passengers intoned.

'I wash the wheels of the bus with the blood of Jesus.'

'Blood of Jesus.'

'I soak the driver's eyes with the blood of Jesus.'

'Blood of Jesus.'

'He will see clearly and by your grace, tomorrow morning we will arrive safely in Lagos. We thank you Father.'

'Thank you Lord.'

'We give you all the glory for in Jesus' name we have prayed.'

'Amen.'
'And all God's people said?'
'Amen!'

8

Lagos

'Reports are coming in that the army has destroyed a whole village in Bayelsa State. We need someone to go down there and find out what happened,' Ahmed Bakare said to the senior editorial staff of the *Nigerian Journal*, the paper he had founded and run for the past five years.

They sat in the boardroom, the windows and doors flung open, the KVA of the generator too low for air conditioning. Ties had come undone, buttons were following suit, a moist triangle of chest flesh visible on most of his employees. Ahmed had taken off his jacket but the knot of his tie still pressed against his throat.

'You must see why it's so important that we send somebody down there?' he said.

It was not the first time Ahmed had tried to get one of his journalists to go to the Niger Delta. They felt the shame of reporting what they had not seen, news of oil spills and militants, fleshed out from the dry summaries on Reuters. Yet shame was not enough to risk their lives.

'The men from BBC, CNN, any sign of trouble, they'll send a helicopter to fly them out,' his political editor said to him. 'Can you guarantee that? Can you even afford it?'

'I'll send you a speedboat.'

'With Rambo inside?'

The meeting ended in laughter as the group filed out of the boardroom. They were competent staff, diligent with deadlines and precise in their prose, but they were more interested in the business of newspapers, in ink and paper quality, distribution channels and advert space, than in the ideas that could be read between the lines of the text, the very principles that had propelled him to found this newspaper.

Nigerian news, by Nigerian people, for Nigerian people. Telling our own stories, creating our narratives, emphasising our truths. They were tired mantras but they would have been sparks to people with imagination. Meeting with his staff was like holding a flame to a wet rag. Port Harcourt was only an hour's flight away. He could go and see for himself: charter a boat, take a recorder, a notepad, a toothbrush and some gin. Surely, the militants would welcome him. They must grow tired of these white journalists who mistook their bravado for real menace, missing the irony of the stylised war paint, branding the movement something atavistic. Or they might use him as target practice.

He was an only child: a caution that had sounded in his ears since his sister's death. For his eighteenth birthday, he had wanted to jump out of a plane over the English countryside, a billowing nylon cloud the only barrier between himself and death. His mother had spent two NITEL calling cards crying down a bad phone line. He was indispensable to her. And what of his reporters? Who were they indispensable to? Their wives, their husbands, daughters, elderly parents, younger siblings still in school.

He returned to his office to sift through tomorrow's leaders. He had committed to publishing at least one anti-corruption piece in each issue of the paper and in the five years the *Nigerian Journal* had been open, he had not failed.

The intercom rang.

'Good morning, Mr Bakare. There are some men here to see you from Chief Momoh's office.'

'Show them in,' Ahmed said to his receptionist.

Chief Momoh was a former Minister of Petroleum and a billionaire, two facts that Momoh insisted were unrelated. A few days ago the *Journal* had run a piece on an oil rig that the chief was alleged to own by proxy. Ahmed had been expecting a visit. He picked up a feature on a former Miss Nigeria and stared at the gap in her front teeth, a dark slit in her wide smile.

The men knocked and entered before he said, 'Come in.' There were three, dressed in black, dark caricatures of hired thugs. They filled his office with a sharp, astringent odour.

'Yes, how may I help you?'

'Chief Momoh is not happy with the story you published about him.'

He had gotten phone calls before, but it was the first time anyone had physically been sent to threaten him. He felt a tense excitement as he waited for them to finish their business of intimidation, their presence a validation of his work. There was no place for a gun to hide. Not in their shallow pockets nor in their hands hanging loosely by their sides. They could beat him up but they did not seem inclined to.

'Chief Momoh has told us to warn you to get your facts

straight. You know where his house is. You can come for interview any time you want.'

He did know the mansion in Palmgrove Estate. The chief and his father had rotated in the same circles for a while and when he was younger, he had swum in the pool that occupied half of Momoh's massive garden.

The man closest to the door, his stomach protruding more briefly than the others', reached into a small briefcase that he had not noticed. Ahmed gripped the phone but he did not lift it to his ear. Sudden movement. That was what always killed people in films.

'He also said we should give you this.' The man drew out two envelopes and placed them on the table with a small bow. 'One is for your parents. Chief has been finding it difficult to reach them.'

'Alright. You have delivered your message. Leave my office.'

And they left, the envelopes remaining cream and expensive against the stark white paper that cluttered his desk. He opened the one addressed to Chief Mr and Mrs Bọla Bakare first. He slid a penknife under the envelope flap, careful that his hands did not touch whatever was inside.

The families of
Chief Herbert Momoh
and
Admiral Joseph Ọnabanjọ
kindly request your presence at the union of their children

Jemima and Akin

He remembered Jemima. She had been two years his senior in secondary school. She had big breasts that ballooned out of her school uniform and a sharp mouth that teachers and students alike had suffered. He opened the envelope addressed to him with steady hands. It was an invite also, no death threat slipped inside, no warning. He felt sorry for Akin. He felt sorry for himself. His irrelevance confirmed by a flat, square invitation card.

His father thought him a fool for moving home to start a newspaper. His mother still loved him, a reassurance she had taken to repeating more often these days. How long before he called it a failure?

9

Ahmed's parents' marriage was strong, incongruously so. His father read widely, understood the foreign stock market, conversed with ease. His mother and her friends wore matching clothes to weddings. His parents were rarely seen outside together but in the domestic space they were courteous, loving even, attentive to how many spoons of sugar and how many cubes of ice. It worked for them, especially after the death of his sister.

Morenikẹ's smile sketched outlines on the edges of his memory but he could never recall his sister's face without the aid of a photograph. From her pictures, he knew she had been angular with bulging eyes but the presence of those few hanging photos had not been a reproach to his childhood.

Ahmed wished she were alive, if only to shift the weight of his parents' disappointment. He had left his good job in England. He was not yet married. He insisted on carrying on with this ridiculous newspaper project.

'The media mogul has arrived,' his father said as he walked into their living room. 'What will he drink?'

Once a month, for his mother's sake, he spent a Sunday afternoon with both of them.

'Bọla, stop teasing him,' his mother said.

'I'm not. I read the damn paper. I saw the piece on Chief Momoh's alleged oil rig. Why did it take you so long to get to it?'

'We were gathering material.'

'Is that so? Perhaps you should rename yourself *The Stale Journal*.'

'Bọla, leave the boy alone.'

'I'm just giving him some paternal advice. If he's going to try and embarrass my friends, at least be the first to the story. What are you drinking?'

'Star.'

'We only have Guinness.'

'Guinness then. I'll get it.'

'No. You're a guest now. We see you once a month so we have to be on our best behaviour or your mother says you'll stop coming.'

His father brought the bottle on a tray to him with a slim glass, setting it on a side stool.

'Dearest, what about you?'

'Orange juice. You know we shouldn't be drinking so close to Ramadan.'

'Live and let live, Mariam.'

They drank in silence, his father tapping his feet as he sipped his port. When their glasses were empty his father stood.

'Right. Lunch should be ready. Let's not keep the news-paperman waiting.'

As always, there was too much food. The table was heaped for guests that would never arrive: his dead sister, her imaginary husband and their six obese children. The chairs were stiff-backed, with wrought copper arms uncomfortable to rest on. On the walls were paintings, trite European landscapes in greens and blues, and in the corner an aquarium bubbled softly, the pale fish darting behind its glass walls. He would have preferred to eat in the living room but his mother liked to create an occasion, complete with gold cloth napkins and heavy silver cutlery brought from storage each month.

'You remember Layọ Adenuga?' she said when they had begun eating.

'No.'

'You do. You went to primary school with her. Short, a bit chubby, very light-skinned.'

'Vaguely.'

'She got married last week. Such a beautiful wedding. Her colours were burnt orange and magenta. It was so difficult to find matching shoes. Your wife better pick simple colours.'

'Who will let their daughter marry this newspaperman? He's not trained for this. He's an amateur and it damn well shows.'

Ahmed would not let himself be goaded today.

'When is your next wedding, Mum?'

'Da Silva and Ajayi. Hundred thousand naira for five yards of asọ ebi. These people want to empty our bank accounts. But you know how close Mrs Ajayi and I are. I can't refuse.'

'Yes, this is what your mother spends our retirement funds on.'

His father seemed relieved that he had not risen to the bait. For the next hour, conversation continued with little to disrupt it. At five o'clock Ahmed pushed his chair back from the table.

'Until next month then,' his father said, shaking his hand and leaving the room. His mother walked him to his car, his boot full of yams and plantains from her kitchen. He would give it all to his neighbours once he got home.

'Don't mind him. He just wants you to do well.'

'Yes. I understand.'

'Will you come with me to the Ajayi wedding? You know your father always leaves me to go on my own. And you never know, you might meet someone.'

He had been stunned by these society weddings when he first moved home, dazed by the towering cakes, free champagne, fresh European flowers, chocolate fountains and ice sculptures as cold as the unmarried belles, aloofly desperate, sitting stiffly in their new clothes and lacquered faces, waiting for a 'hello' from a prosperous-looking, preferably unmarried man before they would let themselves thaw. And when you stepped outside for a smoke or a phone call or to talk more deeply to the pretty bridesmaid, you would see the small economy that had grown round the spectacle. There would be beggars waiting for crumbs, touts watching your car, photographers pointing out your pictures taken that day, men selling money in bundles, freshly minted naira to spray on the couple, cash littering the dance floor, the happily ever after turned into a capitalist boom.

'I can't make it. And you won't be on your own, Mum. You'll have all your friends around you.'

'You're a snob. That's your problem. Why can't you marry one of my friends' daughters? Poor people's children marry themselves all the time, so why shouldn't rich people do the same?'

'We don't have the same interests.'

'What interests? Is it newspaper? I've told you, Remi Okunola's daughter has moved back and started a magazine. Let me introduce you. Her mother can bring her to the wedding.'

'You didn't like my last girlfriend.'

'She had dreadlocks for goodness' sakes. And she was Igbo and you could hear it when she spoke.'

'Don't start that.'

'I don't have anything against Igbo people. Mrs Eze is a perfectly charming and—'

'Drop it, Mum.'

'Well, even if it's the gardener's daughter, just bring someone soon. All I ask is she has a degree and knows how to handle a—'

He opened the door and got into his car. Disdain from his father and this biting prattle from his mother. Sometimes his one visit a month felt too frequent.

'Wait, before you go, how are things at work? You know we can never talk seriously when your father is around.'

'Fine, thanks. We're trying to see how we can monetise our website. Traffic on there is encouraging.'

'Just make sure there's no accident.'

'Where?'

'In the traffic that you're talking about.'

'Yes, Mum. We'll try to keep away from accidents.'

'You had better, oko mi.'

'Your husband is waiting for you inside the house.'

'Then hurry up and bring our wife so I'll stop calling you that.'

'I'll see you soon.'

10

The paper was dying. Advert subscriptions had dwindled since the *Journal*'s honest coverage of the last election. There had been eyewitness reports of ballot boxes stuffed like birds, bursting with voters that did not exist. Long after civil society voices had fallen silent and President Hassan had been sworn in, Ahmed's editorials continued to call for a rerun.

Eventually they had moved on but the damage was done. No one would advertise in a paper that was rumoured to be unpopular with the First Family. In a way it was flattering. It meant the politicians in Abuja were reading. PRESIDENT CALLS FOR NATIONAL DAY OF PRAYER: this was the headline his editorial team believed would turn their fortunes.

'But it's not news,' Ahmed had said in that morning's meeting.

'We need advertising.'

'It's not news,' he said again.

'It's midweek paper. There's no news midweek. Just let it pass. His boys will see it. They'll start buying our pages. We need a positive story about the President.'

'And when you find one, we'll publish it.'

Prayer was all the recommendation he heard for Nigeria

these days. For every crisis, eyes were shut, knees engaged, heads pointed to Mecca and backs turned to the matter at hand. He did not remember the country being so religious in his childhood. Faith used to be a part of the landscape, glimpsed in wax rosaries and white celestial robes, in wooden prayer beads and the vivid scarves his mother wore when she went to the mosque. None of this obtrusive proselytising, loudspeakers on every corner, blasting calls to prayer and songs of praise.

It showed a certain tolerance that his street in Surulere should boast both a church and a mosque, tolerance from his neighbours, with whom he should have long since banded to demolish both buildings. He had chosen Surulere because it stood in opposition to everything he had known of Lagos as a child. He had grown up in Ikoyi, an island physically and metaphorically cut off from the city, a quivering bubble of privilege that he had burst out of once he returned to Nigeria.

Surulere wasn't quite a ghetto. His street was affluent, with high walls and rosettes of barbed wire, but close by lay a grittier Lagos that on occasion spilled into their world in the form of armed robberies. The few times his mother had visited, she offered the boys' quarters of their house, done up and ready for him to move in.

'You'd never even have to see us. You'd have your own entrance.'

'But what of my own pride?'

There was always traffic on the way home, as constant as the sunset, a swarm of engines throbbing heat and irritation, the strain of clutch control, poised on the biting point, starting and stopping until his shoulder ached from changing gear. He refused to get a driver, refused at his age to become an oga giving orders to a man who would glance in the rear-view mirror when he thought he was not looking, eyes filled with hate.

Once he got home, he ate his dinner over the sink, his fork clinking against the ceramic, the lonely chime of bachelorhood. Then he began an editorial, congratulating the President on his new role as spiritual adviser to the nation. He wrote in his study, a converted bedroom with wood-carvings on the walls and an adirẹ cover for his desk. Only a select group were allowed to sing through his complicated sound system. Fẹla he played when the comfortable, cud-chewing life in England began to look attractive. Makeba's voice was a running stream he slipped into after meetings with the paper's accountant. And Ndour was his personal gateway into the spirit world, into a trance where ideas moved easily into sentences. There were books everywhere, spines facing outwards, Fanon and Tolstoy, Achebe and Maupassant, piled eclectically on top of each other. It was the study of a modern Pan-Africanist, a room that Nkrumah would have relaxed in, he liked to believe.

The rest of the flat was spacious and bare. It would have been minimalist in England, a glass coffee table, a white sofa, a pine chair and a long flatscreen TV. In Lagos, the room looked like a cell. A cleaner came once a week, sweeping, mopping and polishing, down to the security bars on the windows. Only the study was out of bounds. He sometimes wished for a woman to interrupt his work and drag him to bed.

He had found many women to sleep with in Lagos but none to split his life down the middle for. He ruled out the mercenaries fast, women who approached men like prospectors, striking for rent money, fuel money, weavon money. As for those left, who found his work meaningful and shared his love of black-and-white films, would these slim compatibilities last them forty years? Perhaps his mother was right. He was not looking hard enough. He was too obsessed with his paper. And to what end?

He would not bring down the government with the *Nigerian Journal.* Those days were gone, when newspapermen were feared and hounded and despised and worshipped for their recklessness. When a headline could force a paper underground and audiences risked much to read an editorial. He could no longer be a scourge to the Nigerian establishment but he could be a thorn, a brittle thorn in its buttock. The article on the President was ready. It would run on the weekend. The paper would lose more subscribers. He would run the *Journal* to the ground before he let it become popular reading in government circles.

Abuja

Chief Sandayǫ, the Honourable Minister of Education for the Federal Republic of Nigeria, slid up his drooping agbada sleeves and glanced at his Rolex, gifted to him by his late wife Funkẹ, a twenty-year-old watch, still telling accurate time. Two hours gone already. On the podium, the Minister of Health droned on, stuck on a slide about malaria prevention.

Each minister would give a special presentation to the President in this dome-ceilinged hall with low-hanging chandeliers that caught the sparkle from rings and chains and bangles. The room was cold, the air conditioner set to chill, transporting them to a region where scarves and thick socks were necessary. The President was flanked by his predecessors, four former heads of state, all human rights abusers, lined like sphinxes, inscrutable in their chairs. They had been defanged now, overthrown by one coup or the other, paraded in the capital once a year as 'elder statesmen'.

Chief Sandayǫ turned his eyes to the rest of the room. You could not speak when a minister was presenting but nothing stopped them from looking, sizing each other up, going over the battle lines in their heads. It was like the polygamous household he had grown up in, except the stakes here ran to billions. His late wife would have mocked him for how fast he had learnt to play Abuja politics. He bobbed a greeting to the Senate President, who had just walked in with a cloud of assistants.

As well as the ministers, the room was choked with their ambitious aides, men and women in sharp suits. The aides held files for ministers, they straightened the folds of their clothing and if necessary, they presented for them, careful to ascribe credit where it was due.

Chief Sandayọ had come with two assistants of his own, Harvard MBA and PhD from Warwick. The Agriculture Minister had brought seven to bolster her. She was a new appointee; rushed into a job she had scarce qualification for. During each presentation, her lower lip disappeared into her mouth, emerging more mangled as Petroleum, Defence and Tourism gave their reports. Finally it was Agriculture's turn.

'Your Excellencies, Former Presidents of Nigeria, His Excellency the Senate President, Honourable Ministers, Honourable Chair of the House Committee on Agriculture, Special Adviser to the President on Performance Monitoring, distinguished ladies and gentlemen, all protocols observed.'

She was trembling, her knees touching and untouching like the wires in a faulty cable. Her makeup was bold, provocative even, her lips too red for this hour of the morning. Her fellow ministers were either plain, pot-bellied men or motherly women, past makeup and seduction. Who had she slept with to get her job? Rumours were flying around already. Sandayọ's bet was on President Hassan himself. One of her aides stood and whispered to her.

'Forgive me, Mr President. I omitted you in my opening address.'

She looked ready to display the contents of her breakfast to the room.

'Your Excellency, President of the Federal Republic of Nigeria, Commander in Chief, GCFR—'

'Perhaps we will hear from the Honourable Minister of Agriculture another time,' the President said, cutting her off. 'My honourable predecessors and your brother and sister ministers will agree that it is not fair to expect a presentation at such an early stage of your new job. Chief Sandayọ, if you will proceed for us.'

His ministry, the Ministry of Education, was of little interest to his present audience. A small budget considering the army of teachers, professors and vice chancellors that fell under his command. Education was only of importance when university staff went on strike, demanding higher pay for their worsening services.

Sandayọ breezed through the introduction: observing all protocols, naming all names. The ministry had begun implementation of its five-point agenda on toilet provision in north-eastern Nigeria to increase female pupil attendance. The ministry had made a detailed plan of a three-tiered approach to combating the increase in adolescent dropout rates.

The jargon came easily to Sandayọ now, each technical phrase linked to another, forming a chain of incomprehensibility that passed as knowledge in front of this crowd.

'And what of the Basic Education Fund?' the President asked.

'We are beginning a strategic positioning of how best to direct this new resource.'

'I have high hopes for you and your team. I hear you have done good things in basic education for the Yoruba people. Now I want you to do the same for the rest of Nigeria.'

The President was speaking of Sandayọ's time in the Yoruba People's Congress over a decade ago, a time that Chief Sandayọ seldom remembered in the whirlwind of meetings and gala dinners that was Abuja.

He had joined the group at the invitation of its founder, Francis Ifaleke, a charismatic, simply dressed man, compelling with no manic fundamentalist air around him, the opposite of all he had imagined the YPC to be.

He still remembered the first meeting he attended; brimming with scepticism, ready to walk out at the slightest provocation. YPC members were rumoured thugs, gullible in their violence, obsessed with invincibility charms and amulets. He discovered that first night a mini utopia it seemed, bricklayers and doctors, vulcanisers and bankers all gathered for the good of the Yoruba race. They were committed to education with the zeal of their guide Ọbafẹmi Awolowo. He had been honoured to accept Francis's offer to become the group's Education Officer.

That was over fifteen years ago, a time of slimmer waistlines and larger ideals. As he swung the sleeves of his agbada onto his shoulders, he wondered what most of his former comrades would think if they could see him now.

12

'Mr Wọle Odukọya is here to see you, sir,' Chief Sandayọ's receptionist said into the intercom.

The ministry waiting room overflowed with teachers, students, widows, pastors, market women, journalists, Student Union presidents, principals sacked for indecency, parents with photos of sons expelled for hooliganism, daughters dismissed for pregnancy. Yet no matter who was in line, Wọle Odukọya must be shown through.

Sandayọ knew Odukọya from his YPC days, when the latter had been one of the younger members, flashy but earnest, eager to please.

'Great Yoruba people,' Odukọya said when he swaggered into Sandayọ's office. It struck him anew each time he saw Odukọya how tasteless the man was. Rhinestones glittered down the seams of his agbada and his shoes shone a patent red. Sandayọ did not rise to greet him. Godfather or no, the man was still over a decade younger than him.

'I hope I'm not disturbing you. The work of a minister is not easy.'

People said Odukọya made his money from drugs. He also dealt in philanthropic causes: widows and young girls who couldn't afford their university fees. People said he slept with them. Sandayọ had wondered what Odukọya would demand for passing on his name to the President. A year had gone by and still no requests, not even for one of the smaller ministry contracts. All the man wanted to do was play this 'do you remember' game.

'Do you remember when we went for adult education in Kwara and they didn't want us to enter because some of the women were wearing jeans?'

With the YPC, Sandayọ had set up classes in village clearings, evening schools for city workers, language courses for the culturally estranged children of the rich, children like his son in America who stumbled over the simplest of Yoruba phrases. He had not known himself to be an organiser or a public speaker, gifts hidden from him and all who knew him.

'I was speaking to Mallam the other day about giving my friend an oil block.' Mallam was their code name for the President. 'I know Mallam wants to give him, but that witch that he married is stopping the deal. Between the First Lady and the new marabout Mallam has hired, I don't know who is running this country.'

'There's a new one?' Odukọya often let titbits like this fall; gossip swept up from the corridors of Aso Rock.

'Yes. The old one's prophecies were not big enough. This one has predicted that Mallam will win his second term and he will be honoured internationally when his tenure is up.'

'Wouldn't that be nice.'

'Abi. But on a serious note, Chief, Mallam is expecting big things from you.'

'Is that so?'

Sandayọ's exploits had not been scalable. He had found himself at the head of a body paralysed with bureaucracy, almost laughably so, his orders reaching their destination months after being issued, replies reaching him after a year. He could not find his way to the field of illiterate Nigerians he was supposed to educate, his path blocked by strategy meetings and Powerpoint presentations.

'OK, let me leave you to all these papers,' Odukọya said.

'Yes, I must return to them. Greet your family.'

Odukọya's visits always left Chief Sandayọ with contempt for President Hassan, a man in the pocket of his simpering, vindictive wife. After winning a suspect election, the President now wished to play the reformer on the global stage, desperate for foreign money to flow into the cracked pipes of local industry. Mallam's newest World Bank-approved plan was the Basic Education Fund. Ten million dollars to improve literacy at primary level. Ten million dollars to leak through the bureaucratic holes in his ministry.

The fine teak detail of Sandayọ's table was hidden by a forest of paper, trees pulped and bleached into minutes, memoranda, appendices and addenda. If you bribed his receptionist, she would place your file near the top. In his early days as a minister, he had thought pressing matters were being hidden by this system. He would choose from the bottom, from the middle, from the folders that did not make it to his table and were left in a column by the door. Only to discover that in one way or the other, these crisp A4 sheets were asking for access to ministry money. No matter how innocuous the heading, the end was always the same: funds.

Next, an application for a fifty-man delegation to Scandinavia. The Norsemen had the best education these days. The trip would be all expenses paid. Stipend large enough for tribute: handbags, perfume et cetera. His permanent secretary had signed her approval. He wrote his signature under hers and began gathering his things.

He was scheduled to attend a gala that evening. He would make a quick dip into the hum of the hall, champagne slopping into wine glasses, young carnivorous women flitting around in semi-transparent silks, an excitable MC announcing his entrance, bland food, expensive crockery, handshakes, back slaps and then outside again, his ears relieved from the din. Perhaps he would just go straight home.

13

Two weeks later, after a meeting at Aso Rock, Chief Sandayọ
ran into Senator Danladi, an old friend from university with
whom he had never lost touch. Danladi was a career politician who had swung through every level of politics, a demo-
crat, technocrat and diplomat as the occasion arose.

'Have you put on weight?' Danladi asked, prodding him
in the stomach.

'Have you married a new wife?' Sandayọ parried.

'Four is the limit unfortunately. You really should remarry. Bachelors get up to all sorts in this Abuja. I have some
news for you. Walk with me please.'

Aso Rock was a sprawling complex of offices, halls and
private residences for the President, Vice President and their
families, heavy-set concrete structures with pillars and
domed roofing. There was a mosque and a church on site,
an imam and pastor always on standby. The buildings were
joined by neat gravel, landscaped with shrubs and cut grass,
watered every day, even in the dry season.

'I am afraid you might be fired soon,' Danladi said when
they had wandered behind a Ministry of Transport office.

'Where did you hear that?'

'I have my sources.'

Danladi was a well-known confidant of the President.

'Perhaps not fired exactly,' Danladi added, casting round with his eyes. 'Cabinet reshuffle. You might get another ministry. You might get something else. Maybe a parastatal.'

'It can't be. Odukoya would have told me.'

'Which Odukoya? The drug baron? What does he know about anything?'

'He's the one that recommended me for my job.'

'Who told you that? I was the one that mentioned you.'

'But the President said it was an admirer from my YPC days.'

'I, Shehu Danladi, admired the work you did in the South West. News of it reached us in Kano, backward and illiterate as we are. Kai. You think it's only a Yoruba man that can do you a favour.'

'Then do me a favour again.'

'The President has made up his mind. He can be stubborn when he thinks you want to use your influence to push him.'

'Please arrange for me to speak to him then.'

'No. You can't know of it. I've told you so you can prepare.'

'I'm not leaving.'

'You won't have a choice, Sandy. My advice: start gathering your papers.'

He cancelled all his meetings that day and returned to his mansion, large with small block windows that gave the building a squint. It was an ugly house built on land worth its weight in government contracts. He had little there: a few suitcases, some paintings from his Lagos home, his favourite armchair. It was not his house, only a loan from the government until his ministerial term was up. And yet, it could so easily have belonged to him. These things could be arranged, as could all the other suspect perks of being a minister in Abuja.

He climbed upstairs to his room. The house was empty, his maid and cook gone God knows where. He did not often return this early. He lay flat on the four-poster bed staring at the brocade canopy embroidered with birds in flight. His wife would have hated this master bedroom. It was lit by yellow bulbs that glowed garish from the chandelier. Funkẹ had loved natural light so much, she had designed large glass windows for every room of their house in Lagos, glass windows that had to be covered with metal sheets at night, except for the window of their bedroom, a single bulletproof pane that let her watch the sun rise.

He certainly would not wait to be fired. He would return to his well-lit Lagos home with his suitcases and his armchair and his paintings especially. On the wall hung his favourite Grillo, an indigo long-necked woman, her gele opening like petals around her inscrutable face. It reminded him of Funkẹ when they first met: the elegant, almost scrawny neck, the flamboyant clothes, the pervading mystery in everything she said and did.

If his wife were alive, he would never have taken this job. She hated Abuja with its sterile parks and lit-up avenues, wide freeways that led nowhere. And behind this ordered, meticulous cleanliness, the most unjust, most grotesque, most perverse of transactions. No, Funkẹ's puritan sensibilities would not have withstood the capital and he would not have come without her.

Theirs, in the beginning, had been a fairy tale. The village boy from Ikire; the Lagos girl with no concept of lack. She had not been the most beautiful but she had embodied his aspirations with her foreign education and the English surname he almost regretted her exchanging for his own. And then she had some sort of experience in a church, a vision, a blinding light, an angelic visitation that had changed her. Stopped drinking. Stopped swearing. Begun building celestial houses, four-storey mansions in the sky. It was partly why he had been driven to the YPC where the goals were more solid.

Their marriage had broken down long before he buried her but they had never lived apart. No matter how far he strayed, Funkẹ remained under his roof, a pious, holy, chanting talisman. He would return to the house she had designed at the height of their love for each other, a mansion charming in its unevenness. Let them keep their Abuja. He was going home to Lagos.

14

Between Bayelsa and Lagos

The headlamps shone on an empty highway, the driver barely dropping speed as he swerved round potholes. Chike felt safer watching the road. When a bump appeared, he pressed his foot on the bus floor. When they swung round a car wreck, he tilted his head to the left, his reflexes joined to the driver's. On either side the forest crowded, the arc from the front lights brushing its outermost branches.

All around him was the rhythm of sleep. Gradually, as the driver did not fail and no accident befell them, the road began to lose interest. He brought out his pocket Bible and the emergency torch he always carried with him. The book slid open to the Psalms. *Our soul is escaped as a bird out of the snare of the fowlers: the snare is broken, and we are escaped.* How easy it was to appropriate these words and twist them into something personal. The snare was the army. The fowler was the Colonel. And the bus, where did the bus feature in this nest of metaphors?

The men of his platoon would have been interrogated by now. He hoped they had returned to base before reporting him missing. Not just for his sake. They would need a story with details they could all remember. Even if questioned separately, they would not budge. Or so he hoped. It was misplaced concern. He should have stayed to challenge Benatari and add his corpse to the body count in the Delta.

He turned off his torch and put the Bible away. How long till Lagos? It was like London, they said, everything was new and expensive. Big cars, models you would never see anywhere else in Nigeria. Large houses. Money everywhere. And under these fantastic stories of riches, always a layer of unease: of daylight robberies and mysterious disappearances.

The woman beside him no longer breathed evenly. She gave no other sign she was awake. Her arm remained resting on his, where it had fallen in her sleep. She was crying, he realised.

'Excuse me, is everything alright?' Chike asked.

'I thought everyone was asleep.'

'Do you need a light?'

'I've found what I'm looking for.'

She blew her nose softly, the mucus sliding out in a rasp. He laid his head on the window again and watched the road. A few moments later, she began to cry again.

'Are you sure there's nothing I can do for you?'

'I'm tired but this man's driving won't let me sleep. And I checked before getting on the bus. He looked responsible. How am I going to manage till Lagos?'

'Will it be your first time in the city?' he asked.

'No, but I can't wait to arrive. I tire for this Niger Delta. It's so dangerous these days. Once you step out of your house, you're afraid. If it's not kidnapping, it's armed robbery or assassination.'

'Yes,' Chike said. 'It's becoming something else. I hope you don't mind my asking but if I was trying to find somewhere reasonable to stay in Lagos, where would you advise?'

'You can try Ojota or Ketu. That's around where I'll be staying. I haven't even told my cousin I'm arriving tomorrow morning. I called her number but it's not going through.'

'Do you have an address?' Chike asked.

'Yes of course. I just hope she won't turn me away.'

'I'm sure she won't.'

'Why are you so sure? Nobody knows I'm going to Lagos,' she said, her voice suddenly cracking in a sob. 'I'm running away.'

Chike was the one who had drawn her out into conversation and now he wished he had left her to her tears.

'My husband beats me. Often. My mother said I should prepare his favourite soup for him, ofe nsala with plenty stockfish. My brother says I should beg him. They've all told me to stay. Stay so the police can discover my dead body.'

She blew her nose, a loud snort rushing into her tissue.

'Softly o. No injure yourself,' the driver said.

'Instead of him to focus on what he's driving. I'm going to feel very embarrassed tomorrow. I wish I could make you forget everything I've said.'

'I can tell you my own secret,' Chike said. 'Grown man like me, I'm scared of Lagos.'

'Why? Because there are too many Yorubas?'

'And how do you know I'm not Yoruba?'

'You just have this Igbo look about you. And anyway what's a Yoruba man doing in Bayelsa if he's not in the army?'

How had she guessed, Chike wondered? Was there something about him that spoke of death? Over a decade in the military not so easily disguised by plain clothes?

'As for me,' she continued, 'the first time I arrived in Lagos, stepping down at the motor park was a shock. I grew up in the East so to have everybody crowding around you, speaking this language you don't understand, I fear o. Somebody can sell you in the market, you won't know.'

'I speak enough Yoruba but Lagos just has this reputation.'

'Armed robbers. Ritual killers. Drug dealers. It's like that and it's not like that. I always enjoy my visits. There's something always happening there. Ngwanu, let us sleep. You don't want to be tired when you get to Lagos. Good night.'

'Thanks. Good night.'

Chike put his temple on the window and continued to watch the road. A year ago, he would never have believed he could leave the army, so set was he in the routine of military life. Yet here he was on his way to Lagos. He was not too old to adopt and adapt new methods. There was a new life waiting for him in Lagos. He would make his way.

II

Monday Morning in Lagos

15

Lagos bus parks attract an assortment of individuals. There are those who wish to make honest money, lifting bread and bananas to the newcomers as they fall out of buses; charging prices that would make black skin blush. Those who wish to steal from the arrivés, offering to carry bags and promptly disappearing. And of course those who are there solely for entertainment: to chase a thief, to fetch petrol for burning if the thief is caught and to fall into any diversion that comes their way.

As for the newcomers, two types only: a JJC with a destination and a JJC whose ambition saw no further than reaching the city. At first, they are indistinguishable. They both study the bus park with a dazed expression, taking in the hawkers with large trays of groundnuts wobbling on their heads, the young boys walking aimlessly in groups. Lagos is no different from anywhere, except there are more people, and more noise, and more. But when they are done marvelling at the sameness of it all, one type continues on his way and the other remembers that he has nowhere to go.

Nigerian Journal editorial

Chike had slept fitfully and yet even in that shallow surface sleep, his dreams had been violent, of hands clutching him from behind, of being buried under a wall of water, eyes fixed on a sky that was burning. There was a time he looked for symbols in his dreams, oneirology of the most absurd kind. The phase had ended when he found himself pondering over a recurring bucket. The bucket meant nothing as it would have meant nothing if he had seen it when awake, broken and disused on the side of the road.

He knew these memories of Bayelsa would gradually recede and then disappear from both his conscious and subconscious. When he killed his first man, in Jos, he had thought the image of the man jerking backwards, blood pouring from his mouth, would never leave him. And now, years later, the features were indistinct, blurred into caricature. He remembered a bald head and a large scar on his cheek. Or perhaps that was the second man he killed. Memories were deceptive.

The woman from last night was awake but she had not spoken to him. They had smiled at each other at the filling station in Ọrẹ, her top teeth resting attractively on her bottom lip. Their approach to the city did not interest her. She stared down at her lap, ignoring the billboards that welcomed them to Lagos.

Bournvita Welcomes You to Lagos:
the Centre of Excellence.

Welcome to Lagos.
Pay Your Tax.
Eko o ni bajẹ.

Welcome to Lagos.
Stuck in Traffic? Only One Station to Listen to:
Rhythmic 94.8 FM

Who would he be in this new city? His experience would be of little use here. When the bus slowed in traffic, he had scanned ahead for an ambush, a useless precaution now. The sun was rising over the city. People were already amove, dashing across the expressways in their office clothes, hurdling over cement barriers and dashing to safety again. Women in bright overalls sprouted like fluorescent lichen along the highway, sweeping dust into piles blown away by rushing traffic. There were roadside saplings planted at precise intervals, a regimented attempt at beauty. Near the state boundary, they passed three statues, white stone men in flowing robes, their fists clenched, their heads covered with square caps. The men stared away from the city towards the newcomers, menace in their stance.

'Who are they?' Chike asked the driver.

'We call them Aro Mẹta. The three wise men of Lagos.'

'What are they saying?'

'Shine your eye.'

*

Oma climbed down from the bus a step behind the man from last night. Her husband would be looking for her by now, going through the rooms in their house, opening and shutting drawers, locking and unlocking doors. He would call her brother and her mother, then he would call her 'friends', that tight circle of wives whose husbands were professionals in Yenagoa.

Her husband IK loved her, in the way you loved expensive shoes, to be polished and glossed but, at the end of the day, to be trodden on. He would never believe she would dare board a bus to Lagos and sit beside a strange man with their legs touching.

Yesterday, she had woken up beside her husband, planning to spend her morning in the salon. IK liked her to look a certain way, hair curled, eyebrows shaped and skin the colour of building sand. She served his breakfast of steaming yams, body-temperature eggs and a glass of watermelon juice, blended minutes before IK sat down. At the door, he had noticed his footprints from last night, dark tracks she had not yet mopped away.

'You sit at home and do nothing. At least you can make sure this place doesn't turn into a pig sty.'

As he walked towards her, she thought, he'll be late to work and in the evening, that'll be my fault too. When he was gone, she spat out the blood, a red trickle she rinsed carefully from the basin. Then she arranged her possessions in the bag that now sat on her lap, brushing against the stranger from last night.

'Brother Chike, good morning,' a young girl said when they disembarked. She was filthy, almost deliberately ungroomed. IK would have sniggered at her matted hair and clothes smeared with dirt. There were two other men with this Chike.

'Good morning. I hope you slept well. I didn't introduce myself yesterday. I'm Chike.'

74

'Ifeoma. But everyone calls me Oma. What are you doing now?'

'Taking my friend Isoken home.'

'You know what. My cousin may not be awake yet. Maybe ... I was thinking that ... I said that I would help you find somewhere to stay. How about I follow you to drop Isoken, if the place is not too far, then I'll show you a good area.'

'I don't want to disturb your plans.'

'Not at all. I need to be doing something while I'm waiting for my cousin.'

On the strength of a midnight conversation, Oma trusted this man who did not know enough of Lagos to threaten her. Better to walk with Chike than remain in the bus park until touts began to circle her.

They boarded a bus, a metal carcass on wheels with a floor like a grater, coin-size holes through which you could see the road streaking by. She would find a space for herself in this city. Even if her cousin should turn her away, Lagos was big enough.

'Owa,' the girl said. The bus slowed for them to disembark.

*

I am an orphan. The thought came unbidden to Isoken as she stood in front of her apartment. The door was worn with age and termites. Termites were of the

Kingdom: Animalia
Phylum: Arthropoda

Class: Insecta
Sub-class: Pterygota

The syllabus had not demanded you know past Phylum but she had crammed it all anyway. Isoken: the virgin geek, sat with her legs crossed because she wanted to marry a suit man, read her textbooks because she wanted to be a pharmacist, invent drugs and name them after herself, Edwina, her Christian name.

'Is this the place?' Chike asked.

'Yes.'

She was still wearing the jeans that the villagers thought an abomination, that her mother said made her bum shoot out, that she wasn't going to change because some dunces felt a woman shouldn't wear man's clothes. If ever men set upon you, you would want to be wearing the tightest trousers in your wardrobe, trousers that stuck to you and cut off your circulation, trousers that neither you nor a stranger could slide off without a struggle.

'Won't you knock?' Chike said.

Knocking: a colloquial term for the introduction of the groom's family to the bride's. She did not know the origins of the practice. Only that virgins were preferred, fresh ground where no one else had trod. Knocking: present continuous verb for the repeat application of one's knuckle to a hard surface to produce a rapping sound. The door shuddered, termites scuttling, alarmed and incensed by this assault on their food.

'Who is making noise?'

It was her landlord running down the stairs in his singlet

and boxers. He had made a pass at her once, lunging for her chest, missing and squeezing the flesh over her ribcage.

'My parents' number, Mr Alabi.'

'Is that why you're disturbing everyone? And you can't greet? You see somebody in the morning and is that the first thing you say?'

'Good morning, sir,' Chike said. 'As you can see the girl is in distress. She's been unable to locate her parents.'

'And who are you?'

'A friend of the family.'

'You said her parents are missing. I thought they all travelled together. Wait, I will bring my phone. You will find them. Stop crying.'

Her parents' number did not go through on Mr Alabi's phone. If they were alive, they would be crying too, secreting salt water from their lachrymal glands. Her parents did not know the word 'gland' nor 'lachrymal' nor 'didactic' nor 'encyclopaedic'. With her mother, she wore her education loosely but her father revelled in her vocabulary.

'Your English can break rocks,' he would say, when she dropped a word of five syllables or longer into a sentence. She would imagine a sledgehammer joined to her tongue by a thick artery, grinding anything that stood in its way.

'Open the door, let me take my things,' she said to Mr Alabi.

'I would have said you should stay in the house and wait for them but you know your rent is due.'

Her clothes were in a metal chest. She left all her skirts, flimsy things that would betray you. She took her mother's shoes, worn in the heels but still glamorous. She took her father's workbox, full of tongs and combs and bright plastic rollers. She slid her hand into the pillow foam and felt the empty space. They had taken all their money to Bayelsa.

*

Chike did not know how he had come to exchange the command of one platoon for another. There was Yẹmi, constantly running his mouth, and the girl, on the verge of crying into her rice, and the boy who had somehow attached himself to them, asking to borrow money for his meal. Oma was the only person he did not feel responsible for. She had gone to meet her cousin, promising to return and show them a place to stay. She shook his hand when she said goodbye and it had felt permanent, a small panic rising in him as she walked away.

When he saw her on the other side of the road, loose skirt billowing from the rushing cars, he felt the kind of gratitude he had not known since his childhood when his mother shook him from his dreams.

'Oma, welcome. If you can just give us directions, we'll find our way.'

'The place is called Tamara Inn. I'm going there too.'

'But your cousin—'

'She doesn't live there again. I don't know her new address.'

'A number?'

'I foolishly left my phone behind.'

They passed through a neighbourhood of small businesses and modest houses, the industrial rumble of generators filling the air. Roadside food was there for the foraging, suya skewered and grilling, meat pies trapped in lit-up glass cages, golden nuggets of puffpuff bobbing in vats of hot oil, boli and groundnut to be mashed together in one mouthful.

The hotel's electronic sign flashed from afar, the letters expanding and contracting, restless on the building's facade. There was no one else in Tamara Inn. The dining room was empty, the TV tuned to CNN at odds with the shabby cloth napkins, folded into collapsing shapes, waiting for guests to shake them free. They would all share one room. Chike and Oma would split the cost. Yẹmi took him aside before he paid.

'Which kain thing be this? Maybe she wan' use us for ritual o.'

'She can't kill all of us at the same time.'

'No be joke matter.'

They were led to their room by torchlight, single file down the corridor, Chike last in the column, stumbling in the dark. Their room lights were working, thankfully. He noticed the room's curtains first: a pale yellow that showed the dirt from the countless fingers that had twitched them aside. A concrete view lay behind the mesh of mosquito netting nailed to the wooden window frames. The bed was large enough for three, four with imagination, not that Oma or Isoken would imagine such a thing.

Isoken went to the bathroom and locked the door. They heard the gush of running water and then the sound of bathing, rain crashing on zinc. Oma stripped the pillows, baring their lumpy foam bodies. She turned their cases

79

inside out and began to dress them again, stuffing them into their sacks.

'Are you going to do that for the sheets as well?' Chike asked.

'Should I?'

'I don't know. I was joking.'

In the bathroom, Isoken was crying, the sound passing through the door and into the room.

'What's the matter with her?' Oma asked, holding a pillow to her body like a baby.

'A difficult time recently,' Chike said.

'Well whatever the matter is, there's no use crying for so long. We've all had difficult times.'

She grasped the edge of the sheet and tore it off the bed.

'Difficult times are made better with good music,' Fineboy sang.

'That's one of the jingles from Bayelsa Beats, isn't it?' Oma said.

'Yup. I used to work there.'

'Really? I've never heard of any presenter called Fineboy.'

'I did the opening lines. Like: "You're listening to High Life Monday on Bayelsa Beats FM. Don't touch that dial."'

'Chineke! It's like the radio is inside the room. Isn't that marvellous,' she said turning to Chike.

'Yes,' he said. 'There are many marvellous things about Fineboy.'

'How do you know each other?'

'We met while we were working,' Chike said.

'You worked in radio as well?'

'No. I was a government worker.'

'I hope I'm not asking too many questions.'

The mattress lay exposed. In its centre was a large brown stain, some waste product excreted or blood released, the mark too spread out to be ordinary menses. Blood from a deflowering perhaps, a quaking teenager and his girlfriend, fumbling until they soiled the sheets. Oma began to lift the mattress.

'Please come and help me. It's heavy.'

Chike and Yẹmi joined her. Only Fineboy remained aloof on the floor.

'Don't bother,' the boy said when the mattress stood straight, needing only a push to be flipped over.

'Why?'

'The other side is worse.'

Chike walked round and saw the green growth, spiralling in all directions.

'You don't want to see,' he said to Oma. 'Let's just put it back the way it was.'

Isoken came out of the bathroom in cleaner, freer clothes and they took their sleeping positions. Women on the bed, men on the floor, Fineboy as far away from the women as possible.

Chike woke up at three in the morning, the time ticking on his watch face. His platoon would be on night patrol, creeping through the Delta.

'Yẹmi. Are you sleeping?'

'Wetin?'

'Your family nkọ?' Chike asked.

'My mother is dead. My father dey for Ijẹbu.'

81

'Why didn't you go there?'

'I no fit stay for his house. I have junior ones at home he is feeding and work plenty in Lagos pass Ijẹbu. I even get family members for this Lagos. They are useless people. If I visit them, they go say they wan' help me, that make I come do houseboy work. How I go dey wash toilet for person wey get the same surname as me.'

'So what will you do?'

'Maybe driver. You nkọ?'

'I don't know.'

When the army had offered to sponsor his university degree, so certain had he been that he would always be a soldier, he had chosen zoology out of his interest in animals. And now of what use was his knowledge of the migratory patterns of West African birds? Who would hire him for being able to distinguish a dolphin from a porpoise? Most importantly, the certificate that could prove his higher education was locked in his trunk in Bayelsa.

'I'll find something,' Chike said. 'I'm not worried.'

16

With the UK charity Jobs Plus estimating that over two million people are unemployed in Lagos, the jobless of this city outnumber the populations of Gabon, Luxembourg and Kiribati combined. The Lagos State Commissioner for Job Creation, Wasiu Balogun, stated that these new figures were 'rubbish lies'.

'Jobs Extra, or whatever their name is, should go back to the UK and face their own problems,' he said in an interview granted to the *Nigerian Journal*. 'In their country, jobless people will just sit down at home and be collecting money from government. We don't have that dangerous system here. Who is really unemployed in Lagos? You might not wear suit and tie but no matter how small, our people will always find something doing. Go to Mile 12 Market; you'll see boys there washing mud from your feet as you're leaving. They're collecting money for that, you know? So they too, are they unemployed? If a female graduate can't find any work, she can begin to make jewelleries, do makeup, tie gele and all that stuff. The only thing is all these people are making money and not paying taxes. Maybe that's why those people are saying they are unemployed. There's no record of their money.'

Nigerian Journal

Someone had left hairs in the drain. Oma picked out the curly, possibly pubic strands, stark against the white tissue. A bucket stood in the cracked zinc tub. She had grown accustomed to hotels with continental breakfasts and satellite TV, to service on silver trays and in-house dry cleaning. On her honeymoon in Dubai, there had been a king-sized bed strewn with dark rose petals, a clichéd touch she had secretly relished.

She bathed quickly but carefully, not wanting water to splash back from the walls. She dried her body with her nightie, disdaining the threadbare towels the men had left unused. Her toilette remained unchanged. She had packed lotion, roll-on, face cream, toothbrush, toothpaste, a bottle of perfume, three shaving sticks, changes of underwear, six sets of clothes and yet no phone. It was a fastidious show of impracticality.

She strode out into the room with the scent of lemon under her arms. The men had left but the girl still lay on the bed, the covers pulled over her head.

'Isabel, you're not going to get up today? Isabel, I'm talking to you. You must be awake by now. The bathroom is free for you.'

She moved closer.

'Isabel, did you hear me?'

The girl slid the covering off her face. Her eyes were red and there was dirt on her lashes.

'My name is Isoken,' she said and disappeared under the blanket again.

'Not our class,' IK would have said after one glance at this Isoken. And it wasn't just the girl. Chike's right-hand man could not speak standard English and the other young man, despite his pretensions, was not quite authentic. She had seen Fineboy's feet when he came out of the bathroom. Hard with tough skin around the cuticles, his toes irregularly thick, dirt crowded under cracked nails. She did not know where the boy had acquired his accent but it was not in America.

Chike alone did she trust, if only for his strong and gentle manner. He was handsome. IK for all his money and expensive clothes was not. 'Monkey in a suit,' her grandmother had said at their wedding, the first time she saw IK.

'For a much younger bride,' her brother's wife said when Oma was zipped into her snow-white wedding dress, tulle frothing around her, paste jewels sparkling in her ears.

'I'm going to find some food,' she said to the shroud on the bed. No reply. Was she expected to feed Chike's hangers-on as well? In the empty dining room, she looked through the laminated menu. She had grown used to ignoring prices. Fifty thousand naira was all the cash she had found in the house. She had not bothered to wonder if it was theft. She had only wished for more as she rifled through IK's trousers, looking for the stray naira he always forgot in his pockets.

'I left something in my room. I'm coming,' she said to the waiter who had appeared by her side with a pen.

Even in this rundown hotel, she could not afford lunch. She stepped out of the building and into the sun. She spotted a Mister Biggs, the yellow B of its logo blazoned above the traffic. It was an uncomfortable and dangerous distance to walk, no pavement to speak of, her back to traffic; any moment a vehicle might knock her down. The effect of her bath evaporated in minutes. Inside the restaurant, the afternoon retreated under the blast of ACs, the lights clinical and fluorescent. It had the feel of a morgue.

'Who's next?'

The attendant's forehead was shiny, like he had just emerged from a deep fryer.

'One meat pie, one beef burger and a bottle of water please.'

She sat down at a red plastic table, covering her tray with serviettes before she unwrapped her food. The pie looked substantial, the burger less so, a sliver of meat cowering between two hunks of bread. 'For what I am about to receive, Lord make me thankful.'

*

Isoken had refused to get up from her bed that morning. Now was not the time for the girl to have a breakdown, Chike thought as he and Yẹmi left the room. She had reason to pass the white sheet over her head and lie still as a corpse but now was not the time. He too wished he could find a flat bed and a blank ceiling with a soft-spoken psychiatrist whom he would tell of his year in the Delta.

Chike walked with his head down, a posture he was not used to. You were supposed to be able to spot an officer in a crowd, something in his bearing and carriage and the way he lifted his feet that should mark him out like a well-bred horse. But every face he passed might be a classmate from military school or a colleague from Jos. He had not felt so exposed since his last posting. In the Delta, there had always been bush to crouch behind but in Jos, only the hilly grassland. From a vantage, you could see a checkpoint for miles. They were sent to calm the local population, to stop the cow herders from setting fire to the Christians and the Christians from setting fire to the cow herders.

It was dull work, flagging down cars at random, opening boots, looking under vehicles, with moments of acute danger, petrol bombs, gun caches, armed mobs they were ordered to disperse with gunfire. He was made for more than checkpoints, he said to his major. The Delta was the closest he would get to a war, his major had replied and so he had applied to be reposted to the Niger Delta.

'Ọgbẹni comot for road,' a motorcycle rider said, swerving round Chike, the passenger's foot brushing his leg. Lagos would kill you if you wasted time on yesterday. The city was full of a palpable distrust, in the way the bus conductor this morning had counted their fare once, then twice, then thrice.

Their first job enquiry was at a bakery with a vacancy sign in the window. Walking into the store had been like stepping into the centre of a warm, fresh loaf. Rows of golden bread lined the shelves like ingots. Beneath the glass counter were frosted pastries and sugared doughnuts and cupcakes glittering with edible silver stars. Neither he nor Yẹmi had eaten that morning.

'Good morning. How may I help you, sir?' the attendant asked, smiling.

'Morning. We saw the vacancy in the window for drivers. Are the positions still available?'

'Yes but you enter through the back. This place is for

87

customers. The manager's office is the first door on the right. He's Mr Badmus.'

'Thank you.'

Chike and Yẹmi walked out and round to a second door that opened onto a dirty corridor. A bin overflowed with food waste and delirious flies. Chike knocked at Mr Badmus's door.

'Who is that? Come in.'

They entered a room, more cupboard than office. Mr Badmus sat at his desk, clipping his nails with a shiny clipper attached to a key ring.

'Yes, what is it? Shut the door. The AC is on.'

'Good morning, sir. My name is Chike Ameobi and this is Yẹmi Ọkẹ. We saw the recruitment sign for drivers. We would like to make an application.'

'All this English for driver? Oya where are your references.'

'We don't have them.'

'Is this your first job?'

'No, but my last employer does not live in Lagos,' Chike said in a moment of inspiration.

'What of you?' Mr Badmus asked, pointing at Yẹmi.

'My last Oga no dey live for Lagos.'

'I can't hire you without references. If you can get it, come back. Please shut the door as you're going.'

It had been a similar story with the bank and the restaurant. A reference was needed, two if possible, three ideally. Chike had driven a general round a parade ground, turning the corners so smoothly, General Ezeaka had commented. How to get that in writing?

They would find work of some sort in the end, something menial that would blister their hands before attacking their minds. He saw the bare-chested men with head pans of cement, their torsos chalky from the mix of limestone and water. That would be them soon. The baker's words had stung him. He was intelligent and well-spoken enough to be a banker or a civil servant or at least a teacher but he had no proof of his university education.

All the way back to the Inn, he worried. *The Lord is my Shepherd, I shall not want.* He had read the psalm that morning and it had given him hope. Now the words seemed a mockery.

'Kedu k'ihe si aga?' Oma said when they entered the room.

It was a type of solidarity Chike did not want established. He replied in English.

'We didn't have luck today. Hopefully tomorrow. Where is Isoken?' he asked.

'I gave her some money to go and buy food. She hadn't eaten all day.'

'And what about Fineboy?'

'He too went to buy food. Separately from her.'

'You don't have to do that for them.'

'What could I do? The girl has no money and Fineboy said his is coming soon. Once he starts in a radio station in Lagos, he'll pay me back double. I felt sorry for him. He has the voice but he doesn't look the part. I wouldn't give him a job as a cleaner, talkless of a presenter.'

Chike watched Oma discreetly as she busied herself for the next hour, making work out of nothing; unfolding and folding her clothes, rearranging the contents of her bag, re-positioning her shoes on the carpet. All the while, she sang softly to herself. This particular song, Chike's mother had sung whenever he woke from a nightmare, still thrashing in her embrace. She would sing until he was calm.

Atulegwu. Nwoke atulegwu.
Atulegwu. Nwanyi atulegwu.
Atulegwu. Nwanta atulegwu
Atulegwu. Nwenu Okwukwe.
Nihi na Chineke n'edu gi si gi atulujo.

Be courageous. Men, be courageous. They were words his mother had sung in the Biafran War when planes flew over her village and dropped bombs in the lanes. Be courageous. Women, be courageous. Sometimes they would bring the wounded to her house, and his mother would help his grandmother, a nurse, dig out bullets with a kitchen knife made sterile over a flame. Be courageous. Children, be courageous. This was the line for him, always sung louder than the rest.

Harcourt Whyte, the songwriter, had been a leper, his mother told him. Every morning Whyte woke with a body further rotted away. This was why he had written 'be courageous', not 'be brave'. Bravery was to dash out of the bomb shelter and grab the child left crying on the veranda. Courage was to go to the stream the day after a bomb had scattered your friend on that path because water must be fetched to sustain the life that was left. Everyone saw bravery but courage was in secret. She would lay him back on his pillow and leave him alone in the room.

17

The underside of bridges are multipurpose spaces: shade and shelter, house and office, church and mosque with cement pillars as grand as those in any mansion, grand and bare like an unfinished mansion. Touts roam these spaces, colonising them at will, extracting dues from anyone foolish enough to linger. There is a strange chaotic order to these places. Every food seller, every hairdresser, even every beggar has paid their levy and they expect security in return.

'Nobody dey steal for here,' one area boy says proudly. 'Under the bridge, our government dey work.'

'Lagos Snapshots', *Nigerian Journal*

Fineboy suggested they try the beach. He had seen whole families crawling into pits in the sand and the common sense of their location had struck him. The beach was close to the business district, to the tall buildings with mirrored facades, to the suited workers going somewhere with their lives. The others were not convinced. Who wanted to go and live in a damp hole, fearful the tide would wash you away in your sleep?

Isoken mentioned the pedestrian crossings that vaulted over the expressways, used by livestock and humans alike. People slept under their awnings that would shelter one from most of the rain. But a group their size would be a nuisance in such a narrow space.

Under a bridge was the most obvious choice, yet it was the last suggested. No condition was permanent except that of the drug addicts and other scum that embraced homelessness and lay down beneath the concrete pillars every night. Better to sleep standing than to wake with the weight of a cement sky above your head.

At checkout, the receptionist showed Oma her dull teeth before saying, 'Hope to see you soon.' To leave here and become homeless. It seemed too drastic.

She did not have to go with the others to the bridge, at least not yet. She could manage alone for a few more weeks. By the time she went to look for them, they would have disappeared into Lagos, moved on to another bridge, been hit by a bus, drowned in the lagoon. Go with them now or never again. To stretch out to sleep knowing there were no walls around you; to bare the soles of your feet to passing strangers; to wake and show your face immediately to the world.

That morning, Oma had felt a wave of nausea swimming up her throat, and then her dinner of beans and crayfish had rushed into the toilet bowl. She had not gotten pregnant in almost a year. IK's job meant that he spent three weeks on land, three weeks off shore, living like an amphibian to please his masters at the Dutch oil company. His visits did not always match the erratic release of her precious, dwindling eggs. Just when Oma's acceptance of childlessness had set in, here was this nausea that could be rotten crayfish or a tiny foetus, burrowing into her body.

A pregnancy test was easily bought. If she were not pregnant, she would return to Bayelsa, hanging her head and casting down her eyes and after the worst had happened, for he would not kill her, she would crawl back into the space by IK's side. It was obvious that the adventure was over. But if she were pregnant? If the plastic stick said yes? She could not risk going back when a stray blow from IK could dislodge the foetus. It had happened before.

Let time decide. If there were a baby, it would show. And if there were none, that would also soon become apparent. Let time decide if she would return to her husband. For now she would go with the others to the bridge. She would stop trying to protect her soft belly of vanity. No one she knew would ever see her there and even if they saw her, they wouldn't recognise her.

*

In the afternoon, a steady flow of noise and footfall made Chike at ease with leaving Isoken and Oma to their devices. The bridge arched above them all, vaulting as high as the roof of a cathedral, shading them from the sun. Their new home might as well have been a market: hawkers sauntered by, holding their wares to passing traffic while traders sat beside fresh fruit and vegetables, waiting for customers to beckon. Thin, agile conductors hung from moving danfos, calling for passengers. Students in packs of brown, green and purple uniforms ambled home, buttons undone, shirttails flapping.

By evening, when he and Yẹmi returned, cars still clogged the road but the nature of the pedestrians had changed.

Men, young men, shirtless for the most part with trousers that sagged and showed pelvic contours, strutted about. The women were sitting where Chike had left them, leaning against a pillar covered with film posters. They were 'the women' in his head, a block unit to give preference to and evacuate first. Isoken's elbows were hugging her knees and Oma was scanning the road.

'Nnọ,' she said when she saw him.

'Daalu.'

He did not wish to make a habit of speaking Igbo with her but there was something soothing in being welcomed, even to a home as derelict as this.

'How was it?' she asked.

'Nothing.'

Fineboy had still not come back. Perhaps the boy would cut his losses and go and burrow into the beach like a crab.

'Some men came to meet us. They said we have to pay someone called Chairman before we can sleep here.'

'What kind of men?'

'They looked like touts. I told them that my husband would speak to them when he returned. I didn't want it to look like we were two women on our own.'

'Yes, that was wise. How much did they say we have to pay?'

'Four hundred naira per person.'

'Whose funeral?' It was Fineboy. The boy had returned.

'We thought you weren't coming back.'

'How can? Y'all are my Lagos crew.'

'There's a problem. We have to pay to sleep here. Two thousand naira in total.'

'Are you kidding me? I knew we should have gone to the beach. I guess we gotta pay the money, Oma.'

'Why are you calling her name?'

'Because she's the only one that has up to that amount.'

It was probably true. Between him and Yẹmi was just over one thousand and whatever money Fineboy had would remain in his pocket as long as someone else could pay.

'Take,' Oma said. He had not seen where she had brought the cash from and he hoped neither had Fineboy.

'Stay here with the women,' Chike said to Fineboy.

'No, let me come with you. I know how such people think.'

Chairman was a middle-aged man with a torso running to flab. He must have been a prizefighter in his day. Past battles were mapped over his arms and chest, archipelagos of scar tissue, marks of a life spent in violent straits. A barrier of testosterone milled around him. These boys would move instinctively on Chairman's orders, a shoal, darting with one mind.

'Chairman,' Fineboy said, prostrating himself flat on the ground.

'Who are you?'

'Fineboy nah the name my mama give me. Your boys talk say we must greet you before we fit sleep here.'

'Your friend nkọ? He does not greet?'

'Good evening,' Chike said.

'What's your name?'

'Emeka.'

'Ah, ọmọ Íbò tiẹ ni ẹ. That's why you don't have respect. My boys told me there are two women and three men. You will pay two thousand naira for all of you. For security. We're stopping armed robbers and bad people from coming to this place.'

'Sah, we don't have the money complete,' Fineboy said.

'You must have it before you sleep. You don't want to know what will happen if you don't.'

The army shielded you from other men's egos. It was civilians that begged and bribed, kneeling with faces pressed to the dust, not minding their fine clothes and new shoes. Even this Chairman would learn to grovel if Chike had come with a small section of his platoon.

'Please—'

'Please sah—' Fineboy continued for him, 'we have come from far. From the Niger Delta.'

'Is that so? Wetin you dey do there?'

'Freedom fighting.'

'You don't mean it. Shake me. I so much believe in what you are doing there. You people are still looking when a real freedom fighter is in our midst. Dagogo go and bring some bitters.'

'Chairman, the fee.'

'We can't charge a soldier fighting for the freedom of Nigeria.'

'His friends nkọ?'

'How many did you say they are again?'

'Five.'

'Five is too much. Ìbá jẹ́ pé ẹyin mẹta pérẹ́ ni . . .'

'Let's pay for only two then. Give us three for free,' Fineboy said. How had the boy picked up Yoruba so quickly?

'We don't normally do our things like that but just because of respect I have for what you're doing.'

Chairman's thug made a show of writing out a receipt, a neat tabulation that included the price before and after the discount. He was ashamed to give Oma her change, proof that the men in the group could not protect them from the idiosyncrasies of this city. Where else must one pay to be homeless?

'Fineboy got us a discount. I'm sorry we had to pay at all.'

'It's better. Let's just follow their rules.'

She had worn a nightie on top of her clothes, its lace frills crawling down her chest and disappearing into the folds of her wrapper. She was another man's wife, a man who had not thought much of her, beautiful as she was. He would make something of himself in this city so that people like Chairman could not so easily trample on him. When Oma began to sing, a reedlike melody in the dark, he joined at a lower octave.

'Atulegwu. Nwoke atulegwu.'

18

Bola Smoothguy, male, twenty-eight. Tall, dark and handsome. I'm a God-fearing, single, mature guy. I work in a
bank and I'm looking for a graduate in her early twenties, of
medium height, who can cook and is ready for marriage.
                    Personal advertisement, *Nigerian Journal*

It was two weeks since they'd moved to the bridge and each
night, Oma had fallen asleep facing Chike. He had never
slept so close to a woman he was not romantically involved
with. He liked to watch her in the mornings, when she
combed her hair that fell over her shoulders, then wiped her
face with a wet flannel before smoothing over her eyebrows,
licking her index finger and slicking them down. Then she
put the flannel under her clothes, her hands moving vigorously, lingering under her armpits, and then finally she
passed a second flannel, reserved especially for that purpose
it seemed, between her legs. Sometimes she would inspect
this auxiliary towel, bringing it close to her face. Once it
came away with blood and Oma had begun to cry. He had
turned away at this inexplicable grief over her menses. He
was no voyeur.

She was older than him, though he could not say by how

many years. Sometimes he guessed a decade, other times, when she sang, he thought less. He would have liked to have met her in other circumstances, to have sat down on the opposite end of a narrow table and asked where she had grown up and what her favourite colours were, a plate of food in front of each one of them. He had learnt in his first year of university that these cheap ingredients, rice, chicken and attention, were enough to seduce a woman.

And then he had learnt he did not like the kind of woman for whom repeated offerings of carbohydrates and protein were enough to sleep with him. Celibacy had crept up on him: first in reaction to the slim pickings and then as a response to the brothel trips of barrack life. And now? If he offered himself to Oma, would she take him, a penniless ex-soldier?

Watching her in the mornings was his only moment of calm. His search for a job had become frantic, almost panicked. He and Yẹmi ranged the city, tramping where they could, taking buses when they could not, riding into the financial district with its glass buildings that distorted reflections, stretching them into thin, long, powerless creatures. They stood in queues, watching others ushered forward because they bore the right talismans, runic Mercedes symbols sketched on conspicuous keys, chunky gold watches, *no other nexus between man and man than naked self-interest, than callous cash payment.* Marx was writing of Lagos, surely.

The city had begun to pick at his self-discipline. He was like other men, Chike found in these weeks of wandering through Lagos. His officer training made him no better than most male specimens, only more likely to hold his head erect when he was walking. He began to pick fights with strangers weaker than him, reedy men like the vendor who shoved him in the chest for bumping against his wares: VCDs piled in flimsy cardboard casings, cheap, pirated copies of Nollywood movies. Chike grasped the hand that had pushed him, his grip tight enough to snap bones. The man had begun begging, a film of unshed tears glittering in his eyes.

'We go find work,' Yẹmi said as he pulled Chike away.

He had begun reading more psalms, their despair suiting his mood. *Save me, O God, for the waters are come in unto my soul. I sink in deep mire, where there is no standing: I am come into deep waters, where the floods overflow me.* He did not hope much for deliverance, the divine rescue that the psalmist was so sure of, but he understood life in the pit, clawing and clawing and sliding to claw again. Lagos was a jungle, an orderly ecosystem with a ranked food chain, winners and losers decided before they were born.

The rains had come, sweeping through their new home and flooding it, dead smells and creatures rising to the surface. Oma knew best how to cope with the new weather. She fetched rainwater in a bucket. She fashioned raincoats out of nylon bags. She even washed her hair in the rain, working her head into a cloud of suds and letting the sky rinse it clean. Chike wondered if her husband would ever show up to claim her or if Oma herself would grow tired of their bridge life and return of her own will.

Chairman's boys were having a party on the far side of the bridge and he was almost certain Fineboy was with them. Their bonfire threw grim shadows, monstrous shapes that danced up and down the pillars. He sat up and inched forward until he was sitting with his back to the group. Their 'neighbours' were also stretched out in sleep around them.

There were Yusuf and Mahmud, brothers from Kano, refugees after their home was destroyed in a religious riot, teenagers and already working in an abattoir carting chunks of bloody meat to a fridge. Or Clement the welder, with his wife and child, asleep on a bed salvaged from the dump, decadent luxury in these surroundings. The bridge-dwellers spoke different languages, worshipped different gods, supported different premiership teams; but every single one Chike had spoken to was moving out soon, even those who had lived there for years.

It was the Lagos delusion. Each morning he watched workers clamber into danfos, pushing, shoving, crushing against each other, struggling to make it inside where they would sit thigh to thigh, heads drooping out of windows, desperate for fresh air. He envied their energy, the illusion of progress as they kicked and struck out, vigorously treading water. He was too smart and too foolish for Lagos.

He lit a match from the box Oma kept for lighting candles. The flame raced down the matchstick, almost at his fingers before he shook it out.

'What are you doing?' It was Isoken crouched by his side. She smelt of the oil she worked with all day as she plaited, twisted, braided, threaded her customers' hair under the bridge. It was a basic salon: a stool, a hand mirror, some combs tucked into her jeans, but at least she had a job.

Isoken had not initiated a conversation with him since they arrived in Lagos, let alone sought him out. He felt that if he turned, if he even glanced at her, she would skitter off.

'I can't sleep with all that noise,' he said.

'Me too. Bestial swine.'

'Madam grammar.'

'Bestial boisterous bothersome swine.'

'Walking dictionary,' Chike said.

'My father used to call me that.'

Chike struck another match and another.

'Can I try?'

He gave her the box. The flame tapered like a gold leaf and then sped to the curve of her fingertips.

'Drop it,' Chike said.

'Not yet.'

She grasped the charred matchhead with her other hand and let go of the burning end. The fire ate to the bottom of the matchstick and was gone.

'The trick is to hold on till the last possible moment. Do you want to try?'

'Another time. Let's go and sleep before we burn this place down.'

19

We regret to announce the passing of the dancing traffic policeman at Junction 5 Ojuẹlẹgba. Michael Ọbafẹmi (or 'MJ of Ojuẹlẹgba' as he was popularly known) was hit by a speeding vehicle on Friday morning. Eyewitnesses reported that the driver of the red Toyota Corolla did not stop.

Ọbafẹmi was loved by pedestrians and motorists alike. Many a dull traffic hour was livened watching his makossa moves, his breakdance spins or his trademark moonwalk. Whenever Ọbafẹmi was asked what he was dancing to, he would smile and say, 'Celestial music.'

Ọbafẹmi never failed in his duties, controlling the long lines of traffic even as he executed the most complex of dance moves. He is survived by a wife and two children. May the soul of MJ of Ojuẹlẹgba dance in eternity to the music of the stars.

Obituaries page, *Nigerian Journal*

Chike and Yẹmi had found work in the end. Not work that would turn them into labourers nor work that was particularly challenging but it was work nonetheless, and close enough to a military nature to be familiar.

They had been at a crossroads, waiting for a gap for pedestrians, when the traffic warden fell to the ground. Her colleague ran out of their rest hut shouting, 'Bianca o!'

Chike approached. He had a smattering of First Aid knowledge from military school, basic skills in wound dressing and artificial respiration. The male warden waved him away. 'Abeg, help us control traffic.'

He stepped into the centre of the road, self-conscious in his civilian clothes. In Ibadan every morning, at the crossroads near their flat, you would see sacrificial calabashes, spherical and mysterious, dark eggs laid overnight. Once he had kicked one open and seen in its smooth hollow a shrivelling cockscomb, a moulting chick, part down, part feathers, and a heron foot with string knotted to its pectinate claw.

Lagos was too sophisticated for such appeals to the supernatural, it seemed. Only noise and grit at the centre of this crossroads, the impatience of the queuing cars reaching him in an endless sequence of horning. He showed his palm to the moving stream. They obeyed him.

Behind him, the warden was hoisting his colleague into their rest hut. The woman was conscious but she let herself be dragged inside.

'This your uniform too tight.'

'Godwin wetin? You wan' naked me?'

'Wetin concern me with your breast? You dey squash this pikin for inside your stomach.'

'Abeg leave my cloth.'

'I've been telling you Bianca, pregnant woman is no suppose to be doing this work.'

'You nkọ? See your stomach. You no be pregnant man?'

'Bianca, go home to your husband house.'

'Abeg leave me jo. Nah who dey control traffic?'

The woman, Bianca, sat up and called to Chike, 'Oga well done o.'

He turned to acknowledge her greeting. She would have been pretty if her eyes had not been crossed, gazing at each other over her shapely nose. Either she or Godwin had freed her stomach from her uniform and now it rested taut on her knees, her belly button protruding like a small fruit.

'You're doing this work well. If to say you be police man, you can just continue make I go home and rest.'

'Tomorrow nkọ?' Godwin asked. 'If you faint again?'

'I could come tomorrow as well,' Chike said, halting one flow and beginning another. 'Or my friend over there could come.'

'Oh, you are two,' Godwin said. 'What's your name?'

'Yẹmi.'

'And you?'

'Chike.'

'O bu Igbo. Which side are you from?'

'Mbaise.'

'My wife is from there,' Godwin said.

Chike had lost track of how long the right stream had been moving. He put up a hand to halt them.

'Not yet. No, they cannot come again. Just that next time, you will give them chance for longer. Oya make those other people dey come. What work are you doing right now?' Godwin asked.

'We are job searching.'

'If person say you should come do our work, you go 'gree? We go share the salary at the end of the month. Fifty–fifty.'

105

'What will you do instead?'

'Business plenty for Lagos. Today, I suppose go port pick something but I dey here. I get wife for house. No be only yellow fever money she go use rub pancake.'

'Hmmm. Godwin! You dey give your wife money to rub pancake?'

'If I get the money, why I no go give her? My broda, you go 'gree?'

Destinies were exchanged at crossroads. This was why his mother had washed his feet in holy water and anointed them with oil when Chike told her about kicking open the calabash. You could take another man's frustrations that way. There was a thirty-five-year-old man in their block still living with his parents; it was a man like that who would fill a bowl with bird parts and place it at a crossroads. And what if the person that touched it was even worse off, Chike had asked his mother. What if he were a leper or a beggar with two stumps for arms?

'Are you a beggar?' she asked as she broke the seal of the bottle of anointing oil.

Godwin spent two hours going through the hand signals and basic tenets of their new trade. They must never step aside for a car. If the car was old, its bonnet could be banged to slow it down. New cars must never be touched. 'You touch big man car, he can come down and shoot you.'

When they heard a siren convoy, the stream must move until it passed. If they saluted the most impressive car, money might fall from its tinted windows.

'If okada no stop for you, no use force stop him. If you injure okada man, the other ones fit kill you.' Godwin hailed one of the motorcycles and climbed on its saddle.

'So what should we do to stop them?'

'If them no 'gree, comot for road. Unless you wan' die.'

20

A new report by the Lagos State Government has revealed that armed robbery has fallen by twenty per cent in the state. While met with rejoicing in many quarters, some human rights groups have blamed this drop on severe police crack-downs, with illegal arrests and suspected armed robbers kept in custody without trial. Other groups argue that the most effective form of crime fighting is job creation. One resident of the Mushin area said, 'Yes, crime has decrease [*sic*] but we need jobs. The boys in our area have reduced their stealing, so it's time for the government to increase their employment.'

Nigerian Journal

Fineboy lay sprawled in a shed with seven youths the state government would have classified as prone to crime. Cigarette smoke drifted from their midst and rap music crackled from a silver radio. His new friends were menacing enough to the skirt-suit women who clutched their handbags when they saw them but no one who had been in the creeks could take these boys seriously. Their fights were primitive, waged with knives and broken bottles. Fineboy slipped away whenever territorial disputes were brewing. He had not emerged from the Delta unscarred to have his face cut up by some amateur gangsters.

The Lagos boys had a radio. That was why he had joined them. It was radio that had led him into the creeks. Nine months ago he was sitting in a bar when he saw the CNN headline. NIGERIAN MILITANTS TAKE AMERICANS HOS-TAGE. A video played of rebels pointing guns at two white men, kneeling with their heads bowed like Catholics at mass. A man in a balaclava stepped forward and began to list demands in a gruff voice as if unaware the tape would be broadcast to the world. The group needed a spokesperson. Someone with an accent white people could understand.

That was when he had the idea. He would go to the creeks and offer a commander his services on the condition he be identified as Golden Voice each time he spoke, no fool-ish militant name like Foodbasket or Breadboy. After a few months of gaining global notoriety, he would seek amnesty, renounce militancy and become a radio star.

How was he to know that in his entire time in the bush, there would be a drought of kidnappable white oil workers? Instead days in the creeks with little food, running from a Nigerian army whose size seemed to have doubled overnight. They had managed to kidnap a Nigerian engineer but when no one showed interest, they released him.

Fineboy had seen the disbelief on Chike's face when he said he was a presenter and yet he had worked for free in a radio station, had sat in a booth with headphones pressed tightly on his ears, a foam-padded mic before him, a produ-cer behind a glass window, counting down silently with his fingers.

He had been looking for job vacancy signs when he heard the major key of a jingle and saw the group crowded round the radio. He asked for directions to a made-up street and then squatted to hear what the airwaves in Lagos had to offer. The format was basic. Phone in and narrate a story about a bad date. Caller fifteen would win cinema tickets for two.

The boys were trying their luck, passing a small Nokia around, the owner of the phone whining, 'Don't finish my credit.'

'We've got a caller on the line. Hello. It's DY on Flavour FM's "Have Your Say". To whom am I speaking?'

''Ello am I on hair?'

'Yes you are. Tell us your name and where you're calling from.'

'My name is Wasiu and I am calling from Onigbongbo.'

'So, Wasiu, please tell our listeners about your bad date.'

'Yes, one girl I am dating, her name is Ramota. I took her to restaurant and she want to order everything on the menu. So I tell her, Ramota please I am not a millionaire. That is how she look me up and down—'

'Hello? Hello? I think we lost Wasiu. Just when I was looking forward to hearing what Ramota had to say. Guys, if there's anything I've learnt about a Lagos babe, it's: don't tell her what to order. We've got another caller on the line.'

They never got through. If Lagos was anything like Bayelsa, the fifteenth caller was a friend of the presenter, maybe a girl this DY wanted to impress or a cousin he owed a favour.

The leader of the group was a quiet boy who asked why he was back two days later.

'I came to listen to the radio.'

'You are sounding like an Americanah today. How come?'

'I'm training to be a radio presenter. I used to do some studio work back home in Port Harcourt.'

'Oya present for us.'

'Good evening. You're listening to Rivers Radio at 5 p.m. The one-stop station for cool, smooth, relaxing tunes.'

It was a flawed demonstration. He had overly stressed the first syllable of 'Rivers' and the tunes had come out as 'toons' but the boys were easily impressed.

'My guy, you for go radio.'

'Shet. It's like Dan Davies is here.'

'Abeg teach me.'

After that he had no problem dropping in for research. They let him flick through stations undisturbed, unless there was a match. Many of them wanted to be entertainers of some sort: rappers, singers, comedians. Sometimes he helped with their diction. The lessons had not progressed beyond swear words.

'Shit not shet.'

'It's not ferk you. The "u" is sounded like the "u" in um-brella.'

'Not humbrella. Um-brella.'

One day he had come to their meeting place and the shack with its bare earth floor and wooden poles was empty. It had taken patience and a pack of cigarettes to discover their other base, an incomplete building on a cul-de-sac: a roofed bungalow with spaces cut out for doors and windows. Plastic sheets were tacked to the empty squares and raffia mats were spread on the floor. It was surprisingly neat, their small stash of illegal material piled in one corner and covered with a blanket. Knives, a polythene bag of marijuana and a brief glimpse of what seemed to be the butt of a pistol, before their leader twitched the blanket over it.

From then, he had begun seeing the abandoned buildings, his eyes now opened to the unfinished structures that lay all over the city. They were run down, their walls crumbling into grit, but they would be better than living under the bridge. Most were already occupied. He came upon a mad man sleeping in one, stark naked, his locs reaching down to his thighs. The dry walls and sturdy roof were almost worth chasing him away for. Yet, even if he succeeded, the man would return. Mad people in Nigeria were lucidly territorial.

When he found a suitable place, he and the others would move there. They did not trust him, he knew, but they were his last connection to refinement. Without the soldiers, Oma and even Isoken when she could be coaxed into talking, he would sink to the level of these youths, his accent making him a one-eyed king in their toutdom.

21

For sale, four bedroom, four toilet detached house in Gbagada. Starting price N20,000,000. For details call Aliu, 080236578991.

Classified advertisement, Nigerian Journal

The others did not know what Fineboy did with his time. He left in the morning and returned at night. Not even the soldiers would ask. There was a recklessness that clung to him, a swagger of an old militant life that dulled curiosity. 'Just don't bring trouble here,' Chike heard Oma mutter one evening when the boy came back reeking of smoke.

If only they could find a small place to live. Just one room would suffice but rent was pegged at mocking prices. For a few square feet in a slum, fifty thousand a year and a payment of at least six months in advance. Where would he find that on his halved salary? Chike felt Godwin had cheated him that day. He felt it strongly enough to challenge him over the seven thousand naira he had placed in his hand at the end of his first month as a traffic warden.

'The money is not complete. It should be ten thousand, half of twenty.'

'My brother, it's twenty they write on the paper but it's

only fourteen they give me yesterday. Sometimes they can give you the complete salary. Sometimes they'll remove some money, add it to next month's own. That's why it's so difficult to live in this Lagos. You always have to be doing something on the side.'

He had wanted to squeeze Godwin's neck and feel his trachea crumple under his grip. Instead, an hour later, he held up a queue until the driver who had beeped at him slid down his window and began to scream abuse.

'Keep shouting,' Chike said. 'You'll get where you're going on time.'

It was the aggression of the downtrodden, petty but briefly satisfying.

He had a taxonomical tree he was always adding branches to, detailed mental classifications for the other road users, an urban Linnaeus, ordering the world. Pedestrians and motorists were migratory, passing briefly to destinations unknown, delineated by their wealth, the comfort in which they travelled, their relations with the fixtures on the road. Fixtures like the beggars who dealt in blessings, mumbling prayers at their customers as they shuffled through traffic. Hustlers who sold all that was conceivable and some things that were not. The gawkers, waiting for an incident, on hand to form a crowd and proffer expertise on every calamity possible.

The road always smelt of exhaust, a lace of petrol on the atmosphere, smog in each breath. Standing in the open, sometimes Chike would grow afraid. Whenever soldiers drove down his road, casually armed with rifles, clad from head to toe in the uniform he had worn for so long, he would turn his face, breathing shallowly until they were gone. Until, tired of his fear, he had saluted a general's convoy. The jeeps, the sedans, the vans, they all drove past and no one returned his salute. He was far beneath their notice. The transformation was complete.

Their salary meant they could now relieve the women. Fineboy was the only question mark. What the boy added he could not say. He ate their meals with an ever-diminishing stock of table manners. At breakfast, his spoon would corner the largest egg. Come evening, the softest piece of yam would also make its way to his plate. And the boy was proud. Any hints that he should go caused offence but he was never offended enough to leave. He would list his usefulness to the group. 'I'm the one that got us to stay in this place for so cheap.'

'I'm the one who borrowed the stove we are using to cook from Iya Bọsẹ.'

I'm the one, I'm the one, I'm the one.

He was coming towards them now, walking at a pace that was almost a run.

'Brother Chike. You have to come with me now.'

'What's the matter?'

'A place. I've found to stay.'

'What kind of place?'

'Quick. Someone can enter before we get back.'

'You'll have to wait for the women to gather their things.'

'No time for that. You must come, then I'll leave you there and come back for everybody.'

It did not sound promising. Clearly no formal arrangement had been made with the landlord. How many others were racing there even now?

'If you don't want to come, I'll go and stay by myself.'

Finally a chance to be rid of the boy. And if he was telling the truth? What harm would it do to go with him? Should it be a lie, he could confront him away from the group and convince him not to come back, maybe even pay him to go away.

'Alright. Let me finish my water.'

Their destination was two danfo journeys and a ten-minute walk away. They passed a main entrance, lit harshly, with security guards checking cars as they drove in.

'We're not going through there,' Fineboy said.

He followed the boy to a side street where there was a man-sized gap in the perimeter wall.

'We have to go like this, just tonight. From tomorrow we can be walking through the main gate like everyone else.'

It was like Fineboy to go through back doors. They slipped through the hole and into a residential estate, the type that rich people parcelled themselves into all over the country. They passed mansions built close to their walls, satellite dishes growing like tumours on their roofs. Some streets were well lit and wide, paved with smooth tarmac. Others were little more than alleys, dark and lined with weeds. It was to one of these that Fineboy led him. On the plot was an incomplete building, falling apart as they watched it. No roof, no windows, no doors.

'You want us to live here?'

Chike saw the remains of a chain and padlock on the ground, discarded like a broken bracelet.

'Abandoned property is for anybody that finds it. Check

it anywhere in the world. Because there's no roof, I came here thinking I would find something uninhabitable but boy was I wrong.'

A small swamp had grown in what would have been a hallway and he stepped carefully after Fineboy.

'Then I walked into a side room and saw this.'

With a sense of drama, Fineboy paused over the metal opening, an iron door sunk in the ground. It groaned when he lifted it, the hinge rusted beyond redemption. Cut into the ground were steps descending into a black hole. Chike hung back, dawdling close to fresh air. The lights came on.

'A fully furnished two-bedroom basement apartment for us to live in.'

The boy stood in the middle of a parlour, done up to showroom standard. A small herd had been slaughtered to make the leather set that took up most of the room: mothers and calves stitched together for sofas and cushions, settee and footrest. What happened to the men who laid these carpets and hung the wall paintings, dark landscapes and bright market scenes, abstract women without faces, men with no eyes?

'We have to leave. Whoever built this can't be up to any good above ground.'

'Come on. It's been abandoned for years. The TV, when was the last time you saw one so old? Even look at the newspapers on the shelf. 1994. This one 1993. The owner isn't coming back.'

Everywhere Fineboy touched, the shape of his palm remained in the dust.

'Honest people don't build such places.'

'Dishonest people don't need them any more. Everybody knows where all the top militant guys live in Yenagoa. It's small boys like me that have to run from the police.'

The place would need cleaning and airing. Even then, the smell of damp clothes might never leave.

'Let me show you around. Mind your step. A bulb blew when I put on the light and there's still glass on the floor. Kitchen to the left, fully equipped, stove and all that. Toilet here. Bathroom there. Separate which I think is better. The flush is still working. There must be a borehole somewhere on the compound with pipes and everything underground.'

Fineboy demonstrated, flooding the bowl with water. Oma would like that very much.

'I'll go and bring the others.'

'Wait,' Chike said. 'How did you find it?'

'Some guys like this, they live in an abandoned house. When I saw their house, I started looking for incomplete buildings.'

'Which guys? They know of this place?'

'Heck no. Let me go get the others. It's getting late.'

There was something of the miraculous in this, a heady coincidence that threatened to sweep away all rationality. Today he had wished or hoped or prayed fervently for a house and now here was one, unoccupied. To think Fineboy had been the instrument of this. He felt chastised as he picked up a broom lying behind the kitchen door and began to sweep the parlour.

22

Nigerians are the happiest people in the world. We suffer and smile, we dance as we weep, we sing in the deepest mourning, but even the *Homo nigerianicus*, joyful and ebullient as he is, gets depressed.

Extract from 'Health Matters', *Nigerian Journal*

Oma kept the bloodied cloth that had put an end to the question of a pregnancy, carrying it in a plastic bag from the bridge to their new home. She could not bring herself to wash the flannel. The blood had turned a rust brown, a smear that might hold cells, the building blocks of what would have become the organs and limbs and eyelashes of her child. The phantom baby had saved her. Without that wave of nausea, she might well be in IK's house, driven there by those first rough days under the bridge.

Life there had been a battle. Hygiene was not an option. Combing her hair was compulsory. Even spraying perfume became a symbolic ritual, every puff a banner unfurled against decline. Only boredom could not be kept at bay. Most days, after she had performed her ablutions and prepared breakfast, there was nothing else for her to do.

She was woken early in the morning by the cries of the bus

conductors, ringing out like matins: Ojuẹlẹgba, Ojota, Ikeja, Agege, Iyanopaja, Ọbalẹnde. She wished she were brave enough to climb into a danfo and discover a destination but she was not sure she would be able to find her way back to the bridge. She had never been so close to poverty, so close to beggars and open-air defecation. She was shocked by how unpitiable these beggars were, how shrewd and businesslike, how the blind never missed their change; how the woman in a wheelchair carried a baby that never grew older, never cried, never ate. She had shared her suspicions with Chike and he had laughed.

'She can probably walk. I dare you. Tomorrow, run up to her chair and push her out of it.'

She looked forward to his return. Once she had sketched on thicker eyebrows and coloured her lips pink, wiping off the effect before he could see it. There would be young women on his road, strutting around in their brazen, tight clothes, garish Lycra clinging to their bums and thighs. She couldn't bring herself to ask how old he was. Certainly she was walking when he was born, probably talking and making inroads into multiplication. They spoke sometimes of his mother who had raised him and cosseted him and of whom Oma would think, if she were alive, this would be a very difficult mother-in-law.

Some days, after she had waited for hours, Chike would return only to bury his face in his Bible. It happened often enough for her to grow jealous of this book that everyone had read in their childhood. It was useful for learning your left from right but it was nothing to burrow into like an ant disappearing into a hole.

'Read it to me,' she said one evening.

'What?'

'What you're reading that's making you smile.'

'It's just something I didn't expect to find here.'

'Yes?'

'Your stature is like a palm tree and your breasts are like its clusters. I say I will climb the palm tree and lay hold of its fruit.'

And since that evening when he had read those words as if speaking without the proxy of a page, she had asked him to read to her. It reminded her of the times her father would take them outside, nights when the electricity was gone and the room she shared with her brother was too hot to sleep in. Her father had a book, *The Stargazer's Companion to a Midnight Sky*, a slim volume with a forbidden chapter on astrology blacked out in felt pen. Because of her father, Oma knew that the Pleiades were seven slender sisters in Greece, and for the Hausa, Kaza Maiyaya were a mother hen and her brood, and the Japanese turned the constellation into a Subaru, a sturdy motor she had once imagined cruised down the Milky Way at night. When their eyes finally came back to earth, her father would say, 'Only a fool says there's no God.'

Gradually the others would stop and listen when Chike read in his low, steady voice. It became an evening ritual they carried on even now that they finally had this home, this extravagance of kitchen, toilet and foam mattresses. She had survived without things she had once thought essential. The wastefulness of a toaster, an entire lump of metal, fashioned into hidden wires and glowing filaments, just for bronzing bread. An Etruscan jug, its handle bent in the shape of an ear, its body painted with the most fantastic village scene, all for pouring water, when water could be drunk straight out of a plastic bag.

She had been a kitchen worshipper once, a nun in the order of the stove. She knew now that the pillars of her old life were decorative columns, supporting nothing. Yet she gasped when she opened a cupboard in their new home and saw a grater, shaped like a small pagoda, with four different hole sizes dotting its sides. She grasped the ends of a rolling pin and ran it up a wall, imagining a lump of dough, spread flat under its pressure. She did not realise till then how much she had missed her kitchen.

Since they'd moved into the basement two weeks ago, the group had been split into male and female, and Oma was stuck with the density of Isoken's mood. The girl never greeted in the morning; complained Oma's perfume was too strong; left the room pointedly if Oma began to sing; and now she had stopped going to work.

For the last five days, Isoken had lain on their bed without moving. Oma, impatient with her inertia at first, had grown frightened after forty-eight hours had passed and Isoken had gotten up only to shuffle to the toilet and back to the depression that was beginning to form in the mattress. Oma had begun bringing food and water on a tray. Isoken drank the water but touched very little of the food.

'Eat. Please,' Oma said in the tone you would use for a child.

'I'm not hungry,' Isoken replied, turning her face to the wall. Oma placed the tray on the bed beside her but she did not leave as before.

*

'Eat. Please,' that woman said, standing over Isoken in a manner she found distinctly unpleasant.

'I'm not hungry.'

'You haven't taken your bath for five days,' Oma said.

'Is that what is disturbing you?'

Isoken's mother would have slapped her by now, would have dragged her out of the bed and flung her into the bathroom, not leaving until she washed herself clean. But Oma was not her mother, did not share even the remotest similarity with the woman who had breastfed her through infancy and disciplined her through adolescence. Spare the rod and spoil the child. If she had grown up with just her father, she would have been rotten now, decayed from the inside, sprouting mould on her soul.

Isoken's father had always been a little in awe of the daughter who knew so many long, inconsequential words. He would have wept to see her handling other people's hair for a living. He had taught her his trade so she could make pocket money at university, not so her life could shrink to weaving evenly spaced cornrows and twisting a million identical braids. If only her family hadn't gone to Bayelsa.

They had gone searching for the impossible, a herbal cure for breast cancer. Isoken had told her parents of chemotherapy and radiotherapy, treatments she had read about online, but for once the string of syllables made no impression on her father.

'Those ones are for white people,' he said.

In the evenings her mother would go off with a group

of village women. She would return smelling of traditional brew, dark liquids stored in glass bottles, opaque and unknowable. Quack medicine, Isoken had told her parents. Unsterilised. Poisonous. But they believed in it and her mother swore she was getting better.

'What happened?' Oma said, interrupting her thoughts. 'Why did you come back screaming that day?'

'Can't you leave somebody alone?'

'No I cannot. Because if you die here, it is us the police will come and carry. What will we do with your dead body? Do I look like a gravedigger to you?'

The matter was almost too small to mention. Walking to the bus stop, a man had whistled at her, then called after her, then followed her, talking of friendship and wanting to get to know her. She ignored him until he took her hand.

'I screamed and ran back here. That's all,' Isoken said.

'Was there something that happened before that made you react like that? Let me go and get you some tissue.'

'My husband used to beat me,' Oma said when she returned.

'You're married?'

'Am I unmarriageable? I had quite a few toasters when I was your age.'

'I didn't mean—'

'That day we all met on the bus I was running away from him. I don't know how I stayed for so long. Only Chike knows about it. Oya, what happened to you?'

'I can't say it.'

'Say it out loud so it doesn't have power over you again. My husband used to beat me. I only married him because I was afraid of being a spinster for the rest of my life. Say it.'

'I was attacked by some men. They tried to rape me. I can't forget. I've tried everything but I can't forget. Semen everywhere. On my face. On my stomach. In my ears. I can still feel it.'

Isoken's mother had slapped her once for crying on a bus. Tears were precious water, only for family members to see. If outsiders saw your tears, they would drink of your sorrow. And who was her family now?

'Just cry it out,' Oma said. 'There's no shame. You know, for weeks after I left IK's house, I will be wiping my face, or combing my hair, and I will just feel his hands closing on my neck. Until one day I said, enough. He did not kill you. Even now, when I feel that thing rising, I say to it, "Oma is not dead." I say it in Igbo. Oma aka anwuro. Isoken, did you hear me? You are not dead.'

'Nobody will want me.'

Oma took her hand and dragged it down from her face, almost as roughly as her mother would have done. The force would leave scratches.

'You listen to me. You are the one that decides if people will want you or not. Every day you wake up, you decide. Eat your beans or else Fineboy will have it. That boy is too greedy.'

*

The girl was eating again, Oma told Chike when he returned. Whatever wall that stood between Isoken and Oma must have been dissolved in an afternoon of feminine

125

solidarity. She had even woven Oma's hair into black lines that bent and twisted on her head. Isoken would not join their evening meal but she had eaten most of her lunch and fallen asleep afterwards.

'Thank you,' Chike said to Oma. 'I was worried we might have to take her to the hospital.'

'She has gone through a lot. You knew of it?'

'Some, but it is not the kind of thing a young girl can discuss with a man. This hair suits you.'

'Isoken made it. It's time for our daily reading.'

Chike did not know how he had come to this evening ritual that had turned him into a sort of priest for the group. He was the doubter, the one who would place his hands in the side and probe for scars. But to Oma, this nightly reading knitted them closer. It took nothing from him to read from a text he read with pleasure and scepticism. At first, he had jumped from passage to passage looking for the credible. One day, a sermon on the mount. The next a parable from Luke. Until Oma had said, 'Read it in order. The way you're doing it is confusing.'

So he chose the book of John and every night they marched verse by verse, chapter by chapter. Tonight, they had camped on absurdity. It was the story of the feeding of the five thousand, a tale so bloated with exaggeration the kernels of reality had long been lost. At the end he felt it necessary to state his position.

'This is one of those stories that makes the Bible so unbelievable.'

'Why?'

It was Fineboy asking.

'Well, how can five loaves multiply into five thousand?'

'Is it not a miracle?'

In university, Chike had run up against this blind faith in the student pastors, crusaders against the gentle iniquities of his first year – alcohol, miniskirts – and too often silent on the grand evils: the cult boys who would kill you if you stood up to them, the lecturers who failed students who didn't sleep with them.

'It is not such a big miracle,' Fineboy continued. 'I used to go to my grandma's farm in the village. We planted maize there. You put four seeds in the ground and when you came back a few months later, if the soil was good and there was enough rain, a few seeds had multiplied into thousands.'

It was obvious once Fineboy said it. There was an agrarian rhythm to the gospels he had never noticed. Much about seeds and sowing, harvests and threshing, vines and branches: imagery that eluded an urban Ibadan boy like Chike.

He had walked in his first garden when he was ten. His mother was invited to a Christmas party at her boss's home. His mother, he later felt, had been wasted in her secretarial job, but back then he had thought her fulfilled with her shoulder pads and wavy hair, styled every weekend in a salon. At the Christmas party, he had looked at the lumpen managers' wives and thought her the most glamorous of them all.

Chike had tried to befriend the other children but even then, the offspring of managers knew well not to mix with a secretary's son. He had wandered off on his own, taking the gravel paths that wound through the grass until he came upon the iroko, a strange choice for a house garden, with its trunk many metres wide and branches that spanned an airplane's wings, their leaves blocking out the sky. Many hours later, the search party of guests had found him cross-legged under the tree, serene as the young Buddha.

It was an incident his mother recounted often, a favourite episode in the legend of Chike. He had walked at nine months; read by three; won prizes in his military school. He would do all that her husband had not lived to do, go where he had not gone, win what he had not won.

By all accounts his father had been an exceptional officer marked for great things. The accident that killed him at twenty-eight had been caused by witchcraft, an evil spell that sent the bus spinning off the road. His mother was the chief suspect.

Her in-laws had shaved her, scraping the stubble with a blade until her head was as bald and bright as a light bulb. Her hair would never grow back as long and thick. They had put her in a room with his father's body, badly embalmed and leaking water. She went through every funeral rite but she would not allow Chike's uncles to touch her savings.

'The bank let me use one of their lawyers for free. Mr Oketade made sure the lawyer was always there when your father's brothers came.'

Mr Oketade was the man whose garden he had walked in as a child, a man who oversaw five bank branches and for whom his mother typed letters and jotted down memos. It was an exceptional kindness, the gratuitous use of a company lawyer. Kindness to a widow, for merit in heaven, or kindness for favours here on earth. Later, when he was older,

Chike wondered who had given his mother the bottles of European perfumes that stood like glass sculptures on her dressing table: the leaning column of Kenzo, the striped bust of Jean Paul Gaultier.

She had vowed never to remarry. A new husband would hang Chike's father's pictures in the toilet. A new husband would be jealous of Chike, frightened by how deeply she placed her ambitions in him. Top ten per cent at the Nigerian Military School. Upper second-class degree from university.

Regulating Fineboy's radio, drawing up a dishwashing rota, monitoring Isoken's mood, directing traffic and quarrelling with other road users: that was his life now. He had fought a stranger yesterday, a brief flurry of fists and knuckles, before Yemi separated them. The man had been holding a woman against a wall, dousing her in water. She was gasping, screaming, struggling with her eyes closed. He had pulled the man off her and their fight began, unevenly matched, Chike at least a head taller and fifteen kilograms heavier.

'Leave him alone,' the girl screamed until Yemi arrived to pull them apart. People had stopped to watch, pointing at the traffic warden disgracing himself in uniform.

He had misread the scene. The man and the woman were together. This savage trapping against the wall, pinned like a butterfly, half drowning under a litre of Ragolis: it was a way of marking her birthday, another year commemorated with a baptism. He knew the ritual, common in military school amongst boys but he had not seen it with adults, and never between a man and a woman. He apologised.

'I thought she was in trouble,' Chike said.

The woman turned her back to him and wiped her lover's face. Her handkerchief came away with blood spots. Her hair dripped down her soaked T-shirt.

'You need new work,' Yẹmi observed as they walked back to their post. It had been dangerously unmanned for those minutes. 'Your mind is not here. If you dey concentrate, how your eye go reach dat side?'

23

The Economic and Financial Crimes Commission is offering a N10 million reward for reliable information on the
whereabouts of Chief Rẹmi Sandayọ, former Minister of
Education. He was last seen in Maitama, Abuja, at 5 p.m. on
March 22nd. A recent picture is pasted below.

Advertisement, Nigerian Journal

Over a month later, everyone had settled into a groove and a
rhythm. Fineboy alone was without a pattern. He stayed in
the flat some days flicking through a limited range of channels. Afternoon television was dull: Nollywood and pastors.
He listened to their sermons once in a while. He preferred
the American-sounding preachers. They paced up and down
large stages, walking kilometres as they moved from one end
to the other, thundering and whispering into cordless microphones, their gesticulations framed by Italian suits, their
steps encased in Italian shoes. Pastor was good business in
Lagos. Certainly more lucrative than radio presenting, yet
the further his dream moved from him, the more desperately
he desired it. It seemed a lifetime ago that he had sat in a
booth in front of a padded microphone.

He had borrowed some money from Chike to buy a silver

transistor radio. It was a small but powerful device that picked up waves far flung as China. He took it with him wherever he went, draining the battery on his wanderings round the city. He did not like to stay in the flat for too long. He was always in Oma's way.

And he would not think of going to Isoken. She had begun making hair beside a supermarket in the estate. Hair Designz the business was called. He had even made a sign for her, large colourful letters on slick laminated cardboard that drew customers. And yet he could never be sure with her. Some days she would greet him in the morning. On others he did not exist.

He walked around the estate, stopping in front of mansions that struck him, gazing at their pillars and arches and small windows set close together. They had robbed homes like this in Bayelsa, when Godspower's funds were running low. The guards at the estate gates knew him now and greeted him when he passed. They assumed he was a poor relative of a family that lived in the estate. Sometimes he gave them money. Very small, trifling amounts that might be useful one day. He read for free the newspapers of vendors he had made friends with, turning the pages slowly, careful not to leave any marks. He had not returned to visit the touts since they had moved underground. They were useless to him now that he had his own radio.

The soldiers complained it disturbed their sleep at night so he had taken to listening in the parlour, falling asleep with the presenters still talking and waking to discover his battery dead. That night, he fell asleep stretched on the floor, twitching the radio to off just before he closed his eyes.

He woke to the rasp of something heavy being dragged down the steps. He lay still, breathing evenly. To rush to the stairs was to dare his strength against someone who might be armed. To remain on the floor was to lose his surprise. Move like a snake, he heard Godspower's voice saying to him. Keep your stomach on the ground and move like a snake.

*

'Thief!'

Chike heard in his sleep, the word mingling with his dream. The sound of something falling pushed him fully into consciousness. He rushed into the parlour, his hand running over the walls for the switch. He saw Fineboy bent over a man, ready to strike another blow.

'Release him.'

The boy stepped back and allowed the stranger to struggle to his feet.

'You raised your hand to hit me? Who are you?' he asked Chike. 'And what are you doing in my house?'

Like a thief in the night, the owner had returned and they were at a loss. It was what they had all feared, despite Fineboy's reassurances. The man was simply dressed in a starched cotton up-and-down. Understated but rich, down to the slim gold chain that hung close to his thick neck.

'I said who are you?'

'Nah who dey make noise,' Yẹmi said from behind Chike.

'Who else is there?'

'Good evening, sir,' Chike said.

'Don't greet me. Why are you greeting me? Who are you and what are you doing in my house?'

The man was shouting, almost hysterically. The door of the women's room opened.

'Don't come out,' Chike turned and said softly but the man heard.

'There are more of you? What is this?'

'Sir, if you will let me explain—'

'Save it for the police.'

'Please, that will not be necessary. We'll be leaving now.'

'No,' Fineboy said. 'Let him call the police.'

'Shut up,' Chike said. 'We saw this place had been empty for a long time. We haven't taken anything.'

'Leave now. Just get out.'

'Call the police,' Fineboy said again. 'I've seen you in the papers. The Economic and Financial Crimes Commission will be glad to know of your whereabouts, Chief Sandayọ.'

The effect of that name was immediate. The man grasped the handles of his chequered bags and turned to leave but he was too slow for Fineboy. The boy tore a bag from his grip, unzipped and upended it. Crisp dollar notes spilled onto the floor.

*

Fineboy saw in that moment the colour of oil when it lay freshly spilt on water. It was a black that caught the sun and multicolours would appear, the white bellies of dead fish floating like stars in a rainbow constellation. Sitting low in the gunboats, speeding through deserted villages, the creeks had entered him, the grievances of those muggy torrents sloshing into him unawares. A mop leant against the wall where Oma had left it. He took it, feeling the heft of the wooden stick in his hands.

'Have you ever paid a visit to the Niger Delta?' Fineboy said.

'Yes. A beautiful place. Working with government for more development. I'll pay. How much do you want? All of you.'

'Stand back,' Chike said to Fineboy.

'I don't take orders from you.'

'Stand back.'

If not for men like these, Fineboy knew he would be a star, his talent recognised, his diction, his rhythm, his flow, making room for him in the radio industry. But this was no country for his ability.

'Stand back, for the last time, Fineboy.'

He turned his back on the soldier, raising the stick to strike. Chike kicked his legs and Fineboy's knees buckled, pitching him to the ground.

'I give the orders in this group. Don't forget that. Now stand up and do as I say.'

Chike turned to face the minister.

'How did you get here?'

'You're questioning me?'

'Search him for car keys.'

Chief Sandayọ tried to beat Fineboy's hands away but he elbowed him and he subsided. The keys were in his left pocket along with a wallet, bulky with cash.

'Take off your shoes and your socks,' Chike said.

Chief Sandayọ hesitated.

'He can do it for you.'

The man slipped off his shoes and then one sock. He held his right foot awkwardly.

'I have a wound there.'

'Let us see.'

He slid off the sock gently and showed them the bandage, wound round his foot.

'Put your shoes back on. Yẹmi, go to the kitchen and move everything that can be used as a weapon. We are performing a citizen's arrest. Your wallet and those two bags will be confiscated until further notice.'

24

'For a dream cometh through the multitude of business,' or so Solomon says in the book of Ecclesiastes. Some dreams should be binned once you wake up. Their root is last night's supper or yesterday's quarrel. Some dreams, on the other hand, are glimpses of eternity, of the supernatural, of the world to come. To the men and women such dreams come to, arise like King Nebuchadnezzar and seek your Daniel.

Pastor Kọmọlafẹ, religious page, *Nigerian Journal*

That night, Chike dreamt of his former commanding officer. The Colonel was standing in a river, submerged to his knees, a cutlass in his hand, hacking at the muddy surface. There was something in the water, something bleeding each time he struck. When the river was dyed red, Benatari straightened and held out the cutlass to him.

'Take the money.'

It ended like cheap Nollywood cinematography: desperately in need of a sequel to join the frayed ends. To share the money amongst themselves would be a form of resource redistribution, a slogan chanted by every dissatisfied group in the country, including the militants to whom Fineboy had so recently belonged. And to perform a citizen's arrest, what did that signify? He had heard the phrase in university from a law student who joked they should perform one on their vice chancellor. Now they had arrested this chief, what would they do with him? Try him? Had he become a Benatari, judge and jury? And what sentence? Death?

He relieved Yẹmi of his watch at 4 a.m. The private was already asleep but so was the suspect, lying stretched out on his back with his fists clenched over his stomach. That was another jargon he had learnt from the law undergraduates: suspect until proven guilty, even when caught in the act. He settled on the sofa and brought out his Bible.

He soon put it away again. His mind was too restless for reading. What would they do with this Chief Sandayọ? What would they do with his money? There were many things he could think to do with money. A house above ground and a car to move through Lagos with dignity and clothes that did not come already worn by Europeans, flakes of their skin lurking in the seams.

Yet he was no thief. He had never wanted these things enough to steal for them or even do a job he did not like for them. He had known his chances of wealth in the army were slim and yet he had served willingly in defence of Nigeria, his large, fragile country.

And yet ... *Money answers all things*, said the Bible held between his thumb and index finger.

How to make something of yourself in Lagos?

Money.

How to marry a woman used to finer things?

Money.

To get any respect in this city?

Money.

It all came down to the money that Chief Sandayọ had brought into their flat.

*

The recently deposed Minister of Education, Ręmi Sandayọ, woke and saw the face of a man, partly lit and pressed close to a book. It was the face of a bookish man, his small eyes peering at the text, his forehead wide and sloping into the shadows. It was the man who had seized his belongings.

'What is your name?'

'I did not know you were awake.'

'I'm not used to sleeping on a couch. What do you want, Mr . . . ?'

'My name is Chike.'

'Tell me what you want, Chike.'

'What was the money for?'

'I owe you no explanations. You are the ones who have broken into my house. How much? Ten per cent of what is in those bags. Just give me my car keys. I will drop you anywhere you want in Lagos tonight.'

'You think I'm desperate, Mr Sandayọ?'

'*Chief* Sandayọ.'

Sandayọ's year in Abuja had shown him that everyone had their price. The question was in what currency. It was his paintings that had trapped him. Collector's items, each one. Sandayọ had driven them from Abuja to his house in Ikire. Then he had dawdled, planning his next move, reeling from the audacity of what he had done. Days of indecision passed until, switching on the television, he saw himself on the news. He had put on weight in Abuja. He could not leave until that smiling, doughnut-cheeked image of himself disappeared from the media.

There were worse places to be a fugitive. His arrival in Ikire at night passed unnoticed. He had not been home in years. No one was expecting him. The mansion built to flaunt his success was empty and haunted by his late wife. He did not believe in ghosts. Funkẹ was either in heaven or nowhere, but in this dead house they had once occupied she appeared vividly to him, in all stages of her life. Young and supple, as on their wedding night, stern and hard, as in her later years.

It was the loneliness of the place that made him feel that she had just left when he entered a room, or even that some essence of her remained, watching him. She had spoken to him. Not audibly but as ghosts would speak if they existed, bypassing voice boxes and talking straight into the mind. 'What have you gotten yourself into?' his late wife asked. When it was the young Funkẹ speaking, the question was said with a lilting mischief, and when it was the old Funkẹ, who had soaked herself in the vinegar of prayer meetings and night vigils, the question was interrogatory with the edge of a police investigation.

He waited it out, with Funkẹ's ghost, until news of him was stale. He switched cars, taking the newest model in his garage, and began his escape to Ghana. He could have made the trip in one go, speeding through the night until he got to Accra, but the unrelenting line of traffic had tired him. He could not go to his main house but he remembered this hideout, built in the eighties on Francis's advice at the height of the YPC's politicisation.

He wondered how these squatters had looked past the crumbling building and discovered his flat. No matter. He would find their price and currency. Till then, he had his phones clipped to the band of his boxers and his passport wrapped under the bandage on his foot. There was no rush. Whoever was looking for him would be searching outside the country now, Barbados, the Caymans, Dubai, scouring beaches instead of abandoned properties in Lagos.

25

Q. What do you call an honest Lagosian?
A. Dead.

Riddles and jokes page, *Nigerian Journal*

Chike was hot. Underground, the only breeze came from the fan blades, dead since 5 a.m. when the power went out. He hated the heat and the claustrophobia of the flat, the sense of entrapment when he stood in the dark tunnel that joined the rooms, the blinding effect of sunlight as he emerged from their hole each morning like a subterranean rat.

What did Chike want, the Chief had asked. Nothing. Everything. He was tired of running the question through his mind. His shirt was off when Oma walked into the parlour. 'Kedu?' she said, pointing her torch in his direction, the beam striking him in the chest and moving away until it rested neutrally at his feet. 'Is that the man from last night?' She was whispering. He answered her normally.

'Yes. When everyone is awake, we'll decide what to do with him.'

'Na wa. I'll start making breakfast. It may be a bit cold by the time the others are up but since I'm awake I thought let me just do it.'

'I'll come with you.'

At first, he watched as she chopped onions into white chips that stung his eyes. Beyond dishwashing, he had never thought to join her in the kitchen. Hot food appeared and he ate with the others, like Oma was their mother or their slave.

'You don't always have to do the cooking,' he said. 'Or the cleaning for that matter. We should share things more.'

'I'm OK. Housework was my life in Yenagoa. I was good at it. Matching hand towels, scented candles, soap dishes in every toilet, complete china set with gold-rimmed teacups and pink flowers on the saucers. From when I was young, if anything is out of place, my mum will say, "Is this how you will keep your husband's house?"'

'Well, I am not your husband and this is not his house. Please let me help you. Even if it's just today.'

She gave him a knife and a tuber the length of his arm.

'Peel all of it. You know how much Fineboy eats and now we have an extra person.'

As he skinned the yam of its bark, he watched her. She was wearing a wrapper and nothing under, her arms free and exposed, her chest bare to her neck. He wanted to stroke her collarbone that rose in a smooth ridge from her shoulders. She had lost weight, not unattractively. Her buttocks still swelled under her wrapper but the bones in her face had become more pronounced. As she sang softly, changing the shape of her mouth, her profile tautened and relaxed. She came to stand next to him. He was aware of the thin cotton of her wrapper.

'Let me help you finish off.'

He had been working slowly on purpose. They had not spoken so intimately since that first night on the bus to

Lagos. She began slicing the yam into sticks and he saw the thick gold band on her left finger.

'You still wear your ring?'

'Oh. I wear it whenever I go out. People respect you more.'

She took it off and put it on the counter.

'I miss my house. I spent so long choosing the curtains. Dark green brocade. Very heavy material. Curtains for an invalid. Once you closed them, even in the afternoon, it was like night.'

'What else do you miss?'

'Being somebody's wife. Don't look so shocked. The difference between the way my relatives treated me before and after I married IK. I used to live with my brother when I was single. Every day his wife will send their daughter to sing that children's song for me: "When will you marry?" You know it?'

'No.'

'You skip and at the same time you sing: "When will you marry, this year or next year? January, February, March," and so on. And then from the moment I got engaged to IK, this rich man that worked in an oil company, my status completely changed. Well, there's only so much you can take from a man, whether he has money or not.'

She raised her hand to her cheek and wiped it, the knife still in her grip.

'You're very special, with or without IK.'

'Everybody is special. No two human beings alike.'

Deflection was the outer defence of the insecure, the brusque putting aside of approval. Except he did not think Oma was insecure. Just married, the ring on the counter, a circular, metal warning. Outside he heard Sandayọ coughing.

'Let me go and check on him.'

He shone his torch at the Chief and saw that his eyes were open, focused on the ceiling.

'A man with a wife should consider my offer from last night. Surely you want the best for her.'

It was an attractive dream. A wife, older than him and riper for the years. A wife who would bear children who would carry the Ameobi name, a name he had often thought would die with him in the Niger Delta.

Fineboy walked into the room.

'Is he still here?'

'Good morning to you too.'

'Sorry, Brother Chike. Morning.'

'Is that the young man that attacked me yesterday? If so, tell him that he's young to be making enemies.'

'You're in no position to threaten anyone. Fineboy, please open the top door.'

The room was transformed from black to grey, a half-light in which features were partly visible. One by one the others came in, looking at Chike and then the shape of the newcomer.

'Let us eat first. Then we will discuss.'

The Chief would not take the food or even the water Oma offered him. He watched them instead, his eyes lingering on every face.

'This is Chief Sandayọ, whom many of you may have heard breaking in last night.'

'Breaking in? To my own house?'

'He was also the Minister of Education. Fineboy, if you'll tell us about that.'

'Yeah. He basically stole ten million dollars. His pictures were all over the papers a few weeks ago and the government is looking for him. We could be rich if we turned him in. Even if we didn't turn him in, we could still be rich.'

'If this wannabe Americanah wants to steal my money, let him come out and say so, but as for taking me to the police, who is going to give a bunch of squatters credit for finding me? They'll say I was captured on the border, dressed as a woman, or some other likely story. And please warn that boy not to make allegations he cannot back up.'

'Oma, what do you think?'

'It's dangerous to have a politician here.'

'I'm not a politician. I'm a minister. You understand the difference?'

'Don't teach me the constitution,' Oma said. 'I studied political science and I know the difference between an appointed thief and an elected one. You should all be in jail. But if we take him to the police, there's a high chance the money will disappear. Maybe they will even arrest us too so nobody will know about it.'

'At least one of you is sensible,' the Chief said.

'Is the money still here?'

It was Isoken asking, the least mercenary of the group.

'Yes. Why?'

'If it's for education, then somebody should use it for education.'

'Somebody like who?' Chike asked.

'Like me. Like you. I don't know.'

'Use your own money to do charity,' Chief Sandayọ said.

'What about you, Brother Chike?' Fineboy asked. 'What

do you think we should do?'

There was a time when Chike's answer would have been out before the question was fully asked, when even to hesitate would have brought him shame. Yẹmi granted him a reprieve.

'All this talk-talk, we go late for work,' the private said.

'You're right. The Chief will come with us and you too, Fineboy.'

'If I'm going, the women are going too. Nobody is staying alone with that money.'

'It is in your family that there are thieves,' Oma said.

'You don't know shit about my family,' said Fineboy.

'Isi ewu.'

'What did you call me?'

'Ha pu ya biko,' Chike said to Oma, before turning to face Fineboy. 'I've asked you to come because we'll need help guarding the Chief while we're working.'

'Excuse me. I'm not going outside. I might be recognised.'

'Once we give you a different set of clothes, you will look just like anyone else.'

'I'll wear my own clothes.'

'They'll give you away.'

'Then I won't go.'

'That's not an option. Don't make us use force.'

When the Chief stood in a pair of Chike's trousers, rolled up because they were too long, and some secondhand sandals Chike had bought at a stall, Sandayọ looked like any old man. His pot belly, once a sign of wealth, was now proof of a cheap, starchy diet.

'Poverty no get face,' Yẹmi said.

147

26

Despite the fiery youth calling for the dissolution of our polity, it would be the chiefest of all follies to break up Nigeria today. Where once, sundering our country was a matter of dividing friends and acquaintances, with every passing year it becomes a matter of separating mothers from daughters, fathers from sons, husbands from wives.

Professor Okeke in 'The Elder's Corner',
Nigerian Journal

'No condition is permanent', Chike read off a lorry that drove past him, its side panels preaching the Lagos dream of sudden changes in fortune, the wheel always turning, none secure, top wobbling, bottom grasping, middle squeezed. Chief Sandayọ's money was the quicksilver hand of fate. Grasp it or watch this chance evaporate.

He waved a green Toyota Camry past before ordering the line to stop. The driver with her windows down, wilting from heat and exhaust fumes, did not acknowledge his kindness.

Who in this place would turn down such an offer? Lagos chewed you to the gristle, ground you to the grist, passed you through a sieve and then threw the chaff-like substance of your life to the winds. No one would admire him for his honesty here. They would think him a fool not to take the money. And perhaps they would be right.

He stepped out of the way of an okada rider who showed no sign of pressing his handle brakes. He glimpsed the man's face, approaching middle age, tribal marks on each cheek, gouged like permanent tears. What would a life spent as a rider in Lagos look like? What privations and indignities and embarrassments? The answers would be worse for a traffic warden living on half wages.

Ten years from now, twenty years from now, he would still be plodding away at a job like this, worries of food and shelter plaguing his mind. He did not know what he would do with Sandayọ's money if they split it – perhaps start an auto business or open a nightclub – but he knew what he would become with a fifth of ten million dollars to his name, a person of substance and dignity, someone worthy of respect.

Even Oma, most opposed to the Chief, did not think much would come from handing him in. Isoken, young and romantic, felt they should fix some schools. He could not guess Yẹmi's opinion. Sometimes, his friend's mind seemed a shallow pond filled with small fish and microscopic impressions. Other times, his pronouncements were as deep as an oracle's.

Fineboy he understood. The boy was a Lagosian before he set foot in Lagos, filled with that acidic zest for life that corroded everything in its way. Fineboy would disappear with the cash, no questions asked. And he, Chike, what would he do?

If he took the money, then in a few months the city had turned him into an automaton, powerless to choose anything but grasping survival. And if he didn't take this chance, he had lost the glittering world of possibility that opened when Sandayọ stumbled into their flat holding a bag of new beginnings.

*

Chief Sandayọ sat in the traffic wardens' hexagonal rest hut, painted the canary yellow of the telecoms sponsor that built it and placed it in the centre of the crossroads, a few feet from where the wardens directed traffic. It was a shoddy job. The plank floor was rotting and the wooden bench that ran round the walls might as well have been made of iron.

He was hemmed in between Chike and Fineboy, sweating like a Christmas goat. It was hot in the hut. Hot outside. Hot everywhere. He had drunk four sachets of Pure Water already, biting with distaste into the plastic bags handed to him by the dirty hands of a hawker.

Chike had paid. He was the kindest of the three men but Sandayọ sensed he was also the most inflexible, a rigid morality underlying his mildness. Fineboy he could not work with. Apart from the fact that the boy had assaulted him, he was too eager to run off with the money. Yẹmi was the only unknown entity. The man had given no opinion on his presence.

Sandayọ watched Yẹmi now, dancing as he controlled traffic, naira notes fluttering out of cars when the drivers were entertained. Yẹmi's routine was repetitive but effective.

150

He slid across the road like a clunkier Michael Jackson or he spun like a coin when he beckoned for a lane to move forward. Sandayọ had met many men like Yẹmi in his YPC days. Joyful, unlettered creatures, possessing village shrewdness but lacking natural intelligence. They had always been easily swayed.

'Kúuṣẹ́,' Sandayọ said when Yẹmi returned from his shift, breathing heavily with his earnings crumpled in his fist.

'Ẹ ṣé.'

Sandayọ let some time pass before he spoke to him again.

'This work you're doing is not easy. And on top you're dancing and directing traffic. Who taught you?'

'Nah me teach myself. I dey learn some new moves I go soon display.'

'Chike doesn't seem to dance,' Sandayọ said.

'No o. You dey look him face think he's a small boy but inside nah old man.'

'It's like he didn't really like the dancing.'

'Nah so he talk? He no sabi better thing.'

'Of course. The two of you won't be able to see eye to eye. Irú ọ̀rẹ́ wo l'ọmọ Yorùbá nṣe pẹ̀lú ọmọ Íbò?'

Sandayọ's question could not be posed in English. It would be robbed of the solidarity he was trying to build.

'Yẹmi,' he said, after the pause had extended beyond hope of reply, 'Ṣé o gbọ́ Yorùbá?'

'Yes I speak my mother tongue but in the army, they have teach us for national unity, everybody must be speaking English.'

Fineboy laughed.

'You think he's fucking stupid? What? Are you going to try and speak Ijaw to me next? I don't need your permission to take that money. I'll kill you and take it if I want.'

'Who is killing who?'

It was Chike returned from his shift. Yẹmi got up and went back to the crossroads, leaving Chike to slot himself into the small space next to Sandayọ. He was numb from the wooden bench and he needed to piss. He had seen men ignoring the DO NOT URINATE HERE signs painted on walls but he was not an animal to relieve himself in the open.

'That girl over there,' Chike pointed. 'Can you see her? In the blue skirt, running beside that danfo with Pure Water.'

'What about her?'

'She's only five.'

'Are you some sort of moron? Am I her mother that sent her to hawk when primary education in the South West is free since the time of the great Awolowo?'

Chief Sandayọ snapped his fingers at a newspaper vendor. 'Give me *This Day*.'

'Oga e don finish.'

'Wetin remain?'

'E get this one dey call *Nigerian Journal*.'

Sandayọ had heard vaguely of this *Nigerian Journal*, liberal but small.

'How much?' he asked the vendor.

'One-fifty naira.'

'Bring it.'

He reached into his pocket and withdrew his hand.

'As you've taken my money, be so kind as to pay.'

Sandayọ found news of himself on page twenty. People he

knew were denouncing him in the piece: his permanent secretary, his special adviser, even his friend Senator Danladi. His friendship with Danladi was a known fact and to save himself, Danladi must denounce him strongly. Yet the words were uncomfortable to read. He was not an opportunist.

'Shit man. That's an ugly picture of you.'

'Says the baboon whose mother called him Fineboy.'

'At least I'm not a thief.'

'Ask the young man if he's ever been to Abuja before. Tell him that over there, I have witnessed first-hand the theft that has destroyed his homeland. He should not look to me for his troubles.'

'I'm not your go-between,' Chike said. 'Lunch time. Fineboy, watch him until I return. If he gives trouble, use the stick.'

Sandayọ knew how to create a mob in seconds. 'Olé!' was the hypnotic command. The corn seller fanning her cobs, the itinerant tailor with his clacking machine, the hawkers carrying supermarket aisles in their arms: all would be transformed into a violent horde ready to destroy the thieves. Petrol would be fetched along with tyres to ring the necks of his captors. A match would be struck, its slim flame thrown in their faces, instant combustion, human bonfires that blazed and dwindled into charred bones and teeth. He would slip away in the chaos, get his money and cross the border. And if he was recognised? If that young bread seller with her narrow hips and large eyes said, 'Aren't you Chief Sandayọ?'

27

Thank you for your article on the conditions of Government Secondary Schools in Nigeria. I'm a reader abroad and I've been contemplating sending my son to my alma mater Government College Ibarapo. My brother told me the standards are still relatively high but thanks to your exposé, I now see that his 'relative' and mine are not the same. I won't be putting my son through that torture. If he ever goes to school in Nigeria, he's going private.

'Ajala the Traveller', letters page, *Nigerian Journal*

They sat in the basement arranged in a horseshoe with Chike at the bottom of the curve. Chief Sandayọ's paintings bore witness from the walls. The light was half current, dimmed yellow bulbs casting secrecy on their gathering. The fan was working anaemically, its blades moving at quarter speed, warm streams of air reaching them in turn. Sandayọ was locked in the men's room with a litre of water and a covered plate of food, an incarceration he had protested loudly against.

'We will use the money to renovate schools,' Chike said, opening their second meeting on the Chief.

'Just like that? You've decided?' Fineboy said.

'What do you propose?'

'I don't see why we can't share it amongst ourselves.'

'Because that's stealing,' said Isoken.

'The only time something is wrong in Nigeria is when you're caught.'

'Devil's advocate,' Oma said. 'Do you think any of us can escape with that money? You leave here carrying two million dollars in cash and what next? Do you have a bank account? Where will you spend it? Who's going to change it into naira for you? The first person that sees you with that money will kill you.'

'Why are you so lazy?' Isoken added. 'I'm working every day, doing hair to save money to go back to school. If you have something you want to do, go and get a job. That money is for children who are suffering.'

The two women were against Fineboy.

'I have suffered,' Fineboy said. 'You don't know suffering until you see what I have suffered. From when I was a child, you can't even breathe properly because of the gas flaring. And the water most places, totally undrink—'

'Please let me hear word,' Isoken said, cutting him off. 'Kidnapping and causing mayhem in the Niger Delta, is that one suffering?'

'Kidnapping people?' Oma asked, shifting away from the boy. 'You, Fineboy? A militant? You knew of this?' she said, turning to Chike. 'You all knew of this? Jesus. In the same house with a criminal.'

'I vouch for him,' Chike said.

'Where do you know him from? You were a militant too?'

'It doesn't matter what I was. No one has ever harmed you. Nobody has assaulted you. I will go to the first school tomorrow. Fineboy, you and Yẹmi will stay behind to guard the Chief.'

'Our work nkọ?' Yẹmi said.

'I've given our notice.'

'You think we dey for army? If you give order, I go just say yes sah? Nah who tell you say I wan' leave my job?'

'OK then. You're free to stay and continue your work. Godwin only has to replace me.'

'No. I go guard Chief. Just that you go ask me before you come take that kain decision. No be say you go give command.'

'We should take a vote,' Fineboy said.

'I agree,' said Isoken. 'All in favour of handing Chief Sandayọ over to the authorities.'

Oma.

'All in favour of keeping the money.'

Fineboy.

'All in favour of redistribution.'

Chike and Isoken.

'Yẹmi?'

'Nah my right not to vote.'

'A majority of one,' Fineboy said. 'That's not enough.'

'We have a run-off,' said Isoken. 'That means we must vote again.'

'I change my mind,' Oma said. 'I go with Chike and Isoken.'

'Right. Y'all have won. So who are we going to say the money is from?'

'We?' Isoken said to Fineboy. 'You've joined the winning side already?'

'Whatever we decide, I'm loyal.'

'I haven't thought of anything,' Chike said. 'Maybe I'll say I'm from the Ministry of Education.'

'They'll ask for ID,' said Oma.

'Just say a mystery benefactor sent you and he doesn't want to be named. It happens in films all the time,' Fineboy said.

*

That night Chike read from the story of the rich man and Lazarus. The rich man, corpulent and grotesque, draped in purple and feasting each night. Lazarus begging by his gates, equally grotesque, with sores licked by the stray dogs of Jerusalem. And then in death, their roles somewhat reversed. The rich man roasting in a lake of fire and poor Lazarus, held in the bosom of Abraham, still needing to be carried.

'You're going to burn in hell,' Fineboy said to the Chief when the parable was over.

'Tell the young man: that may very well be so, but I can assure you he'll be burning next to me.'

28

If you prefer sitting in traffic to sitting at your desk, if you pass office hours waiting for closing time, if you spend more time on Facebook than you do attending to important emails then perhaps it's time for you to consider quitting your job. Before you resign however, plan your next career move and if possible, already have your new job or business waiting. Don't take any major decisions without the support of your nearest and dearest. If your spouse says no, no is no.

From 'Careers with Kunle', *Nigerian Journal*

Chike entered the compound of Kudirat Shagamu Primary School without challenge. Inside, the dim corridors had an odour of sweat and latrines. The students were crowded into classrooms, packed on their benches, elbows and knees pressing into each other. Chalk clicked on blackboards, tapping out like Morse code, white symbols on dark slate. Along with fractions and long division, they would soon learn the equations of inequality, inverse proportion, the rich getting richer, the poor sliding into abjection.

'Yes, how may I help you?'

There was a woman observing his progress.

'Good morning, madam. My name is Chike Okeke and

I'm here to speak to the principal of this school.'

'You are speaking to her. Come into my office. Please sit down. What can I do for you?'

'My boss passes this school on her way to work every morning and she wants to see Kudirat Shagamu transformed. She asks only that you write a shopping list of everything you need to achieve that.'

'Who is this woman?'

'Her one condition is that she remains anonymous.'

'Has she spoken to anyone in government?'

'She wants to deal with you and your school alone.'

'I see. You want me to collect money from you without informing my zonal supervisor? If it's stolen nkọ?'

'Principal, I can assure you that this money is meant for your school.'

'I've written to my superintendent so many times. We need a block extension to accommodate all our pupils. We need at least one computer so we can stop using textbooks to teach Computer Science. And what does he say? Be patient, Mrs Amadi. These things have been budgeted for and will come after the due process. Due process.'

He imagined that even outside the tight walls of her office, she would always speak as if addressing an assembly, no space for interruptions from the floor. Her hair was more grey than black; her age closer to sixty than fifty. She was used to making do, he saw from the broken wooden ruler on her table, held together by clear sellotape. The photograph of the President, framed with yellow metal, was the newest thing in the room.

'Well, here's a copy of the list I have been submitting for

five years. If your employer can help us with some of these items. Good day.'

Outside, the children had come out to play. They were thin but energetic. Stones flew through the air; fights broke out on the edges of the red clearing on which nothing grew. Their screams took him back to the Delta, his mind travelling to the night he left the army, flames on the thatched roofs, the tinder smell of palm fronds burning, the gauze of smoke, the night, orange and ablaze.

The principal's list asked for textbooks, computers, desks, whiteboards, fans, but there was no mention of swings or slides. He would buy them anyway. There was power in his gaze; the all-seeing donor who could grant wishes and change lives. They would be a sort of atonement for those children he had watched career into a line of gunfire. He shut the school gates and began his journey home.

*

'Get me some water,' the Chief said to the circle around his television glued to a Nigerian film. The lead actress's husband had just died and her in-laws had arrived to throw her things out of the house, hurling her suitcase across the screen. The men ignored his request but the woman got up and went to the kitchen. When she returned with the cold water, he thanked her, noting her slim wrists and the way she walked lightly on her feet.

'Chike must be proud.'

'Why do you say so?'

'Any man would be proud of such a beautiful wife.'

'Oh, Chike is not my husband.'

'Beautiful lover then.'

'We're not—'

'Where did your children go to school?' Fineboy said, turning from the screen. 'I can bet they didn't school in Nigeria.'

Sandayọ and his wife had sent their son to America with money earned from publishing and printing, long before he became a minister.

'Please tell that young man I will not be exasperated by his stupidity today.'

'Tell me yourself,' Fineboy said.

'I only talk to human beings.'

'You must have been silent in Abuja then. Bloody beasts of no nation.'

'Basket mouth wan' start to leak again o,' Yẹmi sang, keeping his eyes on the TV.

'Yes, it's good you referenced Fẹla. He would have had a lot to say about the Niger Delta. That bunch of thugs running around claiming to be freedom fighters. If you know how many of them the President has paid off, you'll go and become a militant right now.'

'Who has he paid off?'

'Wouldn't you like to know?'

Sandayọ turned his face to a painting of the Lagos waterfront, an orange fire burning in the foreground, the blue-grey ocean receding into the horizon. He needed to find a way to escape. Fast.

29

Stop complaining about this country. Do something.
'Morenikẹ the Motivator', *Nigerian Journal*

After their daily reading, Fineboy whispered to Chike that he wanted to talk outside. Chike had noticed his restlessness since they decided that the money would go to schools. Fineboy was always restless but there was a brooding, silent quality to his fidgeting these days. Above ground, the air was moist from the afternoon's rain. Chike had cleared the trapdoor area of algae but after such heavy rainfall, it would sprout again. They walked out into the dusk, damp grass rising up their legs. Fineboy lit a cigarette.

'I smoke when my mind is busy.'

'Just don't let Oma see you.'

'Yeah, before she poisons my food.'

The boy inhaled deeply, oxygen and nicotine rushing to his brain.

'I want to bring a journalist. Chief Sandayọ was talking about the secret deals that go on in Aso Rock. It's news for the whole Nigeria. We can't keep it to ourselves.'

Chike did not know what he had been expecting but it was not this quest for the dissemination of knowledge.

Motives were not immediately apparent. Yet it was Fineboy. There must be a motive.

'Do you have anyone in mind?'

'Yes. One newspaper that's very professional.'

'You know somebody that works there?'

'Not yet.'

'It could be dangerous.'

'I won't bring anyone we can't trust.'

'I'll leave it to you then.'

Some minds were always searching for patterns, joining threads until life was a carpet of recurring shapes and symbols. And even if you weren't of that bent, it was impossible not to attach some significance to Fineboy. The boy had found them a home; saved them from eviction. Who knew what this idea of his would bring? He trusted the boy not to harm them. Beyond that, Fineboy was Fineboy.

Chike remained outside after the boy had left, tilting his head to the sky. For the first time since he arrived in Lagos, he felt he had a place in the world again, a mooring in this spinning planet. From the hotel, to the bridge, to the crossroads, to their underground flat, he had tumbled along with chance. Even this family of five had sprung together by circumstance. But now, he had stood up to fate. MAN FINDS TEN MILLION DOLLARS IN LAGOS. DONATES IT TO SCHOOLS. Who would believe it?

He would never be a somebody in this city, never make his mark in any public way. He would have Yẹmi's respect and Oma's and Isoken's and on most days, he believed, Fineboy's as well. Most importantly, he would have Chike Ameobi's respect. That would have to be enough.

Isoken came with him to the schools, his partner in do-gooding. She left her hairdressing to weekends now, bussing from school to school during the week, drawing up lists in her neat, tight handwriting.

Principals always asked for textbooks, desks and computers, the trinity that would solve all their problems. As for the students, they subscribed to the trinity but they also believed in other gods: microscopes, internet access, air conditioning, school buses, flushing toilets, basketball courts, sanitary bins, swimming pools, tennis courts, new equipment for a band. Some wishes they could not grant. A young girl had run up to Isoken after a focus group and whispered, 'We need new teachers.'

They took danfos, the rough and tumble of public transport endured for the higher cause of 'education transformation', a term Isoken had started using for their work of two weeks. Yet it was she who was most transformed, lifted to a new stage in her life cycle, from dormant pupa to this alert, darting creature, drawing up plans and strategies and back-ups. Sometimes in the evenings, they went through self-defence moves, elbow in groin, palm smack, foot stamp.

He did not know what the Chief thought of their use of the money. He seemed to have submitted to his incarceration. Oma mentioned that he complimented her excessively when Chike was gone, praising her cooking and looks.

'Maybe he thinks both of you can become lovers and escape with the money,' Chike said to her.

'He's too short for me.'

'What's your type?'

'People who don't ask too many questions.'

'Like me?'

She had laughed, showing her teeth to her molars and the strong, slim trunk of her neck. *Surely the lines are fallen for me in pleasant places*, he thought as he turned to go back inside.

30

TNJ: Why is it that you only date light-skinned girls?

JJ: (laughs) Who told you that? Well it's true, I prefer our fairer sisters. Not because I'm hating on the chocolate or anything. If you're beautiful, you're beautiful but you know how it is. You want the latest Range, the newest Blackberry and the hottest light-skinned chic. That's Naija for you. We're too materialistic.

Extract from interview with
MC James Java, *Nigerian Journal*

'Mr Bakare will see you now.'

Fineboy had sat sweating in the reception of the *Nigerian Journal* for an hour. When he asked the receptionist to switch on the air conditioning, her reply had been terse.

'We're using the small generator. It can't carry AC.'

She was certainly bleaching. Although whatever cream she was using must be good. It was the ears that gave her away. Standing over her at the desk, he spotted them, coal against her caramel face.

If Chike had divided the money, Fineboy would have taken his share and disappeared. No matter what Oma said, it couldn't be that hard. Two million dollars would have set up his own radio station, an entire media empire if he wanted, Fineboy Communications: Entertainment of the people, by the people, for the people.

But Chike had not shared the money and you could not attack a man that had saved your life. You would be forever cursed and Fineboy knew about curses. His grandfather had committed suicide after cuckolding a river god. The aggrieved deity had risen above the waves and walked on land for the first time in millennia, shrimp and small fish sliding out of his clothing as he made his way to Fineboy's grandfather's hut. A curse had been placed on their male line, cutting them off before forty. Fineboy's father had committed suicide. His older brother had committed suicide but he, Fineboy, would not kill himself.

He had been taken for deliverance in a church where demons were routinely cast out and mammywaters flopped in the aisles, their gills shrivelling under the onslaught of prayer. The curse had been ripped out of him with shouting and convulsing that left him bedridden for a whole day. The matter had been sealed when his mother took him to a medicine man. There were two deep incisions on his chest to ward off death by his own hand.

He fingered the scars through his shirt now as the receptionist motioned him to a door. He had picked the *Nigerian Journal* because its pages were free of the adverts that took up the other papers, adverts congratulating men like Chief Sandayọ. The paper itself looked sleek and professional, standing out from the rest on display. He had not expected the office to be so small.

Chike would not understand why Fineboy was here. It

was true that he would have taken the money if given the chance but it was also true that he believed that Nigerians should know what went on in Aso Rock. The two impulses lived in him peacefully and with one thwarted, the other naturally came to the fore.

He knocked and entered Mr Bakare's office. There were headlines hung on the walls, framed in dark wood, the room shouting with bold block sentences. Mr Bakare was a young man, trendy in his navy blue suit and gold watch face, large as a pocket mirror. The room was cold, the air conditioning denied Fineboy in the waiting room on full blast here.

'Good afternoon. How may I help you, Mr Fineman?'

'Fineboy.'

'Yes. My receptionist Chidinma said you'd come on business of a confidential nature. Apologies you were kept waiting. It's been a busy day. Did she give you something to drink?'

'No.'

'I've warned her many times. I must apologise again. I would offer you something but I don't want to keep you. It appears you have a news story for me.'

'Yes I do.'

'And what is it?'

'News that will make every Nigerian want to read your newspaper.'

'I'll settle for advert subscriptions. The only things Nigerians read are the captions under wedding photos.'

'If you run this story, you'll sell so many newspapers, you won't need adverts.'

'I'm listening, Mr Fineboy.'

'I know where Chief Sandayọ is.'

Under his calm exterior, the editor of the *Nigerian Journal* was an excitable man. He took off his suit jacket and tossed it up to the ceiling, sleeves flapping, silk lining flashing as it rose and fell to the ground. Then he picked up a phone on his desk and said, 'Chidinma, bring this boy a drink and cancel all my meetings for today.'

*

As they moved through traffic, Ahmed Bakare wondered if he was driving into a trap. Lagos was filled with chancers like this young man complete with dubious American accent. He had hesitated at the door of his car, wondering whether to get in with Fineboy or not. No one would know where he had gone, his receptionist filing her nails at the desk and barely looking up when he passed, the last person to see him alive. He could not trust any of his employees. He paid them well but not well enough for such a secret. It was a story that could turn the country upside down or at least bump sales over the ten thousand mark. Five years of the *Nigerian Journal* had made him increasingly modest in his ambitions.

He slowed at the estate entrance for the guards to look into his car.

'Good evening sah. You're here to see . . . ?'

'Aniekan Isong. Kingsley Road. He's expecting me.'

Aniekan as far as he knew was in Canada but these guards would not know. They waved him in. He drove past the large concrete mansions, built like bunkers, the pillars and trellised balconies that decorated them added as afterthoughts.

'Straight down,' Fineboy said. 'Turn left ... Turn right ...
It's this house.'

'Here?' Ahmed asked.

'Yes.'

Chief Sandayọ living in an abandoned building like a beggar? He drove past the broken-down house and parked away
from it.

'Is this the place? Are you sure?'

'Just come with me.'

Ahmed had not decided on the manner to adopt with
Sandayọ. His editors told him he was too direct, too sparse
in his questioning style, shunning the tangential approach
that gave a story body.

'You're sure this is the place?' he asked again, when they
stepped into the waist-high grass, uncut in years. If it were
a trap, no one would find his body here. His mother would
fret about her lost son forever. When they reached a door
sunk in the ground, Fineboy stopped.

'What's the matter? Have you told him we're here?'

'It's not only Chief Sandayọ living here, but you must
only write about the Chief.'

'Do you want me to sign something?'

'Yeah, that's a cool idea.'

He tore out a page from his notebook and wrote in his
slanted hand, 'I, Ahmed Bakare, promise to mention only
Chief Sandayọ in my articles and to protect the identity of
everyone else in this flat.' He dated, signed and gave the slip
to the boy.

'OK. Follow me.'

31

For our fuller-figured readers, stripes can be slimming. Just make sure they're going in the right direction. Vertical stripes make your body appear longer and slimmer. Horizontal stripes can add pounds.

'Fashion Forward', *Nigerian Journal*

The journalist Fineboy brought was a well-dressed man, his suit cut to his shape, the dark fabric resting on his leather shoes. The effect was softened by his lack of a tie. His neck rose out of his collar to meet a smoothly shaven chin, the only hair on his face a clipped moustache that curved round his upper lip. Fineboy had found this elegant journalist too soon, Chike thought. He had not even had time to tell the others of the plan.

'Good evening all. My name is Ahmed Bakare. I'm the editor in chief of the *Nigerian Journal*. Please may I ask where you are keeping Chief Sandayọ?'

'Wetin I tell una? Poverty no get face.'

'We are not hiding him anywhere,' Chike said. 'He is in front of you.'

'Chief Sandayọ, I presume,' the journalist said, after looking them all in the eye. He walked towards the Chief, his hand outstretched like a signpost.

'Who else would it be? You must be foolish if you cannot tell a minister of the Federal Republic from these ruffians.'

'I have some questions for you.'

'Go ahead. Who is stopping you from asking?

Fineboy had chosen well, Chike thought. Only this Ahmed Bakare, suave and wealthy, could have drawn so defensive a response from Chief Sandayọ. They had incarcerated the Chief, seized his money, kept him under surveillance and yet every evening, Sandayọ sat on the sofa like a lord, giving orders to Oma and complaining about her food. Only one of Sandayọ's class could, with one innocent question, pierce straight to his pale, quivering ego.

'Ask him,' Isoken said when the journalist was seated, 'ask him why my school which was built for five hundred students had over two thousand.'

'And while you're asking,' Oma said, 'in my own university lecturers used to force girls to sleep with them or else they will fail them. What did he do about that?'

'Please, you must let me ask the questions,' Ahmed said in an accent Chike recognised as elite, a Nigerian voice diluted with a foreign crispness that spoke each word separately, consonants sounded out, none linked to the other. Ahmed brought out a notebook and a pen and then a dictaphone, which he placed on his lap. He was neat in his movements and very slow.

'Good evening, Mr Sandayọ.'

'*Chief* Sandayọ.'

'I'm going to ask you a few questions and if you would be so kind as to answer.'

'I don't owe you any kindness.'

'You sent the young man to fetch me. I assume it is because you want to tell your side of the story.'

'Is that what they taught you in journalism school? To be assuming? If I sent the boy, why would I ask him to bring somebody from the *Nigerian Journal*? I've seen your paper. Nobody reads it.'

'Alright. Did you take the money?'

'Hakim or whatever your name is—'

'Ahmed.'

'Ahmed, which money are you talking about?'

'The ten million dollars released by the Federal Government for the Basic Education Fund.'

'OK, Ahmed. Let's suppose I know something about this money. Supposing I know. Suppose.'

'No be suppose anything,' Yẹmi said. 'No be the money you bring come?'

'The money is here?'

'Of course not,' Chike said. 'We seized it and removed it for safe keeping.'

'Who is "we"?'

'The terms of the interview,' Fineboy said. 'Focus on the Chief.'

'Yes, focus on me and the money you are supposing I know something of. What is ten million dollars? I was in Aso Rock two months ago and I saw the Central Bank governor himself, taking to the President an amount of foreign currency that would make you weep for Nigeria.'

'I did not come here for allegations against Dr Garba.'

'Why not? When you leave this place, phone CBN and

tell the governor you know his secret.'

'I am not interested in blackmail.'

'You should be. What's your circulation?'

'Eight thousand.'

'You can't be making much from selling to your family members. That boy over there, did he tell you he's from the Niger Delta?'

'I don't see what that has to do with the ten million dollars that has gone missing.'

'Do you know how many of these militant groups are in the pay of the presidency? Sometimes they come to pick up the money in Aso Rock. In the middle of the night. They take it, go quiet for a while and when they've blown everything, they start causing trouble again.'

'Like who?' Fineboy asked Sandayọ.

'It's difficult to remember your strange names. Tomboy, obviously he's the most famous. Edward Clark. Boniface. Many others.'

'Godspower?'

'Maybe. But that's just small stuff. If you want to know about the real corruption, find out how you get allocated an oil block. The First Lady's favourite colour is purple. Very useful information.'

'The money, Chief Sandayọ,' Ahmed said.

'Your mind is too one-track.'

'So how do you get an oil block?' Fineboy asked.

'Befriend the First Lady. Buy her purple things. Purple bags, purple Benzes, purple houses in France. Depends how much you want it.'

'Have you met her before?' Oma said.

'Yes of course.'

'From what I've seen of her on TV,' Isoken said, 'she's a fashionable lady. Classy.'

'How won't she be well dressed? There are three accounts in Dubai that you pay into if you want a favour done in Abuja. That money goes straight to her and it's for shoes and handbags only. I can give you account details for one.'

'Who has paid into it?'

'Oh, so, Mr Journalist, now you're interested?'

The Chief cared what this journalist thought about him, cared enough to tarnish others' reputations, to offer what would have been an explanation in a humbler man. If only Ahmed had stuck to his first line of questioning, Chike thought. The money, Chief Sandayọ. The money. But he had been seduced by gossip. He was a journalist after all. Nothing more would be said of the money, hidden in parcels throughout the flat.

'I'm sorry but you'll have to leave,' Chike said when it was midnight.

'I can't make a story out of this. He hasn't answered me properly.'

'You can always come back.'

32

No matter how sharp your writing or how fresh the scoop, you'll only be producing creative non-fiction if you don't check your facts.

'So You Want to Be a Journalist?', *Nigerian Journal*

Sitting in that crowded basement, with the Chief spewing out allegation after allegation, Ahmed had wanted to do something that would shock this very comfortable man. Tread on his foot or slap him or throw a glass of water in his face. How would he publish such a story? Aso Rock gossip. Titbits swept up from the corridors of power. There was no way to confirm anything the Chief had said.

Tayọ Cole was the only person he could call. During the early years of the *Nigerian Journal*, Uncle Tayọ had been his guide, from renting their office space to securing their first big interview with an opposition presidential candidate. For Ahmed, Tayọ Cole was more than a mentor. He was an ideal, down to his rheumy eyes weakened by repeat exposure to tear gas.

'Uncle Tayọ, good evening.'

'Ahmed, is this you? We haven't heard from you in a while.'

'I'm sorry. How is Aunty? And how are the boys?'

'You didn't call to ask about them. What's new?'

'I have a scoop. A lot of dirt on people in government. Problem is I don't know how to verify anything my source has said.'

'How good is the source?'

'Good. You don't get closer to power than this.'

'Give me an example.'

'OK. The First Lady has three accounts in Dubai. Shoe and handbag accounts.'

'I heard it was two.'

'You know about it?'

'Everybody knows about it. You pick up these things in Abuja. I've told you severally. Activate your bush radio. Your content is good but you're slow in getting to the story. Find the gossip. Then do your research.'

'But that's the problem. It will take me months to research everything this man has said. By the time I finish fact-checking, these people might be dead.'

'You could do an allegation piece. Print it as he's said it.'

'They'll sue me.'

'Not if you've called already and asked for their side of the story. Then you can write: We called so-and-so over *x* allegation and they refused to comment.'

'And if they deny everything?'

'They won't. They won't even take your call. Who are you to get the First Lady of Nigeria to comment? I have to go. Someone is on the other line.'

'Wait. Since when do you know so much about Abuja?'

'Ahmed, I'm an ex-journalist. Just because I'm running

a media consulting company doesn't mean I've turned off my bush radio. And anyway, I have to pass through the capital sometimes. I fought too long for democracy to lose my head there. Trust your Uncle Tayọ. Text me when you run the story. Don't be subtle with the headline.'

'I won't. Greet Aunty for me.'

Ahmed put down the phone. Uncle Tayọ's new familiarity with Abuja was worrying. Should he have trusted him? Had he said too much? The transcript of the interview lay in front of him, painstakingly typed over two days. Ahmed had been surprised at how reedy his voice was on tape. It was not the confrontation he had hoped for, the piercing gaze of the press ranged against the dull forces of corruption. He had been worn out by the Chief's deflections, all thirteen pages of them. The pressure of carrying such a secret was beginning to show. He had stopped sleeping and he could feel the ache in his gums that was the first sign of stress, the ache before they began to bleed.

A mask of Ọrunmila stared down at him from the wall, or at least the artist in Oṣogbo had said the large, hollow eyes belonged to the god of wisdom. His mother would have been horrified by the serene wooden face, angered even, by what she would dub apostasy.

When he prayed, he prayed to Allah the most merciful. But what was he to do with all these gods and goddesses and spirits and ancestors that had peopled his village in Kwara before the first cleric arrived with a Koran? He did not worship Ọrunmila but he thought to him, this wooden embodiment of wisdom hung on his wall.

In the background, Ola's distinct breathy voice came

through the speakers. She was a British singer, allowed into his study on the technicality that her absentee father was Nigerian. She was singing of freedom, of breaking chains and moving walls.

Was he brave enough to run this article? Could he even imagine the consequences? The incendiary days of blowing up journalists were gone. Maybe in some obscure Eastern backwater, or in the lawless Delta, such things still happened, but not in Lagos. And not when the newspaper publisher had a well-connected father. How much his father's name had shielded him from becoming a casualty of free speech, he would never know. It was ironic. His father hated the very existence of his paper but it was his surname that had kept the *Nigerian Journal* open and unhampered for so long.

33

It is my belief that the corrupt in this country exist because
of the goodwill, support and cooperation of large segments
of the population. It is alright to be a thief, as long as one is a
thief who shares.

Editorial, Nigerian Journal

It was many days now since Chief Sandayọ's interview with
the journalist. He stayed underground, watching Chike,
Fineboy and Isoken leave each morning, marching out before the sun rose. They came back secretive, huddling to
discuss the day's work. It was his money they were using to
generate all this good feeling in themselves, this confident
self-righteousness reflected in the passages Chike read from
each night. *It is easier for a camel to go through the eye of a
needle than for a rich man to enter the kingdom of God.*

Sandayọ worried he had been indiscreet with the journalist. He had spent his forties railing against the government,
shaking his fists at the authorities before crowds who never
failed to respond with their own clenched anger. And now he
had joined the ranks of those worthy of denouncing, or so the
journalist seemed to imply with his questions. He had found
himself trying to put whatever he was accused of in perspect-

ive, sharing Odukọya's gossip with the wide-eyed naïf claiming to be a reporter. It was justification he now regretted.

He had seen the man's publication, with its Western layout and aspirations. Ahmed would need weeks of fact-checking, if not months, to verify what he had said. Even Sandayọ did not know if what he said was true. He hoped this foreign attention to detail would give him the time he needed to escape.

He had considered escaping without help. During the day, there were only three: Yẹmi, Oma and himself. Overpowering them was not inconceivable but he was naturally averse to doing violence with his own hands.

Late at night he crouched in the kitchen, reading slowly through his contacts list, charging the phones if there was power, shielding their screens with his hands so no light would escape. They did not know of his phones. He was still guarded but Fineboy and Yẹmi had grown lax. They fell asleep on their watches, leaving him to puzzle over who to call. He would not call Gbenga, his son in America, a doctor with a white wife and three children. They had spoken a week ago. He had climbed to the top of the stairs where reception was best, talking softly.

'Dad. Thank God it's you. They've been calling me. They got my house number from a phonebook.'

'Who?'

'Police from Nigeria. They keep asking if I know where you are.'

'What do you say?'

'Nothing. I drop the phone. They have no jurisdiction in the United States. It's not true, is it?'

'Of course it's a lie.'

'I knew it. I just want you to know that I, Ruth and the kids are behind you.'

To what purpose? Of what use to him were his half-caste grandchildren who greeted him 'Hi Grandpa,' the few times he had passed through Tennessee to spend a night in their cavernous house. On Funkẹ's insistence, he had sent their son abroad when he was nine, funnelled millions of naira into an education that had turned the boy into a stranger, a stranger he was fond of, even proud of, and whom he would never let become entangled in this mess.

Far more practical to have raised a son like Ṣẹgun, head of his bodyguard when he was a member of the Yoruba People's Congress. Those had been heady days. When his name was on every government list, when death threats came in a steady stream. He remembered the democracy marches, protected by the safety of their numbers, steered away from danger by area boys who flung the exploding canisters of tear gas back at the soldiers, giving the rest of them time to escape. He had been so involved in the YPC. He had even fought with their leader, Francis, who had felt threatened by Sandayọ's growing estimation in south-western Nigeria.

He did not know now why it had been so important. To build a Yoruba nation, to make Oduduwa's people great, to return the western region to its glory under Awolowo, their owl-spectacled deity, who stared down at them from the wall during every meeting. And after all their rhetoric and bombast it had come to this: who to call for help.

Ṣẹgun was still in the bodyguard business. They spoke from time to time. Sandayọ did not like the idea of men with guns knowing the location of this flat; it would mean the end of its usefulness. Others like it could be built. The squatters would not come to any serious harm.

He was standing in the toilet, two black bars in the corner of his phone, just enough signal to make the call. He dialled and kept his number private.

'Ṣẹgun.'

'Speaking. Who is this?'

'Chief Sandayọ.'

'Who? I can't hear you.'

'Rẹmi Sandayọ.'

'Afternoon sah. You're still in Nigeria? I thought you would have left the country by now.'

'Come and meet me in my house tonight, you and your boys. I'll pay. Trust me. Come with some guns. I have a job for you.'

'Your house in Lagos? Ikẹja?'

Of course, he did not know this place.

'Lagos yes but not Ikẹja. The address is Plot 15, Ekweme Road, Ojodo Estate.'

'I can't hear you. The line is breaking.'

'I said—'

There was a loud banging on the door.

'Who you dey talk to?'

'No one.'

He cut the phone and flushed the toilet.

'Chief Sandayọ, come out. It's me, Ahmed. The article was published this morning, front page of the *Nigerian Journal*, and it's already making waves.'

'You fool!' He flung the door open. 'You absolute bloody fool!'

34

Thunder Bassey Beats Jimmy Giant in Knockout Seven
Rounds.

Sports page, *Nigerian Journal*

Chief Sandayọ was taller and heavier but Ahmed Bakare
moved faster. Two strikes to Chief Sandayọ's every one
but as he did not hit very hard, the two were evenly
matched.

'Oya separate yourselves,' Yẹmi said coming in between
them.

'Let me see what you wrote.' The Chief picked up the
newspaper from the floor where it had fallen.

EXCLUSIVE: CHIEF SANDAYỌ REVEALS ALL FROM
SECRET HIDEOUT

He skimmed the prose for names. Senator Okpara,
Governor Adeniyi, the First Lady. And there in bold, the
number of an account in Dubai.

'There's nothing in there that you didn't tell me.'

Chief Sandayọ was almost certain that Ṣegun had been
able to hear him. No matter how much he offered Ṣegun,
Senator Okpara would double it. The senator was not a man
you crossed with only ten million dollars. Ṣegun was call-

ing back. He switched off his phone. The journalist's phone rang.

'Hello Ronkẹ. You liked the piece? Thank you. Yes, we need to start holding these criminals to account. I'm just doing my job. Yes, we hope so. Indeed. Thanks again. OK. Greet the boys.'

The journalist's phone rang again.

'Hello Chidinma. Who is this? What are you doing with my receptionist's phone? Yes I want to speak to her. Hello Chidinma. Chidinma, calm down. They can't do anything to you. Once I drop the line, I'm going to call the police. Chidinma, hello, Chidinma. Chidinma!'

The journalist held the phone away from his ear, staring at the screen.

'They shot her. I must get the police.'

'Are you mad? You write an article about Governor Adeniyi in his own state and you expect the police to help you?'

'What should I do?'

'It's too late. One of your employees is dead. You don't know Senator Okpara. She's just the first.'

'Maybe they never shoot her,' Yẹmi said. 'They just shoot the gun in the air to scare you before they cut the line. Nah soldier tactic.'

'Shot who?' Oma came out of the kitchen.

'I have to go to my office,' Ahmed said. 'I have to go,' but he remained standing in the middle of the room.

'Take public transport. If someone is watching for your car, they won't spot you,' Chief Sandayọ said.

'I must go,' Ahmed said. He took out a notebook from his pocket and wrote something down. 'Please call this number if you don't hear from me by tomorrow morning. It's my father's number.'

Sandayọ almost felt sorry for this journalist, naïve enough to be shocked by brutality, a fact of life for most in this country. This was how his son, Gbenga, would be if he ever moved back to Nigeria, a bumbling, principled idiot.

'What happened?' Oma asked, when Ahmed was gone.

'Nothing. Don't worry about it,' Sandayọ found himself saying. 'We'll sort it out amongst ourselves.'

Oma went back to the kitchen and he and Yẹmi were left alone.

'Nah who you dey talk for that phone?'

'My son.'

'That one is OK but you must bring the phone sha. Chike no go like it.'

He handed one phone to Yẹmi, the other in the band of his trousers.

'Why you go shoot somebody over newspaper? Most people only dey look football section. You look like say you wan' faint. Make I bring water?'

'I'm fine.'

Run and leave them. And where would he go without his car keys, his clothes, his money? His wife would have been praying by now. She would have knelt down and bowed her head; shut her eyes and clasped her hands, prayer by the text-book. But for him, there was no one to turn to.

35

The homeless in this city abound.

Nigerian Journal

Ahmed returned the next morning, holding a small suitcase.

'They burnt my office,' he said, after Isoken let him in. 'Nothing but charcoal. They didn't shoot my receptionist, or at least the bullet didn't kill her. My maiguard saw her being pushed into their car. I can't go home and I don't want to put any of my friends in danger. Please let me stay for a few days.'

He lay down in his suit, his green cotton socks pushing over the leather arms of the couch. Nothing could wake him, not even Fineboy's swearing when Isoken spilled tea on him. When he finally opened his eyes, Chief Sandayọ was on the other sofa, reading.

'Is this flat yours?'

'You're still asking me questions.'

'It has quite an art collection. That's a Glover, isn't it? My mother doesn't understand art like this. She'd say too much colour and you can't see the people properly.'

'Your family is new money? I only ask because I used to be the same. Once I had a bit of cash, I filled my house with paintings of fields and flocks of geese. It was my wife that showed me how to look at art, how to consume it. She was so European in some ways. Ate ẹba with a fork, when she ate it at all, but she laughed at people whose tastes she felt were too oyinbo. People who named their children Diana. Nouveau, she would say. Her grandfather went to Oxford. Three generations of money makes it ancient, doesn't it. Are you married?'

'No.'

'I didn't think so. Your wife will want a smarter job than this newspaper outfit you run. You are like my son. I can hear it in your accent. You would find it difficult to marry someone who doesn't have the same international experiences as you. Those kind of women have many lofty ideals but they don't come cheap. Where did you school?'

'Such sudden interest in my life.'

'I don't have a lot of people to talk to. Chike is not so bad but he's out most of the time with the other girl and that foolish young man that thinks he's American. This one they put to guard me is an illiterate obviously. Oma has gotten over her initial hostility to me but she's forever going to the market or locked up in the kitchen. She refuses to be emancipated, that one.'

'So Yẹmi is guarding you. This is a house arrest then. What are they going to do with you?'

'Eat me perhaps. Evil, fat politicians make good soup. Where did you go to school?'

'Charterhouse from thirteen and then Loughborough University.'

'My son went to America. Still lives there. Funkẹ wanted

to send him to England but I would not allow it. It was part of her colonial mentality. Why send him to a dead empire when one is alive? Your parents must have a lot of money to send you abroad for so long.'

'My father was a civil servant in the eighties.'

'Name?'

'Bọla Bakare.'

'Perm. sec. in the Ministry of Petroleum?'

'Yes.'

'So you're disturbing me when you have thieves in your family?'

'I sent a piece to the *Guardian* in 2001, anonymously. They weren't interested in fraud that had happened so long ago.'

'Did you complain when your father was paying your fees?'

'Do you know Nigeria has one of the highest numbers of children out of school in the world? Millions.'

'Stop parroting things you've read off the internet to me. Open your eyes and see what's on ground. Let's say this money I allegedly stole was budgeted for primary schools. If it hadn't disappeared with me, it would have disappeared with my second in command; if not him, then the principals of those same primary schools. Whichever way, the money would not reach where it was meant to go.'

'So it might as well be you.'

'Supposing I took the money, then yes.'

36

Two days ago, before a thousand praise singers and break-dancers, General Wasiu Akinpelu donated N20 million to build a hospital in his hometown in Oyo State. General Akinpelu has unresolved corruption allegations hanging over his head from past military regimes. No matter how hard it tries, the soup a vulture cooks will always smell rotten.

Victor Ehikhamenor, columnist, *Nigerian Journal*

Chike could not deny he gave in too easily to these Lagos traders that greeted you warmly and then proceeded to fleece you. Yet he disliked Fineboy's aggression, his trampling of bargaining niceties, ignoring the vendor's pleasantries in his haste to knock down a price. The returns on this roughness were meagre.

Isoken was by far the best pricer but she became combative if the vendor was a young man, her hands militantly akimbo. They were steadily dribbling their way through Chief Sandayọ's money, $100,000 gone already, on four blocks of toilets, a trailer of textbooks and various odds and ends, microscopes, Bunsen burners, light bulbs.

Chike was uncomfortable carrying large amounts of cash. Trips to the black market were frequent. They would find the Northerners who handled foreign currency, discreet in their white kaftans, counting money into neat stacks, forefingers moist with spittle, lips pursed with concentration. And all the while, Fineboy behind him, mumbling that they'd been cheated.

'One dollar for 126 naira is too low. Ask him for 128.'

Two naira difference: for that the boy's veins stood out in his neck as he whispered through his teeth. It would have been more efficient to split up, each person with a lump sum of cash, trusted to find at least two items a day. But he was wary of leaving Isoken alone with Fineboy, he did not want to go with Fineboy and he did not trust Fineboy to go on his own. So they remained locked in a triangle of uneven angles.

Until the Chief announced one morning that he would be going with them.

'Why?' Chike asked.

'Because I'm tired of sitting in this flat. And I want to see how you're spending my money.'

They might as well try Sandayọ, Chike thought. The Chief had the skills and knowledge for the work they were doing earnestly but haphazardly.

'This is inefficient,' Chief Sandayọ said once he heard their routine.

'What do you suggest then?' Chike asked.

'First of all, why change money so often? Change one hundred thousand dollars once and for all.'

'It's dangerous. You leave the market with that kind of money, you've become a target. We use public transport.'

'Take a taxi.'

'We're keeping costs down.'

'Well, we should still split up. Let's go in twos so we can close twice as many deals each day. How can all three of you be going to one vendor? Even the ministry was not this inefficient. Isoken will go with the buffoon and you and I will stick together, Chike.'

'Who you calling a buffoon?'

'I want to go with Brother Chike,' Isoken said.

Chike had taught Isoken enough to defend herself. Not that he believed Fineboy would attack her. The two would probably never be friends but they were no longer enemies. She had trimmed Fineboy's hair the other day, her scissors snipping close to his arteries and leaving him unharmed.

'No. This way works better. Fineboy will hold the money, and Isoken, you'll hold Chief's phone. I'll be calling you throughout the day. Any problems, call me.'

*

'Chike didn't say who was in charge,' Fineboy said to Isoken when they got on the bus.

'Of course I'm in charge. I have the phone ọdẹ.'

'And I have the money. I could just disappear into Lagos right now.'

'You think I won't stop you? Don't try me. I'm a ninja.'

'Ninja kọ?'

They were no longer enemies now, Isoken and Fineboy. How could they be, living and working so closely together? It was not quite forgiveness. She would never know if he had indeed been one of the men, or if it was hearsay he had repeated so flippantly in the forest. She would never trust him as she trusted Chike, never seek him out to talk, but she could work with him, could appraise him dispassionately and see that there was much that was valuable in Fineboy.

'I would never do that, you know,' Fineboy said.

'Do what?'

'Take this money and run. If not for Brother Chike I would have died in Bayelsa. If he says no, I won't do it. For real man.'

'You and this your Americanah phonetics. I am also capable of speaking English that would discombobulate and incapacitate you with its erudition and sophistication but of my own volition, I choose not to. In short, abeg speak normal English let somebody hear word.'

'I'm keeping the dream alive. I know one day I'll get into a radio booth and wow them. Till then, I keep practising. What about you? What's your dream?'

'I want to go back to school.'

She had been away from her textbooks for so long. She wondered if she could still read the secret language of chemistry. She had made up her own mnemonic for the elements of the periodic table, from Ac to Zr. She had also cheated every time she sat JAMB. At the last minute, she would grow afraid, unsure of her workings, and she would copy from a sheet moving through the room, shading answers that she discovered were false on results day. She was more confident now, better able to see that she could have made the pass mark for Pharmacy without expo, as she could survive in Lagos without her parents.

Today she and Fineboy were buying louvres for a school that had gone windowless for years, rain blowing into the classes during the rainy season and flooding the students out. She hoped these glass slats would be treated with care. It might be a decade before they got such a chance again.

At the window shop, she let Fineboy speak to the vendor. He was not so nervous now Chike was not there and he relaxed into a conversational style that got them a good price. The phone rang. It was Chike.

'Hello. How are things over there?'

'We're fine thanks. We're just rounding up,' Isoken said.

'OK. We've also closed our deal in Computer Village. We're going to go to the carpenter now to check on the desk orders. Where next for you two?'

'I want to buy some sanitary towels. For the school nurses to keep and give to girls.'

'Iyama,' Fineboy said. 'I'm not following you to buy pad o.'

'Yes you are. I'm in charge,' Isoken said.

'Give him the phone, let me speak to him,' said Chike.

'OK. Please tell him I'm in charge.'

*

It had come naturally for Chike to delegate to Sandayọ once they got to Computer Village. The Chief knew his way around, striding ahead into the melee. Men hawked monitors as you would fresh fish, thrusting the blank screens at you for inspection. There were one-room stalls, computer mice dangling, tied together by their tails like real rodents. Spare parts for every machine, butchered technology, stock spilling out of stores and onto the pavement, cash and carry.

'We can't go to any of these smaller shops. They won't be able to fill the order but they'll lie and say they can. They'll quote a good price but they'll either disappoint or make up with bad stock from somewhere else. The big shops are no use, these modern ones that have air conditioning and automatic doors. They pass on all their running costs to the consumer. We need something medium.'

They had chanced upon Obianwu Computers, larger on the inside than out, computers and modems stacked from floor to ceiling, wall to wall, cooled by standing fans. Obianwu reminded Chike of his uncles, who visited once a year when he was a child, walking through their small flat in Ibadan, acquisitive as ants, looking at everything they saw with greed. Obianwu sitting on his high stool with his thick gold chain and bright red shoes reminded him very much of Uncle Vincent, who had built on land in Mbaise that should have been Chike's when he came of age.

'Good afternoon. How can I help you?'

'We're here to buy computers.'

'See computer here. Have a look.'

'We want two hundred.'

Obianwu stood up.

'What exactly is it that you're looking for?'

They were paying cash. Ten per cent today. Sixty per cent on delivery. The rest if the schools were happy with the merchandise. A good discount was expected. Twice the Chief began to walk out. Twice Obianwu called out before he reached the door.

'You did well,' Chike said when they left the store, deal closed.

'You know if we were running this thing like the ministry, we'd have had to split that order. Ten computers to an Igbo man, ten to an Ijaw, ten to a Hausa, ten to a Birom, and so on and so forth. You don't know all the ways government can frustrate you. Where to next?' Chief Sandayọ asked.

Numbers had been dialled on the Chief's phone that Yẹmi confiscated. Not only to a son in America but to a certain Ṣẹgun, who continued to text: 'Where are you sir? What is your address?' Sandayọ had tried to betray them. For whatever reason he had failed. Almost certainly, he would try again.

The safest thing to do was turn the Chief in. And how could they turn him in without the money? And how could they lose the money without losing their schools? They could kill him, Chike thought in fanciful moments. Oma's knives were sharp enough for the job. But it was not so easy for Chike to kill a man any more. How had he done it before; coolly and without rancour, shooting strangers his commanding officer believed threatened the Nigerian state? He could imagine killing a man out of rage in Lagos but not in the clinical way he had once done.

They would have to watch the Chief closely, that was all. Use his expertise but watch him closely. *His talk is smooth as butter, yet war is in his heart.*

'Mind your step,' Sandayọ said as they approached a puddle.

37

I decided to devote my life and my wealth to the poor when I saw so much in the world was vanity. It was a decision my wife and family were against at the time. They thought I had run mad but I am glad to say they have now joined me in good works.

Interview with Guru Mahadi, *Nigerian Journal*

It had begun with Chief Sandayọ wanting to win their trust. For what other reason would he go tramping through Lagos, haggling like an Ikire market woman for discounts small and insignificant. His plan was working. They had grown lax, forgetting sometimes he was their prisoner, joking and exchanging stories with him. Not lax enough to leave him unguarded at night, but still, Oma was no longer required to remove the knives from the kitchen at the end of each day.

Walking through Lagos in Yẹmi's clothes, the Chief was truly anonymous. It was not pleasant to be so completely unknown but it was not unpleasant either. In Abuja when he entered into a room, people would begin to scurry, a wind of motion swirling around him, aides running, civil servants leaping ahead to smooth his way. His wife would have mocked him if she had witnessed this sycophancy.

'What's wrong with your hands?' Fụnkẹ would have said. 'Too weak to carry your own briefcase?'

Chief Sandayọ finally let Chike convince him to see a refurbished school. He added a face cap and sunglasses to his disguise only as a precaution. He no longer feared he would be recognised. Although they fed him well, he had lost weight and his face had thinned into a younger version of himself.

He could guess Chike's motives for taking him to the primary school. A change of heart: it was what do-gooders like Chike and his wife always wanted, proselytisers living for the next conversion high. And yet, knowing this, he was still pleased by the students, lined behind their new desks like rows of crops.

'We've done well,' he said, meaning it for a short moment.

In his fourteen months as minister, he had missed his early days in the YPC, the earth and smoke of their village schools, the eagerness of his pupils. He had been a miracle worker back then. Eyes that had once looked upon letters unseeing, opened to the wonders of 'the cat sat on the mat' while 'John put the kettle on the fire'.

He had spent his thirties driving to the remotest parts of the South West, living the national pledge, serving with all his strength so a few could learn to read and write. And to what end? This was a country that could not be dragged out of the mud. Mud became Nigeria. Filth was her natural covering. And if people like Chike did not know this, it was out of wilful ignorance, a delusion dangerous for these children. What would these new chairs do? Or the computers? Or the textbooks? The statistics did not lie. If these children could read it was only to learn that their country was not made to work for them.

He had found a black thread of nihilism in Funkẹ's new religion, a buoyant despair he understood. Before her conversion, calamities upset his wife. She would cry at the aftermath of an earthquake, pipes wrenched out of the ground, homes collapsed with families inside. She was quiet for weeks after they drove past the body of a child, knocked over and dead by the time they swerved to avoid the corpse.

Then Funkẹ had had her religious experience and all suffering had been put in an unsettling perspective. The sooner the world unravelled, the sooner the second coming of her saviour. Earthquakes, famine, war: all signs and precursors to glorious rapture. It was a rationale to explain a world that never got better. Despite one's best efforts, despite one's highest hopes: the world did not change.

38

On this historic day, fresh and independent journalism has come to Nigeria. We say down with the brown envelope. Down with news without intelligent analysis. Down with bad-quality ink on even worse-quality paper. No more the drab arts and culture section, the lifeless politics pages, the cliché-ridden sports section. The *Nigerian Journal*, for the inquisitive mind, has arrived.

Pilot edition, *Nigerian Journal*

Ahmed remained in the flat with people he had grown friendly with yet knew so little of. On that first night, Sandayọ had seemed almost a captive and Chike his head jailer, but now the Chief was part of the group that went out every morning in a four and did not return till evening, speaking in snatches of the day's work. Computers were ready, plumber not cooperating, painter had done a good job: he could not catch the gist of it.

Nor could he grasp what linked them all. Fineboy and Isoken had the rivalry of siblings but were both equally aghast at the thought. Chike and Oma clearly had some sort of relationship but they were not married. Yẹmi was the only one he could place. Chike's loyal retainer, laundry man and shoe polisher.

Then there were the evening sessions where Chike would read from the Bible and they would all listen, rapt as children, even Sandayọ drawn in, Chike's voice bringing to life the sea of Galilee and the demons of Gadarene. And then after a beautiful reading, he would turn and point holes, the agnostic Bible scholar, and Oma would jump to the defence of the passage, and Fineboy would often join her and whatever side he took, Isoken would stand on the opposite and the Chief would say something cutting and Yẹmi would remain neutral. It had something of a family, the large family he had always wanted as an only child, often humoured, often discontented.

Perhaps if Ahmed had stayed in England, he would have a wife and a house in a North London suburb, a patch of grass to tend, his slot of life to live. He had sent his mother a few more texts, brief and to the point. 'I'm still OK. Tell Dad.' And when she replied 'Wer r u?' in the strangely current text language that she was so fond of, he had texted simply, 'Safe.'

They were right. He should not have returned to Nigeria. After five years, what did he have to show? No newspaper. No building. No staff. He had tried to call his former employees and only Kẹmi, a young intern, picked up.

'Mr Bakare, is this you?'

'Yes. Kẹmi, how are you?'

'You're alive.'

'Was anyone hurt in the fire?'

'Most people had already gone home because the men came at five fifteen. They shot in the air and told the few of us that were in the building to leave.'

'What about Chidinma?'

'I don't know. I left.'

'Kẹmi, I'm going to need you to do me a favour. I want you to write a statement. We still have the website. We can continue running underground.'

'Mr Bakare, I can't. My parents have warned me not to even speak to you.'

'Of course. I apologise. Have you started looking for a new job?'

'Yes. I've dropped my CV at MTN and Stavos Air.'

'That's a shame. You'd have made a wonderful journalist.'

'My parents said it's too dangerous. I'm sorry. I have to go now.'

'Of course. Thank you.'

'Bye, Mr Bakare. Stay where you are.'

When his father called him, he had let the phone ring, answering just before the call expired.

'Good afternoon.'

'I knew you were there. Your mother thought you would have come home by now.'

'I didn't want to put you in any danger.'

'It's better this way. It's been a week but you never know who is watching.'

'How's Mum?'

'She's enjoying your notoriety. No hour passes without one of her friends coming to see her. In fact two of them just walked in. These things they tie on their heads get bigger every day.'

'I should go before someone asks who you're talking to.'

'I suppose you knew what you were getting into when you decided to run that article.'

'I had an idea.'

'You had an idea. Do you know your receptionist is still missing? You have many foolish thoughts but no idea of responsibility.'

'I have to go now.'

'Your mother said I should ask you if you want to leave the country. You could go to England for a while, wait there until things calm down.'

'You want me to run away.'

'I want you to act with common sense. You don't know how serious these people are. You think you can just write anything you like in Nigeria?'

'I'll think about it.'

His capitulation robbed his father of his signature rant of rhetorical questions piled swiftly on each other. Are you normal? Are you thinking straight? Am I your mate? What is the meaning of this? Have you lost your senses? In his childhood, by the third question, he would have been reduced to tears.

'Where are you?'

'It's better I don't say.'

'OK. I have a call coming in on the landline. Your mother sends her love.'

To stand in a queue patiently, to draw the blinds at seven, to offer warm beverages to all and sundry, he had lost these domestic British habits. They could be regained as he had regained this brusque manner when he moved back to Lagos.

And what of his receptionist? He had tried her phone. He had sent texts. He would have gone to her house if he knew where she lived. His staying in Nigeria would not bring her back. If no news of her surfaced, he would pay for an advert in *This Day* to be run in a week's time. He would use a picture from an office party, one where she was posing, clutching the curve of her hip and smiling at the lens. If she was alive, she would never forgive him for using a bad picture and perhaps even if she was dead. Missing person's advert: that was the most he could do for Chidinma, then he too would disappear.

III

Water No Get Enemy

39

Every day brought something new for Chike. One morning he might be arguing with an electrician over ceiling fans that turned sluggishly through the air. The next, he might be stacking a library with books, shelves full for the first time.

He had begun meditating to deal with the stress of their work. There was no other name for this teasing apart of the words, prodding and kneading and pulling until his mind grew slack with the meanings he had made and remade from one line of text. The prose of St John suited this sort of mental labour. *In the beginning was the Word, and the Word was with God, and the Word was God.* A riddle, a mystery, a nonsense that he continued to turn over for days, weaving in and out of the words until all he saw when he thought of the verse was a picture of glowing Hebrew script running through a black, unformed universe.

The journalist had left as abruptly as he arrived. Chike had grown used to his slim form stretched out on the sofa, his face covered by the pages of a broadsheet. In his two-week stay, Ahmed had only left the flat to buy newspapers, returning with a wide selection of dailies and news magazines. In his mind perhaps, Ahmed still ran the

Nigerian Journal and needed to know what the competition was saying.

'Where will you go?' Chike had asked him the previous night.

'I'll travel out. England for a month or so. I think the matter has blown over. They've had their revenge but just to be safe. My receptionist is still missing, you know.'

Ahmed did not have any of the pretensions of a rich man. He ate whatever Oma served them and seemed content to sleep on the couch but he belonged to that class of person who flew easily over borders, his passage through the world legal and approved. Chike had always wanted to travel, to pose under McDonald's arches, twin arcs to the triumph of capitalism, and walk on ocean beds amongst the coral and tropical fish he had studied in his textbooks and knew only as dry black-and-white sketches.

To travel overseas took money, of which there was an abundance in the flat. He was the only one who knew where Sandayọ's loot was hidden, a responsibility that waxed and waned in heaviness. Sometimes, his hands trembled as he counted out the cash for the day's expenditure. Other times he was indifferent, as if the dollars were mere paper stamped with a balding Benjamin Franklin.

The journalist would be in the air now, rushing through the sky. Chike had flown once as a child, sitting in the window seat by his mother, their destination now lost to his memory. He remembered the clouds spread below them like a new, white earth, large cumuli that looked firm enough to walk on if only his mother would let him out of the plane.

'You'd fall. You're too heavy,' his mother said.

'I'm lighter than you.'

'Not light enough. I'd need to stretch you and stretch you and stretch you and stretch you till you were as thin as a—'

'Butterfly.'

'Thinner.'

'Mosquito.'

'Thinner.'

'Amoeba.'

'Yes, as thin as an amoeba. And then you wouldn't have any legs to walk on the clouds. You'd just float on top of them, a long, thin, shapeless amoeba.'

She had pulled at his cheeks as she said this and he had laughed, squirming against the cool metal buckle of his seat-belt. That was what he remembered of flying. The sharp air of the cabin, the mountain range of clouds and his cheeks, sore from her pulling and his laughter.

40

'Sir, the captain has asked that seatbelts be worn at this time.'

'Please can I have a glass of wine?'

'Alcohol will be served at meal times. May I ask that you fasten your seatbelt, sir?'

'What time will the meal be served?'

'The cart will be on its way shortly, sir.'

There were cracks beginning to appear in her makeup that was too thick for this altitude. Ahmed had flown first class with his parents when he was a child. He remembered the air hostesses as slim and tractable. He had stopped flying at his parents' expense in his second year of university. It was also the year he stopped moving with the Nigerian crowd. They had all dated each other and their parents belonged to the same political circles back home but it was the spending that finally separated him.

Mondays to Thursdays were lean days. Ahmed would be almost ascetic, eating simple meals of boiled eggs and noodles because he never knew what Friday would bring. Sometimes they would rent sports cars and drive down to Birmingham or Cardiff, cities with larger clusters of Nigerian students. Once they flew to New York. Half his allowance in one weekend, £2,000. That was when he said: thus far and no further.

Naturally, he had drifted towards the other Africans. The words of Garvey and Fanon, set texts in his first year, had long effaced the worth of his boarding-school friendships. Once he stopped moving with the Nigerians, he began to notice the Somalians, Eritreans, Ugandans, Zimbabweans, Sudanese. They were markedly political. Mobutu. Mugabe. Mengistu. Mandela: names that never left their conversations.

'What's it like living under a dictator?' Farida, their un-elected president, asked once. She was a devout Kenyan Muslim, never seen without a scarf hugging her scalp, always scowling when she saw him drinking beer. Ahmed used to wish he could send her to purdah.

'It's only the West that will tell you every military ruler is a dictator. They want to impose democracy on us.' He had stood firm in his father's words.

'What about Bubaginda's human rights record? Who killed the journalist Deli Giwo?'

'That's not how you pronounce their names,' he had responded foolishly.

That summer he put Farida's questions to his father and some of his own. Perhaps that was the first time he wanted to become a journalist, watching his father evade direct question after question until he finally broke down into straight-forward anger. When he got back to England, he moved out of the flat his parents had rented in Loughborough and got a part-time job in a restaurant. Thereafter, he had always lived his life on his own terms and at his own expense.

Now here he was, returned to his childhood, flying to England courtesy of his father because his mother had felt it was too risky for him to withdraw money from the bank.

'What would you like, madam? Chicken or beef?' The singsong cadence of this air hostess's voice was decidedly northern, somewhere between Manchester and Newcastle.

'What's the difference?' Ahmed's neighbour asked.

'Chicken is like poultry. You might call it fowl in Nigeria.'

'I know what a chicken is. What is it served with? Like rice, potato.'

'Sorry. How silly of me. The chicken comes with a mushroom sauce, mashed potatoes and green peas. The beef comes with rice, tomato stew and some fried plantain.'

'Give me the chicken.'

'And you, sir?'

'I'll have the beef please,' Ahmed said.

When the air hostess had moved a few seats away, his neighbour leaned into him and said, 'These white people, they think we're monkeys. Can you imagine that girl telling me what a chicken is?'

He made a sympathetic noise as he peeled back the foil lid.

'You should have taken the chicken,' she said.

'Yes.'

He looked at his seatmate properly. She was wearing an orange lace shift, maybe in her late forties or early fifties. The gold bracelets on her wrist stirred slightly as she sawed her poultry with the plastic knife. A madam, wife and mother back home but forty thousand feet in the air, only another passenger in economy. He ate the bread but left the sticky toffee dessert.

Someone was patting him awake. Her face was so close, it seemed she would lunge forward and kiss him. Her irises, thin blue rims around very large pupils, stared at him.

'Sir, do you need a landing card?'

'Are you from Manchester?'

'No, I'm an Essex lass. Do you need a landing card, sir?'

'No thank you.'

He had a British passport, his reward for ten years of international fees.

His seatmate stretched over him. 'Excuse my hand,' she said, as she collected the navy blue and white piece of paper. 'Can you borrow me a pen?'

He gave her the one in his breast pocket.

'My son has a British passport. He and his wife and their two children. I'm the only one without one.'

Again he made a sympathetic noise then closed his eyes. He wondered how he would fill his time in London. He had worked on the sales desk in a bank before his Masters in journalism and there was a chance he could resume work. Stanton and Chaney was one of the few still making profits. He checked from time to time. If they asked him about the last five years, he would not mention the *Nigerian Journal*. It was a failed experiment that had eaten away almost all his savings, a cautionary tale for his children.

'Sir, we're approaching landing. Please return your seat to an upright position.'

He watched the air hostess walk away for the last time. With every step, her calves seemed to be sinking further into her ankles. What would become of him in England? What would he do?

41

Chike watched the children walk down the middle of the corridor, careful of the walls that still smelled of fresh paint. Eventually their hands would brush the pale stucco. They would leave dark prints that would be attacked with soapy water the first few times and then left to form new patterns of rounded palms and long fingers.

The school grounds were pleasing, the slides and swing sets shooting out of the earth like metal trees, the beginning of a landscape beneath their feet, saplings planted, grass sprouting. It was insignificant in the grand scheme of derelict schools that crisscrossed the country but it was everything for these children who switched on a computer for the first time, marvelling at the light trapped under the screen, lifting their hands to the glass and drawing them back at a sharp warning from their teacher.

Sandayọ seemed as invested in the work as the rest of them now. If the Chief was acting, he was very committed to his role, staying up till midnight, drawing up detailed timetables for delivery and installation. Perhaps even Sandayọ could not remain unmoved by this work they had done, this creation from nothing. *In the beginning was the Word.*

That night Chike returned to the basement flexing his

shoulders. Oma noticed. She was sensitive to him in the manner of a spouse used to watching for another's needs.

'It's hurting?' she asked after their evening meal.

'Yes. We were stacking shelves.'

'Where? Here?'

She prodded a muscle in his back and he flinched.

'Sit down. Let me give you a massage.'

She sat on the sofa and he sat on the floor in the space between her legs.

'Take off your shirt.'

The others were around and the words were said casually but still his fingers trembled as he undid the buttons. When he was left in his singlet, she began, kneading the nape of his neck, moving round and round on the same spot.

'You're too tense. Relax.'

The parlour flickered into darkness.

'Down NEPA,' Fineboy said.

'Great. We're not going to finish the movie.'

The first time her finger slid under his vest and brushed his nipple, he thought it was an accident. Then she pinched the rubbery flesh until it grew firm under the ball of her thumb.

'Relax.'

She tugged painfully, almost viciously, until all his senses centred on that narrow diameter of skin. Her tongue was a surprise, hot and moist on the back of his neck, travelling until it reached his earlobe, sucking on the dangling fat, nibbling like it was a delicacy.

'Sister Oma, please where did you put your torch? I can't find it.'

'Sorry no battery. I forgot to buy.'

She put her hands on his trousers, fumbling with the button, and then the zip until there was only one layer of clothing left. She hesitated at the band, toying with the elastic, running her finger along it, snapping it this way and that.

'I'm sorry. I can't,' she whispered.

She retreated, running up the cords of his spine and onto the neutrality of his neck, turning his head left and then right.

'I've never been so forward. I've only ever ... with my husband.'

He said nothing. He was impatient for her to be done.

'Finished,' Oma announced loudly. 'Your back should feel better.'

'It does,' he replied, matching her volume. 'Thank you.'

He got up and walked to his room in the dark, following the wall with his hand. He heard Fineboy say to her, 'Me nkọ? I want a massage too or is it only for Chike?'

'You've found work for me abi? Abeg face front.'

Chike shut the door of his room and changed his underwear. She was a flirt, like the most beautiful girls he had known at university, always out of his reach, reserved for the richer boys and their fathers, arousing and withdrawing, teasing and then feigning ignorance.

And yet as he lay stretched out in a clean set of pants, he knew this description did not match what he knew of Oma. She would need divorce papers to feel free of her husband. And not only that, until she had walked down another aisle and made new oaths before God and man, intimacy with him would be impossible. Hers was an ordered world, behaviour fixed into iron channels that he must learn to run in, if there were to be any future.

42

On the Piccadilly Line, Ahmed sat with his suitcase between his knees and his eyes level with a zip that had come undone, revealing nothing lewder than the tail end of a shirt tucked in at the waist. There was no need to tell the slight redhead that her skirt was gaping. No innocence was lost. When he got off at South Kensington, she was still standing unaware, her head swinging to the music in her earphones.

He had planned on staying in a bed and breakfast until he found a modest rental but in the envelope with his ticket, his father had put a copy of the flat keys. It seemed pointlessly scrupulous to refuse. The money that had bought the flat was already stolen. Whether he slept there or not, it would not return to the treasury.

Letters were piled on the doormat when he opened the flat door. He wheeled his case over them, staining the white envelopes. His parents seldom came to England these days. The shopping was better in Dubai and enough society Nigerians holidayed there to recognise his father when he walked past them in a mall. 'Call us when you arrive.' The last thing his father had said to him at the airport.

There was no dial tone on the landline. He would sleep first then find a payphone to call them. His old room smelt stale. No breeze had blown through it for years and he imagined the dead particles, hanging in the air since the last time he slept there. The bed was made. He should strip it and find some clean sheets.

When he woke it was dark. He switched on all the lights and walked through the apartment. Four bedrooms in Kensington. Not a house to be envied by his Nigerian circle but respectable enough. Somewhere to crash when the mansions in Bishops Avenue were occupied by parents who had suddenly flown in from home. His mother had chosen the furniture. You could not take two steps without running into your reflection in a gilt-edged mirror. It was all dated now but it had been the height of fashion once. New money became old.

He slipped his key and wallet into his pocket and stepped outside. London was colder than he remembered. The wind blew up his trouser legs, forcing him to almost jog to the store at the end of their road.

'Do you sell phone cards?'

'Yes. Which one you want?'

'What do you recommend?'

'Where you calling? Nigeria?'

'How do you know?'

'Many Nigerians in this area.'

New ones, he wondered, or still the same old guard, stretching out the money from the military era.

'Phone Home is very good.'

'I'll have that please.'

'Five pounds.'

'Do you have frozen meals?'

'Second aisle on the right.'

He paid and went to the booth near his house. He had forgotten that prostitutes used the space behind the telephone to advertise. They aroused nothing in him. They looked the same, naked and booby with dead, beetle eyes.

'Hello Chike. It's Ahmed. I arrived safely this morning.'

'Good to hear from you. How is London?'

'It's fine. How is everyone?'

'Is that Ahmed?' he heard Fineboy ask in the background.

'Let me speak to him. I want to speak to somebody in London.' It was a woman's voice.

'Ahmed, this is Isoken speaking.'

'Wait,' Chike said, taking the phone from her. 'Let me put him on speaker.' There was the sound of fumbling, then silence.

'Hello Chike, are you there?'

'Yes, he is here. We are all here.'

Their voices were soft but emphatic, like people shouting from afar.

'How is London?'

'It's cold.'

'Nigeria is hot.'

'Is that Oma?'

'Yes. How did you know my voice?'

'How won't the fella know your voice? You guys spent a whole lotta time together.'

'Fineboy.'

'What's up man? How's the United Kingdom?'

'Cold. What of Chief Sandayọ?'

'My whereabouts are none of your business.'

'OK, no finish Ahmed credit with your big grammar.'

'I'm using a payphone but Chike, I'll call you next week with my number, just in case you need to get in touch with me over that matter we discussed. Good night.'

'Bye bye.'

'We miss you.'

'Holla at the Queen for me.'

When he got back to the flat, he trampled on the envelopes again, scattering some further down the hallway. He would call his parents tomorrow when he got a sim card.

43

It had been foolish of Ahmed to think he could slide easily into a job he had left five years ago. His call to his old manager had been embarrassing. Good to hear from you, Alan had said, after having to be reminded which Ahmed Bakare was speaking. There were no openings at the bank. Present conditions, economic climate, you know the forecast.

'You're sounding like a weather man.'

Alan had not laughed. 'We should go out for lunch some time when I'm free.' Ahmed had declined. Now was not the time to be proud, a glance through the business section in *The Times* was enough to show him that. Still things were not so bad that he would, for no foreseeable benefit, lunch with Alan, who condescended as easily as other people said thank you.

For a few days, he had taken to walking round the area, a suburb in the centre of London. One minute, identical houses, door after door, set the same short distance from the street. Then suddenly you would chance on a busy road, with shops and restaurants, then a left turn to take you back to the identical houses and their gated parks. His perambulations had not lasted long. It was too cold to walk slowly and the pace was neither enjoyable nor sustainable.

It was while he was sitting in the living room, eating another pizza microwaved to rubber, that he thought of his friends from university again. Where had their radical crowd dispersed to? They had tried to keep in touch after graduation, meeting for drinks and barbecues, then struggling to weddings and christenings.

He flicked to N in his address book. Njongo Cloete. Living in South Africa now, the shyest member of the group. You would always see him parting his lips like a fish, looking for a moment of quiet to make his point. He did not know the time in Joburg and to call Njongo from England would give his loneliness too great an urgency. The silence in the flat was not the type to send him charging off a bridge. He moved to C. Calvin Sukama. Blunt to the point of rudeness but always practical in a crisis. The last he knew, he was living in London with his Irish wife.

'Hello.'

'Hello, is this Calvin?'

'Yes, Calvin speaking. Who is this?'

'It's Ahmed Bakare, from university.'

If he said 'Good to hear from you,' he would drop the phone.

'Ahmed. Long time no see. Have you been in England all this while?'

'I moved to Nigeria for five years but I'm back for now.'

'Just in time for the recession.'

'How's your wife?' He had gone to their wedding. Only he and Farida were present from their university circle and not even on the same table.

'We're divorced now.'

'I'm sorry to hear that.'

'It was bound to happen, statistically speaking.'

'Are you free some time?'

'For a coffee? Yeah, I'm free tomorrow. Whereabouts are you staying?'

'South Kensington.'

'You've done well for yourself, man. Me too, I'm thinking of moving back home to make some money. Find myself a well-trained African wife. I'll meet you at the station at one. There must be plenty of cafes around there.'

They were predestined to talk about the divorce tomorrow. Calvin could not leave a grievance in the past, but perhaps they would find other things to speak of.

'I don't have a job at the moment,' was the first thing Calvin said when they sat down at a table in the dark coffee shop. It was one of those places typical of London, miserly with space, the rectangular table too slim to cover your knees, strange conversations spilling into your own, the cloying smell of a cinnamon latte clashing with your clean, bitter coffee. This was the cramped life, of low ceilings and narrow expectations, he had moved to Lagos to escape. Calvin unbuttoned his coat but kept it on, ready to leave if he found him unsatisfactory.

'I used to work in insurance. They got rid of the foreigners first. You know how it is in a recession. So which one was it for you: oil or politics?'

'I run a publication business.'

'And you live in South Kensington. Come on. We read the news.'

'It's more media publishing than books.'

224

'Like *Hello!*'

'More highbrow I would hope but there are similarities.'

'So where's your wife? A man living in South Kensington can't be single.'

'I'm not married.'

'Never been?'

'No.'

'Clever fellow. I'm not saying marriage is bad. You know some people can make it work but you need a good African woman to make it work, women like our mothers. Women nowadays are so disrespectful.'

'Do you have any children?'

'No, thank God. They'd have been as rude as their mother.'

And so it went on. It was relatively painless to listen to. Like a preacher, Calvin could talk for hours without response. Hearing him, Ahmed understood why his parents did not visit England often. In Nigeria, he had owned a newspaper, an office building, staff. Here, he was reduced to a sort of agony aunt for this middle-aged man whose belly rested comfortably on his thighs when he sat.

'Who would have thought you would end up printing trashy magazines. You and Farida were always acting like you were going to save the world.'

'That was our whole group.'

'No, you two in particular. Arguing, arguing, back and forth. Like there was nothing in the world to talk about but politics. She asked about you, you know.'

'Really?'

'You still fancy her?'

'I'm just surprised she remembered me.'

What did she say? You couldn't ask Calvin that. He changed the topic.

'So who else do you still talk to?'

'Not many. I can't stand the successful people and who wants to keep in touch with the losers like me. What about you?'

'No one. I want to start though.'

'We should do this again.'

'Yes of course.'

'I can still stand you. Maybe it's because you made your money in Nigeria.'

No newspaper. No building. No staff. If only he knew. He walked him back to the station.

'Do you think she'd mind if I sent her an email?'

'Who? Farida?'

'Yes.'

'She has two kids.'

'I just want to see how she is. Meet up with her for coffee or something.'

'OK, don't raise your voice. It's farida.wagogo@bbc.co.uk.'

'She works for the BBC?'

'Yeah. One of their World Service programmes.'

His Oyster beeped and the barriers clattered open.

'See you.'

44

'Dear Farida' was the most conventional way to begin, even letters to the Home Office began in this fashion, but it seemed to place their friendship on a more intimate footing than it had ever been. 'Hello Farida' was much too casual after an interval of almost a decade. The final draft he felt dissatisfied with but the sixty minutes he had paid for were almost up.

Greetings Farida,

It's Ahmed Bakare from university. I'm in London for a while and have started looking up people from our year. I had coffee with Calvin Sukama the other day. He's put on weight and lost a little hair (a fate which awaits us all) but is otherwise the same. I got your email off him. I hope you don't mind. How are you?

With warm wishes,

Ahmed.

When he returned the next morning, he saw she had replied a few hours later.

Hail Ahmed,

How lovely to hear from you. I always wish I'd kept in touch with more of the group. I can't believe Calvin has had my email address and he's never used it. I work in the BBC, been there for almost six years now. What about you? What have you been up to since the last time we saw?

Xx

The girlish end to her email emboldened him.

There's too much to say in one email. Do you want to meet up for lunch some time this week?

Ahmed

It had taken her a day to reply this time.

Lunch sounds fun. Let's go to Alfonso's. It's this lovely little Italian restaurant on Burleigh Street, just off the Strand. Is Friday at one o'clock any good? I'll make a table booking for one o'clock if you're free. The closest tube station is Temple. Call me if you get lost, 079483829416.

F

He pencilled this new number into his address book beside her name. The conditions for his calling had been stated. He would wait until he saw her.

Alfonso's was not hard to find. She was already seated when he arrived.

'Ahmed.' The scarf was still tightly wound, revealing the entire shape of her head, like she was bald and her skin grew in a gold and green silk pattern.

'Good to see you, Farida.'

She placed her hand on his shoulder and brushed her cheek against his. Their bodies did not touch.

'Sorry to keep you waiting.'

'Don't worry. I came early.'

The menu gave him somewhere to look when she spoke to him. For all her hijab, the shy downward glance was alien to Farida.

'Your email implied that you haven't been in London recently.'

'Yes, I just came in from Nigeria. I moved home five years ago.'

'Good for you. There was an opening recently for a correspondent in Kenya but my girls wouldn't hear of it. In school, when they're asked where they're from, they say Barnet. How can Adla and Afaafa be from Barnet? Stop looking at my left hand. I got divorced three years ago. What about you, Ahmed? I can't see a ring on your wedding finger.'

'I've never been married. Please recommend something for me.'

'The seafood tagliatelle is good.'

He added a glass of wine to his order.

'So what did you do in Nigeria?'

'I owned a newspaper.'

'Owned? Did you sell it and come to London to retire? That would make a fabulous story.'

'No, it was burnt down.'

'Really? Why?'

'I ran a piece about some people in government. They weren't pleased.'

'I think we did a story about that on our website. What was your newspaper called?'

'The *Nigerian Journal*.'

'Wait, let me check on my phone.'

Her nails clicked over the screen.

'We did run a story on that. My goodness, Ahmed, it's you. It says you're in hiding.'

'I suppose I am in hiding. Hiding in Alfonso's off the Strand.'

'No one would have expected you to stay in Nigeria.'

'My staff is still there. I'm hoping my receptionist who was kidnapped is alive and still there.'

'Our correspondent didn't tell us about a receptionist.'

'Yes, her name was Chidinma Ezeanyi. My maiguard saw her being pushed into the arsonists' car before it drove off.'

When their meals came he tried to move away from the topic.

'So how old are your daughters?'

'Four and six. Look, I know the story has gone a little cold but I'm just wondering how you found Remé Sandayọ?'

That's not how you pronounce his name, he thought. He remembered the note he had signed for Fineboy. 'I can't tell you.'

'Do you think he'd talk to the BBC?'

230

'I could ask. I thought you'd be more interested in finding my receptionist.'

'That'd be a story more for agencies in Nigeria, I would have thought.'

'I put an advert in tomorrow's newspaper. With a number to call if anyone's seen her.'

'That was the right thing to do.'

He ate the last of his meal in silence. The shrimps were small and far between. The clams and mussels tasted raw. Black-and-white photos lined the walls, images of dead Italians from the twenties and thirties, gorging on pasta in settings brighter and more appealing than theirs. When the bill came, as he was fumbling for his wallet, Farida slid her card into the machine and tapped in her PIN.

'You're my guest.'

'At least let me leave a tip.'

'It was included.'

He threw a five-pound note on the metal tray.

'If you have money to waste, give it to me. I'm a single mother of two.' She laughed and put the note in her bag.

'That was churlish. Thank you for lunch.'

'My pleasure. It was lovely to see you, Ahmed.'

Again their faces pressed against each other, their bodies remaining distant. 'I'll call you tomorrow to find out if there's any news about Mr Sandayọ.'

45

Saturday morning, 6 a.m., the phone by Chike's pillow rang.

'God punish you,' a woman said. The voice was unknown to him.

He went into the kitchen and shut the door.

'Are you calling about Mr Bakare's receptionist?'

'How dare you put my photo in the papers? You think you can mess with me? You don't know who I am in this Lagos.'

It seemed Ahmed's receptionist had been found. The missing person advert had run today with a picture of the receptionist and a number to call with any information. Ahmed had asked Chike to buy a new sim card for the advert, a number he could use for one day and throw away.

'Your employer informed me that you'd been missing since the *Nigerian Journal* was burnt down.'

'Ahmed is behind this?'

'When calls to your phone were not going through, he assumed the worst.'

He heard her breathing heavily on the other end. Finally, she said at reduced volume, 'I didn't know he was rich enough to run a full-page advert in *This Day* on a Saturday. He was always saying the newspaper was going bankrupt.'

'He'll be glad to know you're safe.'

'They took my phone and said if I tried to get in touch with him, they'd kill me.'

'Of course. Ahmed will understand.'

'So how is he going to make it up to me?'

'I'm afraid he's not in Nigeria at the moment.'

'What about you? I like your voice. Are you tall?'

'Yes, but not very handsome.'

'I'm not too picky. You've seen my picture. Call me.'

He put the phone in his pocket, wondering if this was news Ahmed would want to be woken up with. Good news, yes, that the receptionist was alive, but full-page adverts in *This Day* did not come cheap.

'You scared me,' Oma said, starting at the door of the kitchen.

'Morning. I had a phone call and I didn't want to wake anybody.'

They had not spoken much since the night of the massage. She had grown shy of him, skirting away when they met in the corridor, avoiding him like an adolescent.

'I'm glad you found me here,' Chike said. 'I wanted to talk about—'

The phone's ringing cut him off. Oma took up a crate of eggs and went to the other side of the kitchen.

'Hello.'

'Why the fuck did you put my cousin's picture in *This Day*? What kind of sick person are—'

He cut the line and switched off the phone.

'Who was that?'

'Wrong number. I'll chop the onions for you.'

'No, it's alright, thank you. I'm OK.'

She presented him with the solid wall of her back. He went back to the room he shared with Yẹmi and tried to sleep. On Saturdays the flat emptied. Isoken returned to her salon, Fineboy disappeared into Lagos and Yẹmi too had begun leaving after breakfast, not returning till late. Only he, Chief and Oma remained but she stayed in her room, refusing to come out.

After breakfast, he dialled Ahmed with his own mobile, letting it ring once before he cut the call. Ahmed phoned back immediately.

'Any news?'

'Chidinma is fine. The men took her phone and told her not to contact you but they let her go.'

'Did they take her email address too? She could have sent me a short message. Hi Ahmed, I'm alive. How did you find out?'

'She called this morning. She was quite angry.'

'At least I used a good photo. It'll be good for her market. Is Chief Sandayọ there?'

'Yes, he is.'

'Please let me speak to him.'

Chike took the phone into the parlour. Chief was clipping his fingernails, letting the yellowish translucent crescents fall to the ground.

'Who is that?' Sandayọ asked when he gave him the phone.

'Ahmed. From England.'

Sandayọ took the phone and climbed up the stairs to the entrance door.

'Good morning, Chief Sandayọ.'

'So you've learnt some manners in England.'

'A friend of mine who works in the BBC would like to interview you.'

'You told her where I am?'

'They ran a story on their website when the *Nigerian Journal* was burnt down. They know about the article that caused the arson.'

'Where would my own interview appear? Just on the website?'

'It could be a leading story on the World Service.'

'What does she want to know?'

'She asked if she can contact you directly.'

The Ministers for Information and Petroleum were always being courted by the foreign press but not even a Middle Eastern broadcaster had asked to speak to Chief Sandayọ. He imagined being broadcast around the world. The BBC would show a colour-graded map, white for North Africa, brown in the Sahel, green below the Sahara, with a flag pin-pointing Nigeria and his voice playing over the continent. An interview with the BBC would particularly irritate the President, so careful of his precious, golden image abroad.

'No. Tell her no and don't tell her anything else about me.'

He dropped the phone. It was too risky. His life would be worth very little if he spoke to the BBC while he was still within the country.

'What did he say?' Chike asked.

'None of your business.'

'Just make sure you clear up your fingernails,' Chike said. 'Nobody is your slave here.'

46

Farida had dismissed Ahmed when he called with news of Chief Sandayọ's refusal.

'Not to worry. If he changes his mind just let me know. Thanks.'

Call me when you're of use to me, she should have said. It was not outside the realms of her directness. He had begun drafting a CV after their phone call, starting with his academic qualifications. An A and two Bs at A level, a result that had satisfied his parents without inflating them with pride.

He remembered the struggles of boarding school, the trials of boiled food and boys who did not know where Lagos was, who did not care, dismissing his entire past with a shrug. At his graduation his parents had flown in, wearing matching lace, his mother's gele fanning out and obscuring the view of the parent behind her.

'Excuse me. Please can you take off your hat?'

With all the dignity of a level seventeen civil servant's wife, she had turned to say, 'Does this look like a hat to you?' a reply that had made her a hero in her circle that summer.

Ahmed won the sports prize, a biographical detail too remote for his CV. The house had cheered for the first black student to be awarded the trophy he would later pose awkwardly with on the front steps of the school. At his graduation lunch, his father said in passing, 'It would have been good if you had applied yourself more and won a prize.'

'He did, sir,' his guest, the only other Nigerian in the school, had spoken up. 'He won the sports prize.'

'I meant an academic prize.'

'Bọla, leave your son alone. He's done well. I'm proud of his sports prize.'

'I'm not saying he hasn't done well. As his father, I have the right to tell him where he can do better.'

Three years later, only his mother had come to watch his name being read out with the other upper second-class graduates'.

'Your father sends his love,' she said, looking shrunken without her husband. 'Do you want to have lunch with the Ogunniyis? I don't want you to feel alone at your graduation celebration.'

'Mummy, you don't like Mrs Ogunniyi.'

'I thought you and her daughter were good friends.'

'Not any more.'

'So who do you want to have lunch with?'

He had invited the scholarship students from their African circle. Njongo, Calvin and Farida. None particularly close to him but the others had guardians or parents to celebrate their firsts, reassurance that the exorbitant international fees had not been in vain. Calvin and Njongo had been thankful to be rescued from the sea of flash photography, no lens trained on them. Farida had refused at first.

His mother liked her. She did not cover, claiming in her

generation boys did not stare so boldly, but she appreciated the aesthetic of a well-wound hijab. She and Farida sat next to each other while he, Calvin and Njongo huddled together in a tight triangle. They thought of themselves as men by then and modulated their voices accordingly, roaring when it came to football, dipping low when they spoke of salaries. From a single bank application, hastily sent, he had gotten a job that paid enough to sever all dependency on his parents. The offer letter spread ripples in his plans to start a Masters in Journalism and Media Publishing, a second degree he would have had to take out a loan to pay for.

His screen lit up. One missed call from Chike, who was so expert at flashing that the phone never rang. It was 10 p.m. and he was only three lines into his CV. If Chidinma wanted to sue, it could wait till tomorrow. He returned to the blank sheet of paper.

He had begun softly at Standard Silver, with photocopying and light reading on the Asian markets the bank was trying to break into. The pace had suddenly accelerated. Nine a.m. to twelve to catch the closing hours in Shanghai. Noon to 8 p.m. working on London time, then for the four hours until midnight, struggling to keep up with the best of the oriental brain, his boss used to say. Those who wished to impress stayed longer. Black hearse-like cabs ferried him to work and ferried him home. He slept in his office clothes, sometimes with his shoes on, sometimes with a container of takeaway still on his lap, the oil on the lid hardened to fat by the next day. He had woken up one morning and realised his twenties were passing in front of a screen monitoring share prices, the colourful, jagged graphs brighter and more varied than his life. He began searching for another job.

Stanton and Chaney, a bank that operated almost exclusively in European markets.

'Why do you want to leave Standard Silver?' his interviewer, Alan MacDonald, had asked.

'They work on Hong Kong time.'

Alan had laughed, lettuce from his lunch still wedged between two teeth. Alan was not overly concerned with individual performance so his team took it in turns to coast. During Ahmed's spells of inattention, he took half-days and went to seminars on conflict reporting, flinching at the photos of scattered corpses and severed limbs. He read interviews online and rephrased the questions. He emailed journalists and newspaper editors in Nigeria and all without affecting the team's final output, the only quota that mattered to Alan.

There had been women. A pregnancy scare at twenty-seven that shook him into nastiness. Paternity test. He had insisted and felt only unadulterated relief when the results came out. They would have gotten married if the helices in Denise's daughter had matched his own. He had carried the baby once. Her spine had curved against him, her head resting on his shoulder, her breath leaving a damp patch on his shirt, and he had wished her mother was anyone but Denise.

Childless and wifeless, he had been one of the younger students on his one-year master's degree in Journalism and Media Publishing. It was there he had taken the leap from wanting to be a journalist to wanting to own his own newspaper. Perhaps it was the figures in his account. Two hundred thousand pounds, stowed after a decade in banking, too much capital to go and work under an editor in Nigeria.

His editor pen pals emailed him almost every day. Now was the time. If you ever wanted to get into journalism in Nigeria, now was the time. The military with its stranglehold had been replaced by a democracy that held the press gently by the lapels.

His screen lit up again. Another missed call from Chike. Ten thirty p.m. and he had arrived at the point in his CV where he would either lie or tell the truth. Leaving a five-year gap was unthinkable. No interviewer would overlook the omission.

This time the phone rang for almost a minute, looping the dog bark that was his ringtone into a rabid frenzy. He picked up with apprehension, wondering what could have led Chike to sacrifice his credit.

'Ahmed, this is Chief Sandayọ. Tell your friend to call me right now if she wants her story.'

47

'Put the news for me.'

Chief Sandayọ missed satellite TV and the suave CNN reporters, both male and female made up to a smooth matt finish. These Nigerian newscasters were overweight and leaned heavily over their desks, reading the headlines in a flat monotone that rendered all news dull. He wished for a more modern TV. This one that curved at the ends into a metal box and phased from black and white into colour was from the early nineties. It rendered the newsreader even more un-attractive, her lips thick with lipstick that swung from a lurid purple to a deep black. New Speaker of the House selected; ambulance service commissioned in Lagos; former Educa-tion Minister's house burnt down in suspected arson attack.

The footage was in sepia, dark brown flames surrounding tan walls, a column of cream water cascading too late over the building. Afterwards they showed the wreckage, smoke still drifting from the ruins.

'That's my house.'

It was the house he had lived in with his wife and son, their memories now turned to ashes. They seemed to want to comfort him, the members of this assorted group of squatters. They moved around him silently, watching him as he slowly consumed the rest of his dinner. Who had lit the match? The First Lady famously carried snubs from her childhood, slights preserved and unsealed fresh forty years later. Senator Okpara, the Governor, Madam Ronkẹ, all the names dropped carelessly to the journalist, any could be behind it.

'It's a shame,' Chike said finally. 'The rights and wrongs of these things should be decided in court.'

'Always the great moralist. There is no judge in Nigeria brave enough to decide such a matter. Get me Ahmed on the phone.'

48

The girls were asleep when Farida's phone rang. They were always the girls in her mind, never the distinct entities she knew they would clamour for in a few years. 'Why did you name them like twins?' her ex-husband complained these days. 'When I call Adla Afaafa, she gets upset.'

'If you saw them more often, maybe you wouldn't mix them up.'

It was a lie, a little manipulation for a father who needed to be guilted into seeing his daughters twice a month. He had promised to change so often, she knew his phrases by heart now. Mukhtar was a vacillator, unstable as a nuclear particle. One moment, all children were from Allah. The next, only boys could carry his name. Women should work in modest clothes. Women working was evil. In the early days of love, she had vacillated with him. A lengthy denunciation of Western clothing led to the buying of her first burka. He had recoiled when she stood in the centre of their flat, her pose lost in the volumes of fabric.

'Not for you, baby,' he said, placing his hand on the eye slit and drawing it down to her nose. 'You're not like the women who wear those clothes to seduce men.' So she had worn her scarf and kept her loose trousers until he complained they showed the lines of her pants and drew the eyes of every builder she walked past.

'Not true, Mukti,' she, a first-class graduate, had said, in the baby English she reserved for him. After that, she had bought trousers two sizes too big and held them up with a belt.

He had a son with his new wife now, twelve years younger than him, almost a playmate for Adla. She saw her often, sitting in the car when Mukhtar came to drop the girls. A high, beautiful face, lifted even further by her hijab.

Her phone vibrated. Ahmed was calling. She let it thrum in her pocket until it stopped. Work started early tomorrow. Every day, all day, she cut the news of the day into clips that could be run on air. The ability to divine the best thirty seconds of a speech was a skill she wished she had kept hidden in her early days at the BBC when she was drifting through departments looking for where to settle.

Ahmed's politician was to begin her return to proper journalism. Her phone lit up with a text. It was him again, persistent with whatever he wanted to tell her. After he mentioned the minister's refusal, he had asked if she was free that Saturday. She had been abrupt with her excuse, remembering the extra tip he had flung on the restaurant table. She opened the text.

'Chief Sandayo ready to talk. Call him now. +234808 39501745.'

She couldn't make the call on her mobile. It would cost too much. Leave the girls alone, sleeping, while she dashed to the corner shop for a phone card. Headlines were made of less.

She stepped out onto her street in Colindale, the dead glassy eyes of the parked cars staring at her. She ran under a row of yellow street lamps, the wind cutting through her clothes, her feet pounding recriminations into her head. If Adla had an asthma attack. If Afaafa woke from a nightmare and Mummy was not there.

'Phone card,' she panted at the man in the turban whom she had bought milk from for two years and whose name she still did not know.

'Which would you like?'

'I don't know.'

'Where are you calling?'

'Nigeria.'

'Cobra is very popular for Nigeria. So is Talk Talk. Global Net is also good but if you're calling a landline—'

'Global Net.'

'Five pounds please.'

She snatched the card from his hand, threw a note on the counter and ran out.

When she got home, for a long time she stood in the girls' doorway, her shadow darkening Barbie's curls, faded after many tumbles in the dryer. If Mukhtar were here, she could have walked to the corner shop and waited to hear which phone card was best for Nigeria. If Mukhtar were here, she said to herself as she ran the back of her hand over her eyes, you wouldn't be going out at this time of the night. She shut their door and went to the living room.

The phone rang only once before she heard a voice say on the other end, 'Is this the BBC?'

49

At five the next morning, Richard Brown, the BBC correspondent in Lagos, was woken by Bob Marley's wailing. It
was his boss Edgar on the phone, a Christian who believed
in God and other strange things, who after work hours invited you for drinks and slipped folded pamphlets into your
hands.

'Morning, Richard. We have something for you.'

Ten minutes later, he was in his car, beeping for the watch-
man. This was not an assignment to take his driver on.
Sunday had a wife and six children, too many dependants to
be trusted.

In Ikoyi the streets were still quiet. He drove down the
smooth curve of Bourdillon, named after a popular governor general, the street name mangled to 'Bodylon' by
Lagosian tongues. Then along Osborne, christened for another European. The politics of road signs were largely ignored in this part of the city that had once been a British
reserve, no blacks allowed except as cooks and houseboys,
dumb waiters mixing gin with spit and tonic. Even now,
there were still many whites in Ikoyi, embassy staff mostly,
tethered to their compounds by security warnings, corralled
to a narrow radius of vetted bars and restaurants.

He was more adventurous than most foreigners. His work and love of Afrobeat took him frequently outside Ikoyi and the nearby affluent ghetto of Victoria Island, but he had still not travelled by public transport nor sat astride an okada, those 200cc motorcycles that moved through traffic like flies.

Yet in many ways, he was now a local. After a year in Lagos, he knew how to offer a bribe: never to speak of it directly, looking away when it changed hands, smiling when it was done. Who to offer a bribe: the higher-level officials feigned injury but their staff who granted access were more amenable. When to be familiar and jovial, aping the accents of those around him, breaking into the local patois. When to retreat into his skin and Western training: at press conferences, at checkpoints in the night.

He arrived at the Third Mainland Bridge, a concrete millipede curving over the lagoon for miles, built by an African government, a feat of engineering unnoted by the rest of the world.

Five twenty a.m. and the bridge was teeming with cars, the early drones from the mainland already rushing to work. He let his foot rest heavily on the accelerator, horning at the slightest provocation, the grey lagoon speeding past his right-hand window.

Ojodo. He did not know the place but an okada rider would. Only they could navigate the city. He pulled over after the bridge and beckoned at a rider with a foot dangling over his handlebars.

'Oyinbo good morning.'

Richard was wearing his most inconspicuous clothing.

Sunglasses, long sleeves, khaki shorts and a face cap pressed low. Anyone who saw him would remember a white man had driven past but they would not remember his face.

'Good morning. I'm trying to get to Ojodo Estate. Is it far from here?'

'Very far. I go show you road for two thousand naira.'

'You think I be JJC,' he said, mimicking the hee-hawing of Nigerian speech.

'Oyinbo you sabi pidgin. Oya pay one thousand.'

'Five hundred.'

They agreed on seven hundred naira and the boy gunned his motorcycle and sped off, showing off all the way. He zig-zagged down the straight arrow of Ikorodu Road, crouching forward like a jockey, riding so close to Richard, he worried the boy would take off a wing mirror. He dismissed his guide when he saw from road signs he was getting close and drove past the house when his second okada guide led him to the street.

He called the number he had been given, peering through the gates at the house with no roof, an open mouth gaping at the sky. Surely, Chief Sandayọ could not live here?

Richard did not see where the imposing stranger emerged from. Large-limbed and tall, he seemed to rise from the grass itself, a small tree of a man. Richard tried probing him, phrasing a few statements as questions, but the man was no fool. 'It will be best if you only interview Chief Sandayọ.'

A hot gust of spices wafted out of the ground when his guide threw the trapdoor open. The aroma thickened as they made their way down the stairs and he wondered if they would emerge into an underground restaurant.

'You came without a crew?' were the first words from a disgraced minister dressed for the camera, his pale blue robes spread like sheets around him, a thick gold chain glinting on his neck.

'I have my recording equipment.'

'Alright, sit down.'

The man who had let him into the flat, a sort of bodyguard for the Chief it seemed, retired to a corner of the room with a book.

'Good morning, sir. Richard Brown.' He dipped his head in a slight bow before taking the seat offered. When he met big men in Africa, he exaggerated his courtesy, watching their egos unfurl under the weight of his deference. It was symbolic to them, colonialism upended, black power asserted.

'Yes, yes, good morning. Let's get started.'

Richard placed his pocket tape recorder on a side table.

'Is that all?'

'This is just the pre-interview.'

'That's not what I discussed with Farida. I want it aired as soon as possible.'

It was difficult to explain news management to people who believed their breaking news reached them unglossed. The more exclusive the story, the more careful you were of its hatching. Too soon and it came out sickly and wan, a thing that crawled across people's screens and was soon forgotten. Too late and it grew heavy with details, sinking below the radar.

'Of course, sir. We understand the urgency. Perhaps you could start from when you were appointed Minister of Education.'

He switched the machine on, his eyes flicking often to its blinking red light to make sure Chief Sandayọ's accusations were being stored. Scandal, murder, intrigue. Quintessential African politics. His bosses would be pleased.

*

Chike had never seen a white man up close. On television, the males were mostly brunette with brown eyes and straight teeth. This one was tall and well built but a clash of colours with his red hair and blue eyes and the yellowish tinge of his teeth. He knew something of Nigeria. Not as much as the Lebanese Chike had come across in Ibadan, who spoke Yoruba and cursed if you called them foreigners. But enough to make the Chief feel a big man. As for Sandayọ, he was just as brusque with this white journalist as he had been with Ahmed.

Chike and the Chief had argued over whether or not it was safe to bring the BBC here. The Chief's enemies had burnt Ahmed's office, they had burnt the Chief's house and if they ever found this place, they would burn it down too, crisping them in their beds.

'They won't find us,' Sandayọ had said. 'We'll be discreet and we must not think of our personal safety too much. We began with fixing the schools but what I will reveal might fix Nigeria. You of all people should understand my reasons for doing this. And anyway, it's my house.'

The Chief had almost convinced himself that his was a disinterested crusade against corruption. In this preinterview, Sandayọ had a forthrightness, a rude directness that viewers would assume were the surface attributes of a guileless man. Chike wondered how he would come across in an interview. He had never been much of a public speaker nor a private one.

In the inner corridor, someone flushed a toilet, the gurgle of water reaching them.

'Is anyone else here?' the journalist asked.

'No.'

'I thought I heard flushing.'

'Look, did you come to interview me or do plumber work?'

The interview progressed much as it had done with Ahmed Bakare. Sandayọ shied away from questions of the stolen money, keen to focus on others' crimes. The Chief's accusations had grown even more fantastical. Human sacrifice. Blood covenants. All the macabre details of a Nollywood movie. A confection of lies or the truth?

If their leaders were as depraved as the Chief said, then perhaps this interview, broadcast around the world, would set off a larger chain of events. What could start a revolution in Nigeria? What obscenity would finally sweep the people out into the streets? In the room, the interview was drawing to a close. The journalist had switched off his recording machine and was standing to go.

'Thank you for your time, sir.'

'Don't waste any more of it. Bring the crew on your next visit. My man will show you out.'

50

When Farida called at 8 a.m., for a brief sleep-fogged moment Ahmed did not know her.

'Morning. I hope I'm not waking you. I was wondering if you could come into the office today.'

'Office?'

'My office. The BBC.'

'Ah, it's you, Farida. Have you spoken to Chief Sandayọ?'

'Yes. You didn't save my number?'

'Sorry. Didn't look at the screen.'

'We want a recording of you speaking about Chief Sandayọ. Is that alright?'

'Yes of course.'

The entrance to the BBC was grand, pillared and faintly imperial, built for an age now politically incorrect. Smokers were scattered round the steps and Ahmed wondered why they had not been shooed off until he saw one grind her cigarette under her heel and walk through the revolving doors. These were the staff. If their listeners abroad could see them, perhaps they would sever this last tie with Britannia.

'Ahmed,' Farida said, flowing into the lobby, her wide-sleeved shirt fluttering around her. 'Thank you.'

They touched cheeks and she handed him a laminated name card.

'Everyone is excited to meet you.'

She was voluble, chattering as she led him up the veined marble steps, grasping his arm when he turned the wrong way at a junction, tapping her collarbone when they approached a large group of her colleagues.

'Ahmed,' he said, naming himself repeatedly as hands clutched his again and again. Lucy, Tom, Claire, Alistair. All dropped some token words for him, each more gravely spoken than the last.

'We were very sorry to hear about the fire.'

'Such a shame.'

'A terrible loss for your country.'

At this last, he had smiled like an idiot at a funeral. The greatest day for his paper was its abrupt and entire conflagration.

'Ahmed, we're just going to pop you in front of a camera. Farida has drawn up some questions for you. I'll ask them slowly. Please go into as much detail as you like. We want your answers to be as natural as possible. Makeup!'

He backed away when the dotted foam came towards his face.

'It's just powder,' the makeup artist said.

'Of course.' He submitted his forehead for dabbing.

They placed him on a high stool and he slid to the edge until his feet touched the ground.

'Can you tell us a bit about yourself?'

History graduate. Banker. Newspaper editor in chief and

publisher: an unpredictable trajectory that made him seem like a maverick.

'How did you find Chief Sandayọ?'

No mention of the others, just of a messenger who had led him to the secret flat. 'Saying any more might endanger some people.'

'Did you imagine what the consequences of choosing to print this story might be?'

Here he was matter-of-fact, a manner of speaking which he could already see listeners construing into courage.

'Did you believe the allegations made by Chief Sandayọ were true?'

He found Farida's face. She was pulling a tassel in her scarf, willing him to say what, he could not tell.

'They sent people to burn down my building. You don't take so much trouble over lies.'

His presentation pleased them. They clustered around him afterwards, shaking his hand and murmuring of inspiration and freedom of the press.

'So what's going to happen with the story?' he asked, when Farida led him back to the entrance.

'It's big. We're flying a crew down to Nigeria.'

'I hope it does well.'

She left him on the steps with a new batch of smokers.

51

David West, fifteen-year veteran of the BBC, eponymous star of *West Presents* and owner of a sheepdog left in his ex-wife's care for the next two days, concluded yet again that his new team of researchers were challenged in a way presently undetectable to modern science. How many times must he ask for prose? Simple, English prose, not these nasty bubonic spots breaking up the flow of sentences.

- Former British colony. Gained independence in 1960.
- Largest population on the continent.
- Population evenly split between Muslims and Christians.
- Revenue chiefly from crude oil.

For each point, a subsection of more bullet points to expand. He slammed the sheets on the folding table and an air hostess peered over the divider.

'Sir, is everything alright? Can I get you anything?'

'Another glass of sparkling water.'

The cabin was dark. Most of the other first-class passengers were asleep, stretched out to their full length. A few sat at the bar, talking softly over champagne that would go straight to their heads at this altitude. Six hours between take-off and landing. Six hours to read this mess.

In economy, two thirds of the all-black production crew struggled to find a comfortable sleeping position. West had his own handpicked team who flew with him but this story was sensitive. Their foreign correspondent on the spot, a mediocre journalist, specifically requested that the crew be black. One white man going into a house drew attention. Two raised comment. Five was news.

Taj was a cameraman. No one knew his surname. No one had surnames in Arts and Culture. Mike next to him was the only Nigerian sound technician in the BBC, a distinction he had been unaware of until his programmes editor asked if he would like to travel home for a few days. Tito, hair and makeup, was from Essex but she was black, undeniably so.

The plane had just been buffeted through a section of turbulence, awaking the faithful to prayer.

'Obara Jesus.'

'I shall not die but live.'

'No weapon,' Tito's neighbour said. 'No weapon, no weapon, no weapon.'

'No weapon what?' Tito asked, woken from her shallow sleep.

'No weapon fashioned against us will prosper. My sister, will you join me in prayer?'

'Sorry, I'm not religious.'

Mike was sitting upright in his chair, flicking through their information pack for a summary.

'Have you read this?' he asked Tito.

'Don't need to. Parents are Nigerian.'

'But your name—'

'Tito. Bọlatito.'

The prayers in the cabin were beginning to die down. Taj sat still with his eyes closed, wishing for benzodiazepine. He was still smarting from the woman behind him. The band holding his dreads had snapped, spilling one loc over the back of his seat. 'Dada, don't put lice in my food,' she said, flinging the strand over his headrest and into his eye. The cabin swayed and he gripped both armrests, one of which Mike had long surrendered all claim to.

At the front of the plane, West had given up on Nigeria and moved to the pack on Rẹmi Sandayọ. His researchers had returned to their senses and were writing in full sentences again. Sandayọ had presided over what seemed to be a disastrous year for education. One national strike organised by university staff over pay. One regional protest organised by students over facilities. He moved on to 'Personal Life'. A widower with a son from his first and only marriage. The son was a doctor in America. Married with children. No activity in Nigeria.

'Corruption Allegations. Ten million US dollars missing from the Basic Education Fund, set up to improve reading and writing at primary school level.' David West highlighted this paragraph.

Some colleagues called *West Presents* a talk show because he opened with enquiries into childhood memories and musical tastes, moving in a constricting gyre until he landed on the single question that upset his subject's equilibrium. A Middle Eastern dictator once said it was like discovering the passenger was the one driving. He had given lectures to young journalists all over the world on what he called back seat control.

'Ladies and gentlemen, the captain has asked me to inform you that we will shortly begin our descent into Lagos.'

West stared out of his porthole to catch his first glimpse of Lagos. A rash of electricity spread over the city, an eczema of twinkling lights and street lamps, but mostly the skin of Lagos was a thick sable black. No constant power after decades of independence. No constant water supply. No constant healthcare. A rich African state but, essentially, a failed one. He put his papers away as the plane floated down.

At the tail, once the wheels touched the ground, seatbelts began to ping in release. An air hostess said, 'Please remain seated with your seatbelt fastened until the Fasten Seatbelt sign is turned off.' At the head, they gathered their things slowly; sluggish from their deep sleep and certain they would alight first. West was forced to queue. Usually, when he visited the Third World, he was met at the plane door but this trip was anonymous.

'What is the purpose of your visit?' the man at immigration asked.

'I'm here on business.'

'Of what nature?'

'Social business.'

'Welcome to Nigeria, sir. Hope your trip is fruitful.'

The arrival hall was a cramped space with no air conditioning, more staff than passengers milling around, the African problem of excess manpower apparent. The carousel rotated slowly, passengers thronging around it, jostling for suitcases bloated with foreign junk. He was glad he had no luggage, a small overnight wheeler adequate for the trip. He walked towards the customs officials by the exit.

'Anything to declare?'

'No.'

'Anything for us?'

'I don't have any local currency.'

'We take pounds, dollars, euros.'

The ten-pound note, the smallest he had, caused the man to salaam almost to the floor, his hands hovering above his toes in an exercise pose. He stepped out into the morning air, moist as a damp glove pressed over your face. An arc of African faces peered at him. He was mzungu in Nairobi, obroni in Accra, but he did not know what these people called him.

'You wanna taxi?'

'No thank you,' West said.

'You wanna make phone call?'

'No.'

'You wanna trolley?'

He ignored the tout and looked through the signs held up like stone tablets. The novelty of seeing his name on a placard in a strange capital never wore off.

'That's me,' he said, walking up to the man dressed in brown and orange print, the bright colours making him seem cheerful for this hour.

'Welcome, sir.'

He let the driver take his bag and fell in step behind him. The crew would meet him at the hotel.

52

The journalist's first visit and his impending return filled the flat with expectancy. No one wanted to leave for fear the film crew would arrive and they would be shut out till the interview was over, a calamity that would occasion much weeping and gnashing of teeth.

Chike was increasingly sceptical of this one-man media campaign against the government. Nigerians would not rise up over anything Sandayọ said. The scandal that could rouse people into action did not yet exist. There would be uproar and then things would die down, as they always did.

He could force Chief Sandayọ to call things off. Chief was still in their power, comfortable as he had grown with them. Yet a part of Chike, the part in every human that stopped to gape at crushed automobiles, wanted to watch events unfold. The cameras had been flown from England. The drama must run its course. They would come with their equipment and capture Sandayọ's self-destruction. For, whether now or in a decade, the Chief would pay for granting this interview. Till then, the people in England would have their evening entertainment and the Chief would score a few points, both sides pleased with the results.

'What will I serve them?' Chief Sandayọ asked, growing

giddier as his hour approached.

'There are some soft drinks in the fridge,' Oma said.

'But who will serve them? I can't serve them myself and neither can my right-hand man. Oma, will you do it?'

'I don't want to show on film.'

'Isoken, how about you?'

She looked at Chike.

'I'm the one asking you. What are you looking at him for?'

'How will we explain her being here?' Chike said.

'The maid, of course.'

'But she wasn't here last time. They might ask her questions.'

'I won't answer,' Isoken said. 'They can't force me. Please?'

'Alright. But don't speak at all.'

Two hours before they arrived, Chief Sandayọ began to grow fractious. He asked Oma to sweep the carpet a third time, bending himself to pick invisible specks with his hands. He swapped the positions of two of his paintings and then swapped them back.

'What do you think? They should see this waterfront scene when they enter, shouldn't they? Yes, that's right.'

When the others had retired to the inner rooms, they remained in the parlour in their new roles, minister, bodyguard and maid, until Chike's phone began to buzz in tinny song.

'Don't let me hear any flushing during my interview,' Chief Sandayọ shouted.

Who did the blighter think he was, West wondered as Richard Brown stepped into the stairwell before him. Brown's impudence had begun that afternoon at the hotel, when he had shown up half an hour before their scheduled meeting time. West had refused to come down until the appointed hour, and when he reached the hotel sunroom, he found the correspondent already briefing his crew. They were sitting by a window that looked out on the ocean, their armchairs drawn close in an insubordinate huddle.

'I hope you don't mind that we started without you,' the man said, rising. 'I'm Richard Brown. I've been the correspondent in Lagos for a year.'

'West,' he said, taking the man's hand indifferently.

'A real honour to meet you. I've listened to you lecture on back seat control.'

'Well, Mr Brown, thank you for looking after my crew. Perhaps if you could sit a little way from us while we discuss things. I hear Caucasians draw attention in this place.'

It was the first inkling the crew received of why they had been thus assembled. On the trip to the hotel, they had wondered why a makeup artist from CBBC, an Arts and Culture cameraman and a sound guy for a pilot sitcom should have been drafted into this hurried visit to Nigeria.

'Not here. Look around. It's out there that's an issue.'

There were other white men, now that West did look around. Shorts-and-sandals types in a room full of ties. There were Chinese too, buttoned up in collared shirts and black suits, their professionalism matching the dark wood flooring. A waiter walked past, balancing a tray on his finger-tips. A yacht cut slowly through the water, a sleek, white triangle at least fifty feet from bow to stern. Richard Brown resumed his seat in a comfortable armchair and left the high rattan stool with its low back for West.

'As I was saying about lighting—'

'Before we get into that, I want to meet the crew,' West said.

'Pardon me. I thought you flew down together.'

'He flew first class,' Tito summarised, straining the atmosphere as finely as the orange juice sitting pip-free in her glass.

'BBC policy,' West mumbled.

'Taj,' the dreadlocked man said, placing his hand on his chest, an acquired and now unconscious gesture he made every time he said his name. 'I'm the cameraman.'

'Mike. Sound and lighting.'

'Tito. Makeup.'

'Very nice to meet you all. I'm David West. So,' he said, turning to Richard, 'any new developments in the story?'

'Did you listen to the pre-interview I sent to London?'

'I prefer to approach a subject with fresh eyes.'

'Well, Chief Sandayọ is a typical "big man" around here. Never answers a direct question. Your material may need a little rephrasing if you want to get the most out of him. He made some serious accusations two days ago.'

'I think we'll find my material will be fine.'

'The apartment is quite spacious so there'll be many angles for you to work on, Taj. We're hoping there'll be electricity when we arrive. If not, we'll have to wait it out.'

And so on until it was time to leave and West had made

little input into this exclusive edition of his show. Brown insisted on driving the news van, adamant the local driver could not be trusted.

'Do you have to beep at every car we pass on the road?'

'I swear they can't see you if you don't.'

'Yeah, these Lagosian drivers are mad,' the sound technician said from the back seat as they ran a red light.

West abandoned his notes and looked out of the window at Nigeria. The country had had its share of dictators but none had captured the Western imagination, no cannibals in their ranks. The architecture was Third World concrete, of a style he had seen from Bangladesh to Burundi, square, heavy-set buildings, made for colder climates, hot as coffins inside. Waste spread around them, like Lagos was one giant bin, filled with empty Coca-Cola bottles and cellophane wrappings. There was a bustle and a buzz but not in the purposeful manner of New York or Tokyo. This was the aimless energy of a crowd, static electricity flowing nowhere, sparks rising from too many bodies jostling in too little space. He wrote down 'static electricity' under Ojodo, their destination. It sounded exotic, not to be found in the midst of this squalid city.

Perhaps I should retire after this. It was a thought that came to him before each interview. It was reassuring that despite Brown's manic driving, his mind was calm enough to produce it.

'We're here.'

A tall, imposing man let them into the compound and led them to the derelict building. The light was too dim to see his features.

'Evening. It's better if we don't talk until we get inside. Just in case.'

In case of what? He had no idea what the Nigerian government would do if they were caught. Not much, he expected. Not to a man of his profile. They entered the flat, Brown intolerably preceding him; his subject awaiting like a fat cloud.

53

Chief Sandayọ sat resplendent in a white agbada, a squat, cylindrical cap perched on his head, and resting on his lap, of all things, a flywhisk.

'Rẹmi, I presume,' West said, pushing past Richard. The Chief did not rise.

'Who is this?'

'Evening, sir,' Richard said. 'This is David West from the BBC, flown in specially for this interview.'

'Alright, welcome. Sit down, all of you. Would you like something to drink? There's some juice and soft drinks.'

'We were hoping to get started as soon as possible,' West said.

'It won't take time. Bring some drinks, Isoken,' Chief Sandayọ said.

'Isoken,' Taj murmured.

'I'll just start setting up the camera,' he said softly when she returned with the tray. No one saw the blinking light as the lens began to capture her movement.

With the exception of Taj, they all drank the sweet apple juice. Tito and Mike sat on a single sofa with their knees touching. West and Richard sat on another, as far from each other as the space would allow.

'Did you all fly down from England?'

'Yes,' West said.

'The BBC must think this is a big story.'

'There is some excitement at headquarters. If we could start soon—'

'What's the hurry? I'm not going anywhere. Enjoy your drinks.'

'Power might go at any moment,' Richard said.

'That's true. Isoken, clear these tables.'

'Makeup.'

Hollows brimming with oil soaked up Tito's first layer of powder to Chief Sandayọ's nose.

'So much? Do you want me to look like a masquerade?'

'Your skin is quite oily. You should try an exfoliating face scrub.'

When Mike switched on his equipment, the lights in the room trembled and grew dim.

'Power can't carry everything.'

In the end, neither was adequately lit. He dipped the boom mike, a furry pill-shaped creature, floating in the space between their foreheads.

'Are we ready?'

'Don't call me Rẹmi in the interview. Either Chief Sandayọ or Minister.'

'Action,' Richard said.

'From his secret hideout, Chief Rẹmi Sandayọ, former Minister of Education, is threatening to bring down the Nigerian government. Two months ago, he was removed from his position after corruption charges were levelled against him by Nigeria's Economic and Financial Crimes

Commission. Many expected him to keep a low profile and disappear. Instead, he granted an interview to the editor of the *Nigerian Journal*, in which he accused the First Lady and popular Senator Okpara, amongst many others, of crimes including corruption, drug trafficking and murder. The same day the article was published, the office of the *Nigerian Journal* was burnt down, leaving many wondering if the allegations were true.

'Is Chief Remi Nigeria's first high-profile whistleblower or one of its most corrupt officials yet? I join him in his hideout to find out.

'Good evening, Chief Sandayọ, and welcome to *West Presents*.'

'Thank you, David.'

'You've made some very strong accusations but before we go into that, let's cast our mind to the late forties when you were born. What was it like growing up in colonial Nigeria?'

'Of what relevance is that question?'

'Cut.'

'I want to ease you into the interview.'

'I'm at ease. This is my house.'

'Let's try that again. Please try and answer the questions, Chief,' Richard said. 'Take two, action.'

'Welcome.'

'Thank you, David.'

'You studied literature at the University of Ibadan, started your own printing press at thirty-two and were a successful businessman before being appointed the Minister of Education. How did you make that leap?'

'Your colleague did not ask me any of this.'

'Cut.'

Tito rushed forward to spread powder on Chief Sandayọ's forehead, which was beginning to glow.

'Chief,' Richard said, 'if we stop, we have to start all over again so please, no matter how seemingly trivial, answer West's questions.'

West drew a line through his notes. There was a school that believed driving a subject to refutation was the only way to conduct an interview. It was a kind of hard talking he recoiled from but he had gained some proficiency in the style before discovering back seat control.

'Take three. Action.'

'Welcome, Rẹmi. The government has called you a thief. One newspaper report describes you as "Nigeria's most clueless public official", but we want to know what you say. Who is Rẹmi Sandayọ?'

The Chief visibly swelled under this assault, rising like dough.

'Chief Olurẹmi Sandayọ, the Jagunmolu of Gbongan, is first and foremost a patriot. I have not called you here to carry out a smear campaign. I've called you because I want to speak out against a corrupt government that is destroying this country.'

'But some will ask: why wait until you were sacked to speak out?'

'Who said so? I fought for the democracy we have in this country. Check it anywhere. I marched. I was tear-gassed as a member of the Yoruba People's Congress. I have been speaking out for years.'

'Perhaps against the military, but you've been oddly silent

during your one year as minister. In fact, there has been no recorded criticism from you until now.'

'When you are first appointed to the top of the system, your response is not to throw your hands up and say, "This place is so dirty, I have to run to the papers." You want to clean it up. If you've done your research, you'll see, as a private citizen, I took education to the deepest, most under-developed parts of Yoruba land. They knew me as "Teacher" in those days. But I couldn't duplicate my success in the min-istry. I could not. The rot has gone so deep. Even to the smallest clerk.'

'Let's widen the interview to the accusations you made a month ago. You said, and I read from the now infamous *Ni-gerian Journal* article, "The First Lady has three foreign ac-counts in Dubai. She calls it her shoe and handbag money." How does one know about corruption at the highest levels of state without being part of it?'

And the Chief was ushered into his element. He dropped his voice confidentially when he spoke of sex scandals, his voice rose to prepubescent levels when he mimicked the reckless political wives and finally, in his closing, he thundered against the system.

'Let's move now from allegations concerning others to one closer to home. The ten million dollars, Rẹmi. It has been alleged it was embezzled from the Basic Education Fund. What happened to the money?'

'Before I answer you, Richard, let me ask. Who are you to question me?'

'This is an interview, Chief Sandayọ.'

'In your country, the descendants of the biggest thieves,

are they not the ones making the decisions? Your House of Lords. Who made them so? Was it not by oppressing the poor, by swallowing all the land? Today, we are calling them "my Lord", calling them "Honourable". Your banks built on the slave trade, Lloyds, have they returned any compensation?'

'You're saying the British judiciary of today should pursue centuries-old crimes?'

'What of the ones of today? Where does all the stolen money in Africa go? Your being here is a case of the pot calling the kettle black. And because the pot is bigger, more powerful, better armed, it can talk anyhow to the kettle. But one day, in my lifetime I can assure you, there will be a revolution in the kitchen.'

'That may very well be so but till then, the question remains: is the kettle black? Did you or did you not steal the money, Remi?'

After a pause, West said, 'Chief Sandayo?'

Taj zoomed in on his face, the surface of which was placid.

'I took it.'

'You admit you stole the money.'

'I took it but not for myself. I was tired of seeing projects we designed at the top never trickle down to the bottom. So I decided to become my own personal Ministry of Education, like I was in the days of the YPC. There are over ten schools that my team and I have fully equipped.'

'Your team?'

'Yes. I and a team of committed Nigerians who love this country and believe that she must be great again. In a few weeks we have achieved all I have been trying to in one year in the ministry.'

'Chief Sandayọ, you are aware that your claims are easily verifiable.'

'Mushin High School. Agege Primary School. Mile Two Elementary. Kudirat Shagamu Primary School. Those are some of the names. Check it.'

'We certainly will. Thank you for coming on *West Presents*, Chief Sandayọ.'

'Thank you, David.'

'This is David West from Nigeria, on this exclusive edition of *West Presents*. From me and the team, good night.'

'Cut.'

54

'You and your team fixed the schools?' Chike asked when the journalists had gone, stale excitement left behind, the room warm from their crush of bodies and machines.

'Is that what is bothering you? Isoken, clear this place please.'

'She's not your maid. Sandayọ the benevolent, the great benefactor.'

'What did you want me to say? It was that tall man in the corner who fixed the schools. Hail him. Interview him instead. Is that it? You want to be famous? I can call them back. Tell all with Chief Sandayọ, part two. Chike the brains behind the mission. The brightest—'

'What if you've put those principals in danger?'

'How? Once you take the crew to interview them, it'll be obvious they know nothing about where the money came from.'

'Who is taking them where?'

'You heard what David West said at the end. They want to verify my claims about the schools.'

'No.'

'Isoken can take them.'

'Not me,' she said.

'Fineboy will do it then.'

'Do what?' said Fineboy, stepping out of the corridor and yawning. 'Is it over? How was it?'

'Chief Sandayọ lied and said that he stole the money on purpose to renovate the schools and now the journalists want to go and see the schools that we fixed but Chike has refused to take them,' said Isoken.

'Were they white?'

'What does that have to do with the price of fish in the market?' asked Isoken.

'I've never met a white man before. It wouldn't be so bad if I went,' Fineboy said, turning to Chike. 'Surely it doesn't matter who gets the praise as long as the schools are fixed.'

'Do whatever you think is right,' Chike said. He climbed out of the flat and into the early morning. It would be dawn soon, another day in Lagos, two school deliveries to supervise. There was rain in the air. The soil had opened to receive moisture, a metallic scent rising from the earth.

Chief Sandayọ's words had stung him, perhaps because they were true. If he stopped Fineboy from going to Kudirat Shagamu with a film crew, he would not be doing so out of concern for the principals. No one watching them would ever think they had been party to a conspiracy, not when they thought their benefactor was a woman.

Showing the schools could even bring about some change. International shaming always drew responses from a government sensitive to foreign opinion. More schools might be renovated. More children given a chance at a better future. No, it was not the principals he was worried about.

Let not thy left hand know what thy right hand doeth. That thine alms may be in secret: and thy Father which seeth in secret himself shall reward thee openly. And if you didn't believe in heaven or a Father there? Who would see and know that Chike Ameobi should be credited?

*

In London, they received Taj's editing with mild surprise. At the introduction, instead of West's usual stare down the camera, only his crisp voice rendered anachronistic by the images of the young maid it played over. She was beautiful, like many anonymous Africans who had made their way to the BBC on film reels and photo stills.

'We can't use this,' the producer said after they watched her fill a glass in silence. The room was too dark, almost sinisterly so, the dimness made pronounced by the Chief's white clothes catching what little light there was. He sat like a sage, with his hands folded in his lap or drifting into the air when he wished to emphasise a point. The bitterest accusations were offered in an emphatic, lecturing style that gave weight to his words. On occasion, when West pressed him, he would lurch unsteadily to an answer, the epidermis of composure thinning but never disappearing, even under the most direct questions.

Above all, West's trademark circumspection was missing, replaced by a hungry, inexperienced journalist, so eager to trip his subject up that he opened a new lead at the end of the interview. They could not run this episode without further investigation into the schools Chief Sandayọ claimed he had refurbished. The crew would not be pleased.

*

'You're bloody joking. It's my cousin's wedding this weekend and I'm a bridesmaid,' Tito said, packed and ready to return to England. It was her second trip to Lagos – the first was when she was a toddler – and she was finding the experience unpleasant. The water tasted funny, the food upset her stomach and the staff mumbled, 'Ọrọbọ,' when she walked past, staring at her hips.

'Down with the BBC,' said Taj, whose mortgage was the only thing stopping him from quitting his job and backpacking through Asia. He too felt vaguely harassed by the hotel staff. He had wound his locs into a bun and covered them with a beanie. Still the doorman called out, 'Bob Marley!' every time he passed through the lobby.

'I'm staying. You people have British passports. If they sack me where will I go?' Mike said. His relatives did not know he was in Lagos. He did not want them to.

'We'll find one or two of the schools Chief Sandayọ mentioned. Film a few shots and we're out of there. You'll be able to take the evening flight if you want,' said Richard.

They had accepted by this time that Richard was the leader of their mission. West seemed to be wilting in the heat, water running out of his pores as quickly as he consumed it.

'I left my dog with my ex-wife and she won't keep him for longer than two days.'

276

Chief Sandayọ had declined to take them to the schools himself, instead proposing a man who was rather curiously called Fineboy.

'He'll meet you by Kudirat Shagamu School at nine tomorrow morning.'

55

'Howdy,' Fineboy said, peering into the van full of journ-alists. There were two white men in the back. They would have been worth millions in the Delta, catapulting him to fame as he read out demands in a clear accent, the muzzle of his gun pressed to their heads.

'Good morning. You're the man Chief Sandayọ has sent to take us to the principals?'

'Yup. If you'll just step right out and follow me.'

Fineboy did not know if his accent would impress. The British refused to Americanise, leaving their broadcasts nasal and difficult to understand. He always swung the dial when he landed on the BBC.

'How do we know it's the Chief that sent you?'

It was the only woman in the group speaking, dark with a frizz of blonde extensions scattered around her face.

'I'm here to take you to the principal of this school.'

'My colleague just said that. I'm not going anywhere with this man until he gives us some confirmation. This is Nigeria. People go missing here.'

'We don't need a makeup artist for this section. You can stay in the van if you don't feel like coming, Tito.'

'Who said I don't need makeup? I am sweating like a pig.

You're not the one standing in front of the camera.'

'Look, Chief sent me to meet you. You guys are from the BBC and you're covering the work he's done here. Come with me now or forget about your story.'

'Well I'm not staying in the van. How long have you had this driver?'

The woman climbed out backwards, her jeans sliding down to reveal the lace fringe of underwear. The leather belt lashed to her hips was for show, it seemed. The rest followed with their equipment.

'Let's move fast. We don't want any touts asking questions.'

'You didn't tell us your name,' the woman said.

'Fineboy.'

'Well, at least that's the name the Chief gave us.'

'It fits me, right? Am I not a fine boy?'

She was large for his tastes but it would not hurt to have a girlfriend in London, one stop from America.

The children were outside their classrooms, covering their new swings and slides. They stopped playing when they saw the white men.

'Oyinbo,' a few called out, too shy to come close. Both before and after the renovation, these children were lucky. School for Fineboy had been a paddle away, a dense, terrifying mangrove forest on either side, an empty building at the end of the journey, staff gone off trading in the creeks, supplementing their small incomes. School had been a transistor radio, kept in a box and draped in protective cloth throughout the day, a household shrine cosseted with care and waterproofing. Every evening the black machine would speak like an oracle, prophesying a future of milkshakes and soda pop, jazz and hip hop, freeways and shopping malls. He learnt English from that radio, he learnt how to steal batteries for that radio and the day it died, after his younger brother dropped it into the oily water under their house, he cried more than he would for his father, found dead with neat slashes in his wrists.

'All this is brand new. I'll take you to the principal and she can show you around. I'll be mentioning a guy called Chike a lot. That's Chief Sandayọ's agent.'

'Why isn't he the one showing us around?'

'He's down with a fever.'

Fineboy had overseen this school, down to the last desk delivered and so, in a way, it should be him, not Chike, showing the oyinbos around. He knocked on Principal Amadi's door.

'Fineboy, morning. You saw my text saying that we got the final batch of textbooks. Who are these people? Shut the door,' she said, when she saw the two white men.

'Morning, Principal. Chike sent me with these journalists to see the renovation work that we have been doing here.'

'But he said the donor wants to remain secret.'

'I have a letter of authorisation.'

He gave her the forged note, the signature at the bottom swooping and large. The principal lifted it to the light, like one trained to spot counterfeits.

'Why didn't he come himself?'

'He has fever.'

'How long will it take?'

'Not very long,' one of the white men said. 'Just a few

shots of you talking about the new things you've received and then some footage of the equipment and we'll be off. Don't want to disrupt the school day.'

'Yes. These things can distract the children. I won't give you more than fifteen minutes.'

She showed them desks, one to each child for the first time, and the rows of books, lined like bricks, and lastly the computers, waiting for the arrival of an IT teacher to be switched on.

'It's not that our teachers don't know how to use computer. I myself, I can surf the net and all of that but we want to hire someone that can really use the resource. We've been asking for these things. Government has promised to provide but sometimes the demand is too much. It's good that a concerned Nigerian with the funds has decided to help us. We are hoping for more like her.'

On their way to the next school, Fineboy sat next to the female member of the crew, leaving no space between them, his thigh touching hers.

'So how you finding Nigeria?'

'Hot.'

'Met anybody interesting?'

'Look, I have a boyfriend if that's what you're trying.'

The van laughed as he shifted away.

'Tito!'

'Give the man some hope.'

'Is this how the women are over there?' he asked one of the white journalists. 'So hard?'

'Yes. It's all this feminism, isn't it, Tito?'

'Shut it.'

'You know I'm part of the team that fixed those schools.'

'Really? Chief didn't mention any of your names. We'll pop you in front of a camera then if that's OK with you. Ask a few questions. Are you happy to do that, West?'

The other white journalist, who had been leaning silently against the window, shrugged.

And just like film trick, after the story had been confirmed five times, they pointed the camera at him.

'No, I don't want you to show my face. Just my voice. And I want you to use my presenter name. Golden Voice. I'm a radio guy.'

'OK. Taj, if you shoot in the other direction so we just see the back of his head. Excellent. Rolling.'

'So you're one of Chief Sandayọ's team.'

'Yeah. I sure am.'

'Please tell us why you chose to join him?'

'Education is my passion, my vision and my mission. A country can't have a future if there is no provision for the kids to go to good schools. I met the Chief and I believed in the promotion of his vision and so I signed up. We said the donor was a woman so nobody would suspect us.'

'And what would you say to those who think that it's wrong for you to have adopted this method? That it's a crime for you to take government money and use it in this way.'

'I'd say the Chief is the Minister of Education and he's just doing his job in an unusual way.'

'And cut. That was excellent, Fineboy. You did it like a pro. One take.'

56

The entire production team of *West Presents* was gathered in Meeting Room 12. The inner wall was made entirely of glass, an aquarium design that allowed senior members of staff to peer in without stopping, time-saving on taxpayers' money. A rectangular light wood table took up most of the room. In keeping with his Marxist leanings, the producer sat at neither end. A bold intern, overly bold, was first to speak.

'We can't use this as it is. It's too . . .'

'Too much like propaganda for Rẹmi Sandayọ.'

'People will be bored by an honest African politician.'

'Hardly honest.'

'He robbed the rich to educate the poor.'

'Nigeria's Robin Hood.'

'That's good. We could use that for follow-ups.'

'Someone is sure to be offended.'

'The Nigerian government might sue.'

'It's about time the BBC started offending people again.'

'Easy for you. You're retiring soon.'

'With no pension to speak of.'

'Let's stay on topic please.'

'What are we going to do about the girl at the beginning?'

'Leave her in.'

'Take her out.'

'We'll lose West's introduction.'

'He can record another one when his flight lands tomorrow morning.'

'No, leave it in. It adds something.'

'Atmosphere.'

*

The night *West Presents* aired, Ahmed was invited to the Strand and introduced to the crew. The cameraman he thought affectedly uncouth. His beard grew up his face and into his locked hair but his shoes were leather tapers that spoke of Italy. Tito he would have guessed was Nigerian until she spoke in the singsong accents of the north of England.

'Are you from Manchester?' Ahmed asked.

'Essex.'

He found David West unpleasant. His manner in person was as it was on screen, didactic relieved by bouts of bonhomie.

'How did you find Lagos?' Ahmed asked him.

'Intriguing. In a way it hasn't moved on from its colonial past.'

'How so?'

'The city has expanded on the grid left by empire. It makes the place terribly overcrowded.'

'I see. The planning is colonial.'

'What else? The people seem to bear no memory of having been British. That's the best thing about your country.'

'After one trip, the man's an expert,' Ahmed said, when he was beside Farida again.

'Who, West? It's his job to be an expert.'

'Even to people from the country.'

'Especially to you.'

'It's on.'

The lights went off and Isoken came on screen, laying out bottles and glasses in graceful, balletic movements.

'You know her?'

'Yes.'

'She's very beautiful,' Farida said when Isoken bent to pick up an ice tray.

'More so in person.'

Chief Sandayọ came on next, volumes of white agbada swirling around him like the crisp waves of a meringue.

'I think you're more beautiful,' he whispered to Farida.

'Watch the interview.'

Even though most of the room must have watched it, there was a murmur of excitement when Chief Sandayọ said, 'I took it.'

His candour was insulting. When Ahmed had pressed him about the money, Chief Sandayọ had blustered into anger and threatened to end the interview. At the time, half a story had seemed better than none, so he had done sloppy work this pompous foreigner had gone to finish for him.

'I took it but not for myself,' the Chief said.

There was some brief footage of secondhand computers, then Fineboy's garbled American voice explaining why he joined Chief Sandayọ's 'team' and then the principals, effusive in their praise of the mystery benefactor. The last headteacher, staring earnestly down the lens, said, 'Every day I thank God for our helper. She has saved us from the Education Minister who took the money meant for our children.'

The rascal had landed on his feet.

57

'Arrested today' was all Principal Amadi's text said. Each time Chike called, a cold, remote woman would say, 'I'm sorry. The number you are trying to call is presently unreachable.'

He went and saw the desolation for himself. They had drawn red Xs on the fresh walls and pushed over the swing set, its seats smashed to wood chips. The effort it must have taken to carry out that act of vandalism. Had they come with axes or had they gone through the neighbourhood looking for a firewood cutter to lend them his tools? At the gates he had once walked through freely, a single armed policeman stood guard, holding his rifle against his body like a spear.

'Yes, what are you looking for here?'

'I came to see the principal.'

'What for?'

'My son,' Chike faltered. 'My son attends this school.'

'You can't see her. She's been arrested.'

'Please can you take a message for me?'

'Do I look like a houseboy? My friend, leave this place before I arrest you.'

When he got home, Chief Sandayọ was in his favourite

gallery pose, his hands behind his back, his face close to a painted sunrise, dawn spreading over brown huts and green fields.

'It's you, Chike. Why are you coming down the stairs like a wild animal?'

'Principal Amadi has been arrested. Along with the other principals.'

'Why?'

'Why do you think?'

'I'm not going to play riddles with you.'

The Chief turned back to the Arcadian canvas world, dark, upright figures walking to and fro, masters of their own land. The painting slid off its hook easily and when Chike threw it, it flew like a missile, crashing into the wall and landing on the ground, face down.

'My wife bought that,' Sandayọ said, running and kneeling by its side. 'You tore it!'

Sandayọ lifted it from the ground, gently, like the dead wooden frame could feel his touch. 'It was for our fifth anniversary. Every year, a new anniversary painting. Even when we had stopped living as man and wife, the painting must come on the eighteenth of March. Twenty-seven of these I have.'

The Chief put it back in its place. The rent slit through the sun, a gash in the sky.

'I suppose you think it's my fault. But it was my money we used to fix those schools. How could I know where it would lead?'

The space suddenly felt too small, the room contracting until he felt he would have to kill Sandayọ just to breathe.

Chike left the flat and went above ground. The principals would be sitting in jail now, trying to describe the man who had lured them with his story of a mystery benefactor. If Chike found them and visited them, would they shout as he approached their cells? 'This is the man that brought us the stolen money. This is the man to be locked up.' He was no Christ to give himself for the sins of others. Sandayọ had stolen the money and Sandayọ should be in jail.

The principals would not be released unless Sandayọ was arrested. They were being used as bait to draw him out and were the Chief a more principled man, he would hand himself in. And were pigs a lighter species with hinged wings, they would fly.

58

Ahmed sat opposite Farida in a private booth in Jade Garden, a yellow paper lantern hanging over their heads. There was a shimmer of metal on her eyelids and she was wearing lipstick. It was almost a date.

'Have dinner with me tomorrow,' he had said, the evening before. Her acceptance surprised him.

'You will? OK. Where is best for you?'

'I can't come into central London. The girls.'

'I'll come to you then.'

'But it's too late to find a sitter. Maybe another time.'

This was her way of saying no gently. Her earlier refusals had been curter.

'They can come with us.'

'That would be asking too much.'

'I want to.'

She held the line, breathing so softly he thought she had gone.

'Farida?'

'There is a Chinese restaurant they love and it's very close to our house. But who would I tell them you are?'

'A friend from university.'

Adla, the elder, was Farida. Small with features geometrically precise. Afaafa must look like her father, Farida's ex-husband. They were divorced, legally, although Mukhtar had not seen the need. If he wanted to remarry, a traditional ceremony would suffice.

'He just assumed I would never have another husband.'

'Would you?'

'I don't know.'

All this was said hurriedly while the girls filled their plates. When she drank, her lipstick left the shape of her lower lip on the glass, a full, crimson curve. The girls returned and their conversation moved on. They were engaging but not attention-seeking, leaving him and Farida to discuss how West's episode had been received.

Apart from a poorly punctuated letter asking the BBC to co-operate in apprehending Chief Sandayọ, the Nigerian government had mostly been silent. The story had spurred debate on the internet and comment pieces in national papers, with clips of the interview played and analysed on some other news agencies.

'We'll wait and see where it goes,' Farida said as he helped her into her coat.

He walked them home, glad to amble despite the cold. They could almost have been a family. He hugged her on the doorstep. Their cheeks touched and he felt a slight pressure from her body before she pulled away.

He could be a father, he thought as he walked to the station. He could imagine dropping the girls at school, driving them to away games, teaching them how to eat ẹba with their hands. He was getting ahead of himself. One almost date and he was planning a wedding. His phone thrummed in his pocket. A text from Chike. 'Principal Amadi arrested this afternoon', he read. Ahmed turned and began to make his way back to Farida.

*

'Ahmed, what are you doing here? Did you forget something?' Farida had changed into pyjamas and she pulled her dressing gown closer. Nothing in the evening had suggested sex.

'They've arrested one of the principals David West interviewed. I just got a text from Nigeria. Apparently it happened this afternoon.'

'Please come in.'

He walked in through her narrow hallway, his arm brushing against her satin thigh as he edged past her. The house was in that state of accumulated disarray that showed she did not have many guests. The girls' toys were out, half-clothed dolls with their naked legs splayed, their heads stuck in the crevices of the sofa, books on the floor, washing out to dry, the empty cups of a bra dangling pertly from a radiator. She stood in front of the lacy B cup, still pitifully small after two children.

'Please sit down. Would you like anything to drink? Some juice or a cup of tea?'

'No thanks. I'm fine.'

She called her boss, who was still at his desk, monitoring a protest in Albania. Ahmed, noting her self-consciousness, sat on the arm of the sofa and looked down at the carpet or her bare, swollen ankles. The bra was squashed under her armpit when she dropped the phone.

'He wants me to come to the office. What am I going to do with the girls?'

'Take them with you.'

'They need watching. Adla has asthma and Afaafa doesn't sit still.'

'I'll watch them. We can all go to the BBC and I'll stay in the lobby with them while you do what you have to do.'

'You've already been too kind today.'

The only other option was to drop them at Mukhtar's house. To stand on his doorstep and wait for him to look at her like she had just looked at Ahmed. Perhaps his new wife would come to the door instead, carrying her son on her hip.

'Thank you. I'll just go and get us ready.'

The girls were in bed but still awake. She paused at their door. Sometimes, a quarter of an hour would pass while she eavesdropped but there was no time for that now.

'Adla, Afaafa, we're going into my office tonight. Ahmed will look after you. I want you dressed in five minutes.'

In her room, her clothes from that evening were still spread out on her bed in the outline of a person, like a flat scarecrow. The black cardigan and black jeans had seemed appropriate for a casual meeting with a university friend. The red lipstick was not but it had been a while since she sat opposite a man in a restaurant and he paid for what she ate. She changed and went back to the living room.

'Mum, your hair.'

There was a time she had gone without her hijab, just after the separation from Mukhtar when every week was a new change: new flat, new school for the girls so why not a new look. She did not think God minded her afro, combed out every morning until it stood up straight, swaying only with heavy gusts of wind. But *she* had minded. Minded rushing to mirrors to see if resting against a wall had flattened the back, minded the knots the hair tangled into, minded the community she had stumbled into by not chemically straightening her hair. Adla and Afaafa could choose what to do with their hair but she was too old for new habits.

59

Over the next week, the arrest of the principals made the front page of every national newspaper in Nigeria. One by one, each was taken into a custody that did not permit bail or allow visitors. One anonymous teacher recounted how her principal had been dragged out of a lesson at gunpoint, terrifying the class of six-year-olds. 'THIS IS NOT LIBERIA', the headline had run, causing one Mrs Ene, Liberian wife of Mr Ene, to email a six-page letter of complaint to the editor.

The mood in the flat was growing increasingly oppressive and Yẹmi was glad to escape. Against the statistical odds, he had succeeded in becoming a tourist in Lagos.

First, he paid for his excursions with his savings and when that ran out, with a hundred-dollar bill taken from Sandayọ's loot. He was as deserving a recipient as any primary school. He had left school at eight and the government owed him many years of education.

He would enter a bus, not minding the destination the conductor was calling, riding all over the city. He had been to beaches, sinking into loose sand, gathering shells into his pockets; drawing near the worshippers in white garments that fluttered like wings; stepping at last into the ocean and gasping as the cold water surged round his feet. He had walked in a protected forest, plunging into the emerald silence of seventy-eight hectares of undisturbed habitat, his guide pointing out the reserve's animals: monkeys, snakes and the half-submerged head of an alligator, lying in wait for its prey. He had visited a small village of artists, cane weavers, painters and sculptors, moving through their exhibitions for free.

It was in this manner he came to see the water city. At first it had looked like any slum. The single-storey houses, with corridors that ran from front door to backyard, were of a style common to Lagos. He peered down the shafts that led to the plots of communal living. Naked children stood patiently in buckets while their mothers doused them with water, washed clothes bleached in the sun and in one lot, he saw a streak of silver grey.

'Good afternoon, Ma. How much?' he asked the trader who sat in front of a pile of bronze roasted fish, each bent in a circle, its tail stuffed into its mouth. He spoke to her in Yoruba.

'Three hundred for one.'

He paid without haggling.

'Does this area flood?'

'Sometimes. You know we are near the water.'

'Where is it?'

'Behind the houses.'

'Do you know somebody that can take me there?'

'Junior,' she said, causing a small boy to slide out from under her table.

'Yes Ma.'

'Take this man to see the water and if you see Uncle Sabo,

ask him to take him on the canoe.'

They walked down the narrow alleyways squashed between the buildings. Very quickly, they left the sandy ground and came to soggy swamp crisscrossed with wooden planks. The boy stepped on one and it swayed. Yẹmi held back.

'You no go fall.'

He soon saw his first house. It stood high on its stilts, its wooden ankles bathing in salt water. He had seen villages built on the sea in the Delta but nothing of this magnitude. Everywhere he looked, the grey houses and their rusted roofs spread like a sheet. Lightweight canoes moved between the buildings, their owners paddling lightly to steer. They were selling things, drifting from door to door, passing up plates of food and fresh fruit, sliced and wrapped in cellophane.

'You want to take the canoe?'

'Yes.'

'Let me go and find my uncle.'

Some residents had taken to emptying their waste by their houses and the rubbish drifted together in small islands. The boy had returned with his uncle.

'Afternoon. My name na Sabo.'

'Ẹ káàsan. Yẹmí lorúkọ mi.'

The man switched to Yoruba.

'My son said you want to go on the water. Enter, let me show you around.'

They pushed off slowly, the boy at the front, Yẹmi in the middle and the uncle rowing at the back.

'How long has this place been here?'

'I don't know,' Sabo said, 'but I came to Lagos twenty years ago and even then, it was here.'

Some houses were squat, with doorsteps almost level with the lagoon. Others were two storeys high, relative skyscrapers. Plank bridges ran from building to building and children, adults, even a dog, walked surefootedly across.

'Where do you go to toilet?'

'In the water.'

'Where do you have your bath?'

'In the water. It's enough for everybody.'

'What work do you do here?'

'Many of us are fishermen. Let me show you.'

They left the traffic of canoes and the houses came fewer and further between until they came to a part of the lagoon unbroken by stilts. Scattered along the surface were men standing still as silhouettes in their low-sitting boats. Occasionally a net would be thrown, arcing in slow motion before it sank. Some fishermen had rafts and it was these that caught Yẹmi's eye. They had rigged sails to their platforms and they hovered, cloudlets, above the water.

'What do they use to make them?'

'Plastic bags sewn together.'

The sun was setting and the fishermen were starting to come home. *Okachi Rice*, he read off the corner of a sail before the raft moved by.

'It's time for me to go back to Lagos.'

'Where do you think you are?' Sabo said, turning the canoe around.

When they reached land, Yẹmi offered to pay him but he refused.

'My son told me how much you paid for the fish.'

'What do you call this place?' Yẹmi asked as he stepped out onto a plank.

'Makoko.'

60

Ahmed's phone rang. It was his father.

'We saw you on BBC. You're putting on weight in London.'

'Yes. I should leave the flat more.'

'You should have told us you would continue with the story from over there. You would have saved my time. I went to prostrate for you last week. The dust from that man's shoe entered my mouth for nothing.'

They did not speak for a few moments.

'Come to England,' Ahmed said.

'I have cancer.'

He did not ask how having one meant you could not do the other.

'Since when?'

'Since last year. Prostate. The doctor said it won't kill me.'

'I'm sorry.'

'You're sorry. You don't know what it's like to have a son that is ashamed of you.'

His father had paid the school fees of over sixty people in their village and they would all come for his funeral, lining up in black to show their grief, wearing dark glasses to hide their tears or their conspicuously dry eyes. There would be no surprises by the graveside, no illegitimate children rushing forward as they lowered the corpse into the ground. His father had been faithful to his mother. In that at least, his conduct had been honourable.

'I didn't agree with all your choices.'

'How you can reach your age and still be so like an infant? Maybe it's because I sheltered you. I should have left you in the village like your grandmother was always asking. There are roads in that village because of me. There are graduates. There are widows who did not have to watch their children starve. And my child. My own ingrate child—'

His father's voice cracked.

'I know, Daddy. I know.'

'Ahmed, I am old. One of my children is dead and the other is a stranger to me.'

'Come to England.'

'And join you in your fugitive life? You're lucky these are not the days the military used to kidnap wanted men and smuggle them home. You didn't ask me what happened when I went to prostrate.'

'Did it help?'

'That upstart from Ondo. He watched me lie flat on the floor before telling me he no longer had any clout with the presidency. That he was just a retiree living in seclusion. All the way to Akurẹ to hear such lies.'

'How is Mum?'

'She wants to go to Dubai. She wants to stay at home. She wants to come to London.'

'You should travel. Somewhere.'

'Why? I'm not the one making accusations on BBC.

301

There's been a car parked outside our house for days. Maybe they think you'll show up here one evening. Stay in England.'

'You'll think of coming. It may get dangerous.'

'Yes, yes. I'll talk with your mother. She sends her love. The flat in London that only you stayed in for most of the year: that was my own love.'

*

They would wake and find him gone. Chief Sandayọ had imagined a grand farewell, a personal leave-taking with a message for each one but it was too dangerous. They might not let him go so easily. Some hours after midnight, he stepped over Fineboy and walked into the men's room, careful of Yẹmi's body spread on the floor. He had once seen Chike half under the bed, rooting around for something. It could only have been his money.

He cupped the beam with his hand. It was Oma's kitchen torch, slid into his pocket while no one was looking. The black polythene bag gleamed dully in the far corner. He got his head under and then his neck, then his shoulders, the ridge of the bedstead pressing into his back. Above him, Chike breathed evenly. He stretched his hands and his fingers brushed the thin plastic, then grasped it, then pulled it until both he and the money were out in the open. There was no time for counting.

'What are you doing?' Chike asked.

He turned off the torch.

'Rẹmi.'

'Yes.'

'What are you doing?'

'What do you think?'

He had run from his beloved wife, leaving her for duller women who did not disappear into vigils and trances. He had run from the YPC when the assassination of its leaders began; he had run from Abuja, dragging his money behind him, and now he was running again.

'On top of the wardrobe, under the kitchen sink and in the carton by the staircase. Your phone and car keys are in that bag as well.'

'You won't alert the others?'

'And then what? Renovate more schools? Put more principals in prison? We were going our way before you came and we'll continue when you're gone. That money is tainted. On your head. On your children's heads.'

'I know you don't believe all that.'

He worked fast but carefully, packing the money tight into Oma's market bags. Then he went from room to room stopping briefly by each person with some cash.

'I left something for the women with a note. I even left for Fineboy, obnoxious fool that he is. He began things with the journalist. I'd forgotten how it felt to stand with my head stubbornly against the tide. To be you.'

'Where will you go?'

'I don't know. Accra first and then wherever I feel led. I'll be back in a few years, maybe when this First Lady has gone. Prostrate in front of a few people and things will go back to normal.'

'The others will miss you. We worked well together.'

'And you? Let me leave you something. If you were

ministry staff, you would have earned a salary for what we've done.'

'It's not yours to give.'

'I await your beatification, Chike.'

His car remained as he had parked it, unchanged but for a covering of dust. When he turned the key, the engine whined and died. Perhaps it was a celestial finger pointing him back to the flat. And what good would that do, in heaven or on earth? On the sixth try, the petrol in his cylinder caught fire and the engine began to rotate, humming a single bass note.

*

Chike was lying down awake when Fineboy entered the room.

'Chief is gone.'

'Yes. He left not too long ago.'

'Then we can still catch him.'

'He's driving.'

'You knew.'

'Yes I did. Please go and wake the women and meet me in the living room. Yẹmi, get up.'

After a few minutes, they were assembled. He did not sit and neither did they. He was the Colonel addressing his troops, feet at attention, no one at ease.

'Chief Sandayọ has left with his money. He's heading to Ghana. If we call the police now, they can watch out for him at the border.'

'But he left us money,' Oma said. 'He was our friend.'

'It's not his to give. Those principals will never be released if Sandayọ is not captured.'

'He was our friend,' Oma said again.

The upper door clanged open. They thought it was Sandayọ, returned to find them plotting his downfall. Then a rush of footsteps and the first policeman stepped into the parlour, followed by another and another, in their black plastic hats, pouring in like a swarm of beetles.

'Where is the Chief?'

Their guns were new, their boots gleaming, their faces a stern rictus. As long as you were in khaki, the police were nothing to be afraid of.

'Which chief?'

'Don't be foolish. We have photographs of Chief Rẹmi Sandayọ entering this building.'

'He has gone.'

'Where to?'

'We don't know. He left yesterday.'

'All of you. Your hands behind your head. Search this place,' the unit leader said. They were a disciplined squad. They fanned into the rooms with precision, kicking open each door then jumping to the side, waiting for the on-slaught of bullets that never came.

'Who are you people?'

'We are just squatters. The man you call Chief Sandayọ found us here and left us. He didn't tell us his name. He didn't stay long.'

'Why are you the only one answering? The rest of you, are you dumb? You. Yes, you. Why did he leave?'

'I don't know. He didn't stay long,' Oma said.

'Why did he come here then?'

'Nothing. I don't know.'

He rammed the butt of his rifle into her shoulder and she staggered back.

'Look, there's no need for that,' Chike said, moving towards their leader. The point of the gun swung into his cheek.

'No need for what?'

The man's hands were shaking. He could feel the tremor travelling down the barrel and onto his face. It was some sort of medical condition, a palsy of his nerves, not fear. This man would shoot him and have no recollection of it tomorrow.

'Stop that rubbish,' Chief Sandayọ said from the stairs.

*

He had reached the express when he saw the swirling red and blue of a siren convoy. From his protest days, he knew the terror of a line of black vans, the police inside them sullen and trigger-happy, tear-gas canisters dangling from their fingers. He had seen things from the other side in Abuja, when he had inherited a convoy with darkened windows and grown used to whizzing anonymously through the city.

He parked and kept his head down. Police escorts were banned in Ojodo Estate. It was one of the reasons he had chosen it. Yet this one had driven up to the gates and was now being let in. He drove back to the estate.

'Hey, who let those police in? As a member of the Estate Committee I demand to know why that escort was allowed in. Who is responsible?'

'Sorry, sah. They are not escorting anybody. They came with special warrant. We cannot stop them,' the guard said.

'Where were they going?'

'Macaulay Street, sah.'

'Open this gate.'

They checked the resident sticker he had peeled off a car that morning and waved him in.

On Macaulay Street, the vans were parked and empty. For the first time since his wife's illness, Chief Sandayọ began to pray. His cynicism and disbelief crumbled, like they had fallen apart at the sight of Funkẹ on a hospital bed, wires running through her, feeding, cleaning, monitoring her faltering heartbeat. He had joined her prayers then, cobbling scripture from memory, saying amen to her rambles, much to his wife's amusement and disbelief. That she would see him pray as she lay dying, it was the sort of fatalistic joy that hymns were penned to.

'God of heaven,' a location of no use to the Chief now, 'and of earth,' too vast for his purposes, 'and of Ojodo Estate, please save them all. Do not let them be punished for Christ's sake. Amen.' It was the bargain Funkẹ had always used when petitioning for things.

He waited, the gear stick on reverse.

Do not let them be punished for your *sake.*

It was almost audible, the voice. He was too old to be listening to phantasms in his brain, his fears amplified, his conscience expanded until it brushed against his eardrums. The voice was feminine, reminiscent of his wife. It would be like Funkẹ to leave her eternal work of psalm singing and harp playing to trouble him at this moment. Where was her spirit when he had said yes to a ministerial position that had brought him nothing but shame? Where was she when he had filled those bags, stacking the money like bricks, building towers of greed? Why had her ghost not stayed his hand then?

In the YPC, they had never subscribed to European codes of conduct. The chivalry of 'all for one' was impractical in their situation. They had long agreed that if any of the committee were arrested, the rest would disperse and regroup. No one was to make himself a sacrifice. He switched off his engine and began to make his way towards the building, bags trailing behind him, arguing with himself all the way.

*

'Arrest him,' their commanding officer said. 'Arrest them all.'

The man was short and stocky, a Colonel Benatari in proportions, his face and hands a crosshatch of scars and near misses. He was not used to being challenged. Chike could see he was growing impatient with these interruptions to his authority. Handcuffs were unhooked from belts and stretched wide to receive their wrists. They would be separated in prison, into male and female. The guards might take a liking to the women. Isoken would not survive such an ordeal again.

'Wait,' Sandayọ said, struggling to regain control of the arm that had been seized.

Why had the Chief come back? It was too absurd to believe that this man who had stolen millions would turn inches from escape and fly back into the fowler's net. Unless the Chief had begun to believe the image of himself he had fashioned for the BBC, the burnished idol of Rẹmi Sandayọ.

'Wait. I have something to say. Step back. I have an offer for you. How much did they say I stole? Answer me. How much are you to recover? Ten million dollars, isn't it? There's at least nine million here. Nine million dollars right here but nobody knows that except the people in this room.'

'You can't buy your way out of this. I've radioed the Police Commissioner to say you've been captured.'

'Not me. Let them go and we'll say you only found seven million. I'll swear to it in court. That's two million *dollars* to share. More money than you will ever earn in your lifetime. Any of you.'

'You are very bold for someone under arrest.'

Chike could see the struggle in the commanding officer. There was a gold band on his wedding finger. He would have many dependants. The others were standing still, barely breathing as they watched this drama unfold. Oma's lips were moving without sound. She must be praying.

'Make up your mind,' Chief Sandayọ said. 'They'll be waiting for us at the station.'

'Who said I have to work with you? I can take what I want and still arrest you all.'

'I'll know. The Commissioner of Police will certainly wonder why nobody told him when you were sharing money.'

'Are you threatening me? I can have you killed right now.'

'You'll explain to your superiors what happened between my capture and death.'

'You resisted arrest.'

'Shoot me then.'

If they killed the Chief, they would kill them too. There could be no witnesses. He had seen countless executions. No matter how brave or courageous, at the last moment the sphincter would loosen, soiling the air and tarnishing the reputation. He would never distinguish himself in combat, never marry, never have children, never mumble to Oma that this nervous excitement he felt around her was love, never show Isoken how to break a man's nose, never tell Fineboy that his accent was a nuisance, never thank Yẹmi for the countless services his private had done him.

'Sir, if we're taking this money, we must start dividing it soon.'

It was one of the subordinate officers speaking. They too were watching the drama tensely, calculating how and where and when they would spend their share.

'Alright. Get out.'

Oma bent to pick up her scarf.

'Don't touch anything. It's all evidence. Just go before I change my mind.'

'Thank you,' Chike said when he passed Sandayọ.

'Maybe you'd have done the same for me, St Chike. Don't worry. These are just servants. They can't do anything without orders and I have powerful friends. Did you hear that, Mister Man, I have powerful friends,' the Chief shouted to the commanding officer. Already things were shifting in Sandayọ's direction. The Chief would take care of himself.

At the top of the stairs, Chike turned and saw the police-men kneeling before the money, counting and placing it in stacks. Their commanding officer watched closely, his tremulous hands rising often to stroke his beard. It was their turn to eat. Who knew when next they would be invited to the table?

61

They left through the hole broken in the fence, an ignoble reversal of fortune that saw them worse off than when they had arrived. They were thankful for the escape, thankful they would not be forced into a van with Chief Sandayọ, handcuffed, stifled, fearful, but already they were looking back.

'I wanted to buy a sewing machine,' Oma said. 'Where am I going to find the money for that again? I left what Chief Sandayọ gave us behind.'

'I already make plans. I wan' go Badagry, see the slave something.'

'I have to go back,' said Isoken, the least mercenary of the group. 'It was what I needed for my fees. For when I pass JAMB.'

'The police might have gone. Once they've taken the money, what do they need the flat for?' Oma said.

Leaving would hurt Oma the most. She who had scrubbed the walls and polished the floors and bought new covers for the cushions, how could she not look back, like Lot's wife, turned to a pillar of salt, longing for her crockery, left on the shelves of Gomorrah.

'Anyone who wants can return but as for me, I'm going to the bridge,' Chike said.

They stood hesitant on the roadside, late birds in a migration, unsure whether to leave the comfort of their nest. Fineboy was the first to follow him, crossing the gap with swift, decisive steps. It was a gloomy ride. No one wanted to arrive. They willed the journey to last longer, comfortable in the dark limbo of their danfo. But this night, when they would have been happy to jerk forward, keeping their place in a sea of brake lights, there was little traffic and they sped back to their old home.

The bridge was more awful in fact than in memory. Had they really lived in plain view of passers-by, like animals in a zoo, their every action on display? Had they really slept in this open stink of running sewers and rotten food? First, they greeted Chairman.

'You people have come back. Where you disappear go?'

'We travelled,' Chike said.

'Welcome. The money you paid before is still valid. We don't do things rough here. We are very organised.'

They found a space and sat huddled on the ground, shy of each other once more. Their cardboard bedding had been torn to shreds and discarded, useless in the bounty of the flat. Chike remembered now how close Oma had slept to him, her breathing keeping him awake some nights. The cement was cold and hard when he lay down, harder for his absence.

'Brother Chike.'

It was Fineboy, squatting by his head.

'Yes, what is it?'

The boy placed something rolled and cylindrical in his hand.

313

'What is this?'

'Money.'

From the flat of course. If anyone had been sharp enough to keep hold of their share, it would be Fineboy.

'How much?'

'Three hundred dollars. Everything Chief gave me.'

Sandayọ had been generous in those last moments. Even to Fineboy he would have given more, Chike thought. And who was he to confront the boy? Fineboy was loyal to them, in his own strange, amoral way.

'I know you don't believe I can do something like this.'

'No. You've misunderstood my silence. I am very grateful. We are all grateful.'

62

When Chief Sandayọ was shown to the small room with two camp beds on either side, one already occupied, he had complained immediately.

'As the Minister of Education, I demand a single room.'

'Please come with me.'

He followed the orderly down a passage with cells on either side, putting his wrist to his nostrils, breathing through the perfumed cotton of his sleeve. A torch was shone into a cell. Rows and rows of bald heads shone back. Most of the prisoners were sitting, dozing in that position, their heads hanging between their knees.

'Nah who dey shine that light?'

'God punish dem.'

'This is the standard accommodation here. There are no more single rooms available. If you don't want that place, you stay here. This is not a hotel.'

As if sensing the presence of another human being, Sandayọ's neighbour began speaking soon after he returned to the room. He spoke conversationally, not as a sleeptalker but like a mad man, stringing topic to topic: football, women, the cost of onions in Mile 12. He must be relatively important to have secured such quarters: a 419er, a drug lord, or perhaps a politician whose face he would recognise in the morning.

The room smelled: a warm, faecal smell. Not long after he lay down, his neighbour farted, a moist burp of gas. The window was fastened with a padlock. Death by asphyxiation. Outside a light went on, streaming through the bars and onto a calendar, laminated and waxy, the days of the year numbered and accounted for.

He faced the wall, head cradled in his arm. How had it come to this? His in-laws had always said he would end up in jail, the parvenu whose suspenders matched his red shoes and who travelled abroad for the first time as an adult, exclaiming at snow and the London Underground.

He wondered how long it would take for his son to hear of his arrest. Gbenga was his sole next of kin, his only legally recognised child. He hoped the boy would not be foolish and come to Nigeria. He would be of no use here. All he could do was follow him to court, trailing a step behind his handcuffed father, his soft, confused face on the cover of every daily the next morning. Assuming he had a trial. Resisted arrest: it was not too late for those words to become an excuse for his discreet murder. Nobody knew he was here except Chike, Yẹmi, Fineboy, Oma and Isoken. It pleased him to say their names out loud, adding his voice to his roommate's briefly.

Already he was doubting his 'experience', if you could call the promptings of his conscience that. There was no mystery to what had happened outside the flat. Ruthless as he was, he had principles and they had guided him from within. He had always known that if necessary, he would rise to some sacrifice, some greatness that others, glossing over him and plumbing him superficially, would be amazed at.

63

Chief Sandayọ had been in prison for five days now. Everyone connected with the story was ending up in jail, except Ahmed safely ensconced in South Kensington.

'Very ornate,' Farida said when she visited last weekend, without the girls because they were with their father. He could not have Farida without this ex-husband and his rota of scheduled visits and drop-offs. It was like a supermarket deal.

She had been playful when she came, sitting cross-legged on the sofa, leaning forward to pinch him once, a delicate nip of pain on his upper arm. And then a kiss so brief when she was leaving, he was not certain it had happened, or if the fact his lips had half covered hers meant she had only wished to offer her cheek.

He had not been good company. He was still disappointed with the lack of media interest over the principals, from the BBC and other channels. Their incarceration had coincided with the engagement announcement of a royal.

'There's no space for foreign news in the media right now unless it's a terrorist attack. Especially since she's marrying a black man,' Farida had said to him.

'Yes. We all have tails.'

He had seen a headline three days ago: WE'RE BLACK

AND BLUE, with the photo of the couple, the woman a smiling, undistinguished brunette, the man a mixed-race strain that could hardly be called black, with his green eyes and curly blond hair framing his handsome face. Tucked away in a small paragraph in a minor newspaper, he had seen news of the principals, a still of a woman beaming in front of a row of computers.

'Sometimes a story just sinks,' Farida had said, taking his hand. 'It's nobody's fault. All we can do is hope that some civil society groups will take up their cause in Nigeria.'

She had left soon after that, the handhold, then the half kiss. He could not enter lightly with Farida. These small displays of affection meant more with her than any woman he had been with. To kiss her properly, with his arms around her waist and her body pressed close to his, would be a proposal, a declaration of intent that would include Adla and Afaafa and even Mukhtar, their absent father.

He turned on the TV and found himself watching a live music show with a short, excitable presenter introducing guests like he was calling up circus acts. The bands were passable, the steady dub of average music, the stylised leads blandly good-looking and white.

He had had enough when the presenter said, 'And ladies and gentlemen, to close the show, we have the one, the only, the legendary Ọla. But first, a break. Don't touch that remote control.'

He wanted to see what Ola looked like now, this hero of his adolescence, held up as proof that Nigeria was not irrelevant since it could produce such a star. She had discovered her heritage in her last two albums, spelling her name with a dot under the o, speaking often of her Yoruba roots, tendrils floating across the Atlantic and joining her to the ancient city of Ile-Ifẹ. It was good for the music if managed well, this cosmetic mysticism.

The presenter returned to the screen, more solemn now. They had dimmed the lights and there was a shimmer of smoke on stage, preparation for communion with the ancestors. The camera panned the audience, handpicked it seemed for the fresh, healthy glow they gave off under the yellow studio lighting.

She had aged well, he saw when she walked on with her guitar, loping to the lone stool set out for her. She was still as thin as the Africans on Oxfam appeals, her veins rising like little green bridges over the back of her hands. Her loose brown curls fell down her shoulders.

She strummed the first chord of her song and the audience cheered. They had not whooped so loudly for the other acts. Ahmed felt pride, that curious immigrant pride for the successful whose names twinned yours with their strange consonants, their pasts as obscure as yours.

Ola or Ọla strummed her opening chord again. Was she nervous? He could not tell from her expression, the relaxed, open look of a face used to being followed by paparazzi.

He imagined the producer fidgeting as she played the same chord, wondering whether to scream 'Adverts,' before she upset their strictly rehearsed show. He willed her not to disappoint, to pour out the voice that lifted you on currents of air, floating you into oblivion.

'I dedicate my first song to Rẹmi Sandayọ, a man imprisoned for trying to do good in my fatherland, Nigeria.'

Give me freedom,
Pay my ransom,
Take my kingdom,
For you.

Break my chains,
So I can run again,
I want to walk on water,
With you.
Set me free,
For eternity,
I want to plumb the oceans,
With you.

Give me freedom,
Pay my ransom,
Give me your kingdom,
Give me you.

I'll follow you, deep into the sun,
I'll fly with you, to where the ends of the stars
        have begun,
I'll float with you, over the edge of the world,
If you'll let me
Come with you.

Give me freedom,
Pay my ransom,
Take my kingdom,
For you.

64

The bridge was now a strange place. They had lost the rhythms of the space, the art of sleeping amidst the nightly disturbances. They had forgotten the crude privations, the indignities of furtive squatting, the embarrassment of a buttock exposed. They had forgotten that day was always shaded, sunlight blocked out by the bridge, and night was never night, carousing fires burning till the morning. It did not leave time to think of Chief Sandayọ or wonder how he was faring in prison.

They were absorbed by their resumed hardship, embittered by it, Chike the most so. He could no longer concentrate, take a thought and run it through his mind for hours. All he could feel was that an injustice had been done. He had known contentment in this city. He had found a place and purpose and he had lost it, cast out into chaos, an urban Adam with no garden to tend. The gnawing was back, the longing, the grasping for basic things. He could not look at Oma and Isoken. He had failed them, led them round the wilderness, back to Egypt.

The attack on the bridge took them by surprise. Chairman and his boys had made enemies or perhaps the enemies had always been there, only their battles had been fought further afield. A single gunshot woke them. Chike's reflexes were intact.

'Lie down and stay still.'

Chike counted fifteen, not more than Chairman's boys but surprise on their side. He could see sticks and cutlasses; at least two rifles.

'One by one, we are going to walk slowly until we reach the main road. Nobody stop. Nobody look back. Oma.'

'I can't.'

She was in a panic. Not the heavy-breathing, limb-jerking type that you could coax a man out of with words. It was quiet, leaden, soldered-to-the-ground terror. Isoken was no better. She had covered her face with her hands. Self-defence would not help her here. Not against guns. He could not ask Isoken to go first.

'Oma, please.'

'I'm too afraid to stand up.'

He could not hit her as he had done once or twice to a soldier who would not move, a sharp, stinging blow to bring him out of his paralysis.

'Just think there's a pot of soup on the other side, about to burn if you don't get there now,' Fineboy said.

'As if I would leave soup on fire unattended.'

She was crying, like the first time they met, full circle in her tears. Chike could not think of what could reach her, only that he could use no force, not even to pull her to her feet. He knew too much of her history to lay his hands recklessly on her.

'Make you sing that song for am,' Yẹmi said.

'Which one?'

'Nah for your Igbo language. Aturu something.'

Aturu was sheep. Sing to Oma of sheep? A nursery rhyme? He could not understand the private. And then he remembered his mother's anthem, sung as she cut through life in the lonely, rocking boat of single motherhood, her son clinging to her, a barnacle she could not scrape off.

'Atulegwu. Nwoke atulegwu.'

Oma had left her husband with only a bag and a few sets of clothes, left him for Lagos, a carnivore of a city that swallowed even bones, and yet she had survived, had adapted, had discovered fat in this lean land and thrived.

'Atulegwu. Nwanyi atulegwu.'

This woman whom he loved deeply, anxiously, who could make him grow timid with a glance, whose hands had fed them since they came to Lagos, turning oil and leaves into soup, bruised tomatoes into stew, old yams into pottage, their daily miracle worker.

'Atulegwu. Nwenu Okwukwe.'

He closed his eyes as he sang, willing into his voice a courage that would strengthen Oma's calves, strong and shapely, muscular and slender, legs for walking, for taking life in her stride.

'Your voice is croaking,' she said finally, standing like a

toddler, pushing herself up from the ground with her hands. 'Just keep singing for me. Even when you think I can't hear it.'

But there was no time to indulge this romance of the singing lover. Any moment now they might be seen. 'Isoken,' he said when Oma was about to disappear from sight. The girl made no fuss now someone else had done it. She walked with her head down and her elbows out like he had taught her, in ramming position. She was as tough as a seed, seemingly dead for months, yet put in the right soil she would shoot up, reaching for the world.

'Fineboy.'

The boy was the most blasé, almost drawing attention with his casual saunter. And yet where would they be without him? There was always a way with Fineboy, always a road where others saw the smooth, concrete bricking of a wall.

'Yẹmi.'

'I dey go last.'

'Private, don't question my orders.'

'We no dey for army again.'

'Yẹmi, please.'

When he was alone, Chike waited a few minutes, watching the clashing of sticks and steel, the pop of glass bottles shattering like fireworks over dazed heads. Perhaps they should have joined the fight for their bridge, thrown themselves into the melee with nothing but their fists. It was not a place to risk dying for, this patch of cold cement.

He walked slowly to the others. Oma was still singing. He took her hand and she took Yẹmi's and he took Isoken's and she took Fineboy's and Chike led them down an empty road lit by street lamps, standing guard like tall metal sentries. The city was empty, an architect's model of a place, the pavement stretching barren for miles. Every once in a while, a car would speed by, the driver's eyes flicking anxiously to their group. Only thieves gathered at this hour.

'What now?' Oma said.

'We can call Ahmed. He's overseas. He can help us.'

Chike imagined the world as Fineboy saw it, people lined like instruments in a toolbox, none unusable, not even the ones he had no names for. Why had he not thought to call Ahmed sooner? The man must have a place in Lagos or at least would know people who could house them until they found their feet.

Ahmed answered on the second ring. 'Hello Chike, what's the matter? It's late. Do you want me to call you back?'

'We need somewhere to stay for a few nights. We've had to run away from under the bridge.'

'You're staying under the bridge? For how long? You should have told me.'

'You could have asked. So are you going to help or not? My credit is going.'

'Sorry. Of course. My place is not safe. Please give me fifteen minutes. I'll find something. Where exactly are you?'

Behind them, the bridge was on fire, the flames as tall as a building, new floors rising with each passing breath.

*

If Ahmed called his father now, he might wake him. But there was no one else he could call, no one whose house would absorb five guests at such short notice. He had grown used to independence from Bọla Bakare. Living in the London flat was bad enough and now he would add this favour to a growing debt.

'Ahmed, what's the matter?'

'Good evening, Dad.'

'Is everything OK? Are you in trouble?'

'Not me. Some friends of mine need help.'

'What kind of help? Is it money? Couldn't it wait till morning?'

'Sorry. I shouldn't have called.'

'Well you did. I'm awake now. What is it?'

'They've been made homeless.'

'What kind of people are these?'

'They helped your son when he was in hiding and had nowhere else to go.'

'You must be saddle-sore from riding that your high horse. I just want to know that we can trust them under our roof. Your mother will want their family histories, I'm sure.'

'You can trust them.' Except Fineboy perhaps, but Chike would be there to keep an eye on him.

'Text me the address.'

'There's no real address. They're waiting on the side of the road.'

'Well, text me what road they're on. And if any of them has a phone, put us in touch. Your mother has woken up. Hold on.'

He could not hear his mother's end but he could imagine

it, fretful and needing to be calmed. When Ahmed was a child, long after he was too old, he would creep into their bedroom and lie in the valley between his parents, scared there by a nightmare. Sometimes his father would tell a story of Ijapa, the tortoise who outwitted his friends and enemies alike. Ijapa who swindled the entire animal kingdom and was wanted in nests and burrows for fraud and embezzlement and theft. When Ahmed was older and he understood more of what had been done with the papers that filled his father's study, he recognised the workings of Ijapa in their houses in America and Dubai, his father outsmarting the dull system with ease.

'Can you imagine your mother, wanting to come with me at this time of the night,' his father said, returning to the phone.

'Will it be safe?'

'What else can I do? I'll take the jeep with the tinted windows so no one can see inside. The parked car has left the front of our house but you can't be too careful.'

'Thank you. I'm sorry to drag you into this.'

'I have always cleared up your messes, Ahmed. I'll call you when I've found them.'

*

When Ahmed called to say they could sleep in his parents' boys' quarters, they had expected servant rooms, narrow beds and thin mattresses, rusted bathtubs and a large sink they would all crowd over each morning, jostling for space with cooks and gatemen. They had been at a loss when they saw the cream sheets and felt the cool air blowing from the AC vents: three large rooms between five of them.

For the first time in years, Chike had a room to himself, the smallest of the three. Their meals came on silver trays, brought by a maid who lived off the premises. Their first evening, they had all crowded into Chike's room, Oma and Fineboy bundled in the white towel robes they had found folded on their beds. Their communion had dwindled away under the bridge, too disheartened to sit quietly and listen to Chike read. Now they wished to pick up the story again, a few verses from the crucifixion where they had been cut off.

The soldiers were sharing Christ's clothes in the rough, unsentimental manner he imagined Chairman's boys would have done, when the rap of bones on wood uprooted them from the blood and mud of Golgotha to their clean, airy boys' quarters room.

'Come in.'

It was Ahmed's father.

'Good evening. I hope you're settling down well?'

'Yes we are, thank you. It's more than anything we were expecting.'

'You looked after my son. There's a pool if any of you are interested in swimming. My wife and I don't use it any more but we keep it clean.'

Where did this man with his trimmed greying goatee think they would have learnt to swim? Who could afford swimming lessons and the paraphernalia of goggles and floating armbands?

'I hope I didn't interrupt anything.'

'We were just reading from the Bible.'

'Well, I should leave you to it,' Mr Bakare said but he lingered at the door.

'You can join us,' Chike said.

'We're Muslims, a little lapsed but not enough to attend a Bible study. My wife will be wondering where I am. I told her I'd only be here briefly. I need to lock up.' He stepped out and stepped in again. 'But if you want to come up to the main building sometimes. We don't get many visitors under sixty. Which one of you was it that met Chief Sandayọ?'

'We all did,' Fineboy said.

'That interview was an extraordinary thing. He was a little too flashy in his dressing, not really what you expect of an Education Minister but the man has guts. Did you watch it?'

'In a way,' Chike said.

'I've never really liked the First Lady but I wouldn't dream of taking her on. Although I suppose I am taking her on by having you here. I'll see you tomorrow.'

Chike opened the book to read again but he had lost the thread; the magic of leading them to an unknown conclusion had vanished. The three men on their crosses would die certainly. One would rise arguably. The story would go on, meandering through acts and epistles from apostles, stopping finally at Armageddon, world's end.

'When Jesus therefore had received the vinegar, he said, "It is finished": and he bowed his head and gave up the ghost.'

'That's not a nice place to end,' Isoken said. 'Read a few verses down.'

'You all know how the story ends.'

'Wetin happen? He no die again?'

'No, he died. Then he came alive.'

'How?'

'I don't know.'

'It was a miracle,' Fineboy said.

Except they had read of the abundant miracles in John, of water transforming and bread multiplying, of footsteps on water, the lame walking, the deaf hearing, the blind seeing. This death on a hill in Jerusalem was nothing like that. Unremarkable: with two others dying in the exact same manner. And yet, seismic.

'We'll get to that part tomorrow.'

65

'So some British pop star with a Nigerian name mentions Rẹmi and suddenly he's a cause?' Ahmed said to Farida over the phone.

'Look, are you coming into the studio or not?'

'He stole that money. Don't believe any rubbish about taking it to fix schools.'

'Are you changing your story? Do you have any evidence, a new statement or something like that?'

'Of course I don't.'

'Then we can't use it.'

'Just for a moment take off your journalist scarf and allow me to be disappointed that it is Rẹmi and not those principals who are going to be the star of this story.'

'Those principals.'

'What about them?'

'You keep calling them "those principals". What are their names?'

'I don't know.'

'Well then how do you expect anyone else to?'

'I wasn't the one who interviewed them. It was the BBC. It's your responsibility.'

'Look, Ahmed, I am not the BBC. I am just a very overworked and underpaid journalist who is supposed to be at a parents' evening tonight but instead is phoning up people to join in a panel discussion about the situation in Nigeria.'

'You should have told me.'

'About what? The panel? That's what I'm trying to explain.'

'No, the parents' evening.'

'Why?'

'I don't know. I could have gone and taken notes for you so you wouldn't have to miss it.'

'You're not their father, Ahmed. He's in Enfield with a new wife and a new son and no space in his life for his two daughters. And sometimes—'

'Yes? Sometimes.'

'Sometimes I wake up in the night and I think I still love him. I'll see you tomorrow evening.'

*

Chief Sandayọ did not know what an overnight sensation he had become. He did not know that 'Sandayo Nigeria' was the third most popular search on Google after 'Ola and Sandayo' and 'Ola and Nigerian politician' or that his name had been mentioned in secret cables in fourteen different languages or that men and women with deep consciences were pasting his face onto cardboard squares and preparing to march on Whitehall and Washington with his smiling press photo. All he saw of these converging global forces was that his roommate was ejected and his camp bed replaced by a sturdy wooden frame with a thick mattress.

Apart from these minor conveniences, he was still very obviously in prison. Lunch was dilute egusi, breakfast stale bread and dinner not to be depended on.

He had lost count of how long he had been in this room. Legally, he could not remain in custody without charge for more than forty-eight hours but he knew of people who had slept in cells for months.

Still, they had not charged him. Someone outside must be championing his cause. Perhaps Ahmed or the BBC was putting pressure on the government to release him. His hope of the first few days had grown to a frenzied expectancy. Each time the rusted key grated into the lock and his orderly turned the handle, he felt his heart lurch forwards.

Today, the orderly knocked before he entered.

'Afternoon, sir. I've brought a fan for you.'

'About time. Put it over there, next to the window. Not there, are you blind? I said next to, not in front of.'

He lay down when the orderly left and stared at the calendar on the wall. He almost missed his flatulent roommate, a drug dealer it had turned out. He had no visitors. Not Chike and the others, despite what he had done for them. Not his son, safely in America. Not the loose reel of acquaintances he had made in Abuja. Certainly not his half-siblings.

He was one of twenty-four children. His father had married eight women. His mother, a sickly sixth wife, neither favoured nor beautiful, nor clever, nor scheming, had died when he was nine, leaving him to fend for himself, fighting for the very air he breathed. His stepmother Iya Bọsẹ used to say of him, 'Don't give Rẹmi any advantage. Once you let him in at the gate, he will take over your house.'

Where was the advantage to be pressed here? He could not command his release. Nor would this orderly have the power to return his phones. He would start by ordering lunch: jollof rice and chicken with a cold bottle of malt.

66

There was a painting Chike remembered from Sunday School, a great white throne with sheep and goats on either side, Judgement Day as simple as the sorting of livestock, the whole world split into wool and hair. The sheep had fed the hungry, clothed the naked, cared for the sick and visited the imprisoned. The goats were too busy eating junk to be of use to humanity.

He remembered that parable when he thought of Sandayọ in jail alone. The Chief had given his freedom for theirs, the messianic story subverted and turned on its head, a thief, like the ones who had hung on either side of the cross, claiming to be the main act. Or perhaps he had misjudged the man, the whole of Sandayọ, greater than the scanty parts he knew of him.

He should visit the Chief. He would visit the Chief. He had grown slothful in the Bakare mansion. He had never known this complete leave-taking of work and responsibility, his rumpled sheets straightened daily by another hand, meals served hot or cold, as you liked it. He thought of where they would go when this holiday was over. He did not want to return to the crossroads, to live again in their fringe life with no bank account, no passport, no identity. He was prepared for the job market this time. He could change his name and create a past of documents and certificates, with a string of false recommendations vouching for his work ethic. Or he could be pragmatic and ask Ahmed to find him work, the Bakare name pushing him to the front of the queue.

He read most days, sitting by the window that looked over the garden, a pristine and sterile Eden, lawn clipped, gravel raked, petals floating briefly on the air like bright feathers, swept up soon after they fell to the grass. Yẹmi and Fineboy still went into Lagos, the mansion's walls not high enough to block out the city's pull. Isoken took literally Mr Bakare's injunction to visit the big house and spent most of her time in their library.

Oma's efforts to help out in the kitchen had been rebuffed and now she too read magazines carted off from the Bakare coffee table. They talked often these days, eating their lunches together, walking in the garden at dusk, parting chastely at night after the group reading. It was an old-fashioned courtship, rigorous and slow in its advances, each increment to be cherished. Who knew when they would have this tranquillity again?

He wanted for nothing, except news of the world outside this hermetically sealed compound, where electricity burned twenty-four hours like the sun. The TVs in their rooms showed grey static when switched on, the lines dancing to their own music. Mr Bakare had come to apologise.

'We never connected them to the DSTV. We did up this place for Ahmed, you know. He was working in a bank in the UK. Big bank. And when he said he wanted to move back to Lagos, my wife suggested we renovate because we're close to the financial district. Just to help him settle down at first. We knew he'd want his space but rent is not cheap in this area and if you live far the traffic is horrendous. But he didn't want to live with us and he didn't want to work in a bank. My son the newspaperman. I suppose you know more about that than me.'

The elder Bakare was a lonely man. There was a rift between him and his son, a fault in the family geology. Sandayọ had a son too, waiting somewhere in America for news of his father, sitting by the phone in settings Chike could not imagine. He would visit the Chief soon.

67

The release of Chief Sandayọ and the principals came in parenthesis in the world media. An earthquake in Indonesia, with buildings levelled and dams burst open, made footage of a reduced Sandayọ walking out of a prison seem rather tame. He had only spent twenty-seven days inside, nothing close to the incarceration on Robben Island.

He had hoped that Chike or one of the others would be waiting but perhaps it was still too dangerous to associate with him. Once they sighted him, the local pressmen ran to meet him, dragging their equipment along. He spoke into the bush of microphones that sprouted round his mouth.

No, he had not been tortured. Yes, the food was terrible. Indeed, a victory for democracy. Undoubtedly, the struggle would continue. Certainly, corruption must die. He did not know what he was saying by the end. Only that he felt drunk on his words and the small crowd that gathered felt it too.

'Solidarity forever,' they sang as he stepped into the car that would take him to his home in Ikire. The car had been provided by the Norwegian embassy, a blue Peugeot with a young, clean-shaven driver behind the wheel. They reached traffic on the Lagos–Ibadan express forty-five minutes into their journey. The slow jolting forward made him sick. A siren and a few armed police would have cleared a way through this seemingly unforceable jam but a Peugeot, without even the mystery of tinted glass, must make its way slowly down the road like everyone else.

He lay down on the back seat. He was looking forward to resting in Ikire, not as a fugitive but as a townsman free to walk about. The town had changed a lot since his childhood. They had gone everywhere on foot then, bicycles a rarity, cars an event. A metallic wash of modernity had come over the place now. Tinny motorcycles zipped along the dirt roads and a faltering electricity flickered on and off. Some things had not changed. The town was still famous for its plantain, fried when rotten into black, sticky balls. Funkẹ had craved dodo ikire when she was pregnant, the round lumps dancing through her dreams, sex symbols of a gourmand. He would drive at dangerous speeds to bring back the dish, heaped into a cooler and still warm.

And then when Gbenga was born, as a family, they had driven down to Ikire and walked round the plot of land on which he would build his country seat, a mansion his sons would bring their wives and children to. He would preside over this large family each Christmas, the patriarch Sandayọ. Empty dreams. Gbenga did not come home and Funkẹ had no more children. Gbenga's exit had damaged her womb. His siblings would grow for a few months and then come tumbling out of that hostile organ, small as teaspoons, or large as grapefruit. It did not matter. They would not reach full term.

Then the hocus pocus of abiku and spirit children and curses that pushed his wife into a world without lipstick and red wine, a world of fasting and penance. She had been

340

so beautiful on their wedding night, tipsy and scared but determined, gripping him with her thighs, pinning him between her legs.

'What are you waiting for? Push it in.'

He missed all the Funkẹs. The bride, the mother, the raving evangelist. He would stay in Ikire for a week, long enough to arrange a new passport. The old one had been seized on entrance into the prison, along with his phones. The mobiles had been returned. The passport had gone missing.

His life did not feel in danger, yet for a moment, standing at the desk and demanding his passport, he wondered if he should have taken the Norwegian ambassador's offer of asylum in the embassy premises until he was ready to travel. It would have meant looking overly beholden to a foreign power, a way of thinking he must get used to now.

His phones had been ringing since he left the prison. His ex-assistant had called to say two generals wanted to meet with him; a former president wanted to congratulate him; a godfather wished to discuss his future. He was a new tool, an unknown entity in the political space.

'Tell them you don't know where I am.'

'Where are you, sir?'

'You just don't worry about that. If anyone asks for me, take a message. I'll be available in a week.'

His son in America must have heard of the release because he too had called. He let the call ring out. He was not in the mood for Gbenga and his American solicitousness. From Chike, not even a text. Perhaps the group had already dispersed.

He did not know when he slept. He woke to the sound of banging. It was dark and they were parked on a road that wasn't the express. He saw a hand flattening itself repeatedly against the window, the palm broad and white, the thin glass shaking on each impact.

'What is the meaning of this? Keep driving.'

'Get down from the car,' the driver said. It was the first time he had spoken throughout their journey.

'I will do no such thing.'

The locks clicked but he held on to the handle, struggling with the stranger outside. He was not strong enough. They pulled the door open and dragged him to the ground. The earth was cool and moist on his face. It had rained recently, lightly enough to wet the soil without turning it to mud. In Ikire the farmers would be watching their crops, counting down to the harvest. The grass rustled with wind and small creatures, hurrying through the undergrowth. 'Help!' he shouted as the first blow fell on his back. The Peugeot drove off, its back lights growing smaller and smaller, dwindling stars in a dark night.

68

'They killed him.'

'Who?' Chike said to Ahmed's father, who was standing in his doorway and clutching his forehead.

'I didn't know this kind of thing was still happening. Good Lord. Are we living under Abacha?'

'Who?'

'Your friend. The minister. Sandayọ, whatever his name is. They found him in the bush this morning. Beheaded.'

It would fall to Chike to tell the others. These were his first thoughts. That the Yoruba did not announce death directly. That he did not know what the custom was in Edo and that he would break the news to Oma in Igbo.

'They're sure it's him?'

'Yes. It's been confirmed. It's on TV now. My wife and I, we watched for a while then I thought I should come and tell you.'

'I want to see it for myself, please.'

'Yes of course.'

They moved slowly, their feet crunching the stones of the gravel walkway that led to the Bakare mansion.

'My wife wants us to leave the country tomorrow. She doesn't think we're safe.'

343

'Are you?' Chike asked.

'Before today I would have said yes, of course, but now I'm not so sure. This kind of thing hasn't happened in years. In years.'

'We'll be leaving too then.'

'No. Even if we go, you must stay. For the young girl's sake. What's that her name again?'

'Isoken.'

'Isoken. Yes. A beautiful Bini name. I wanted my wife to see her, to see if she would notice the resemblance between her and our daughter who passed. You believe in the afterlife? This Sandayọ, would he make paradise or heaven or whatever?'

'I don't know.'

Inside the house Mrs Bakare was dressed as if already in mourning, a black kaftan shrouding her to her feet, a rebellious gold embroidery running along the hem.

'Good evening, madam,' Chike said, standing with his hands behind his back. She nodded and turned away.

'Please sit down,' Ahmed's father said. 'His son should be on soon. They announced it before I came to call you.'

Chief Sandayọ's son, even in grief, was evidently sophisticated, speaking in a soft American accent that broke down into tears on air. His father would not have lost composure so, Chike thought as he watched Sandayọ Junior wipe his eyes and then cover his face, his shoulders shaking.

'They should leave the boy,' Mrs Bakare said. 'Don't they know his father just died?'

The presenter put his hand to his earpiece and seemed ready to move on but Sandayọ Junior interrupted him.

'Wait. I have to say— My father loved Nigeria. He gave

344

his best and in return they killed him. They killed you, Dad, but Nigeria has always killed her best. So wherever you are now, I know you're in good company. Rest in peace.'

For a moment, there was quiet in the studio as Sandayọ's son focused on a spot off set. If any words could awaken the ghost of the Chief, it was this last invocation before time ran out. Chief Sandayọ stayed dead. The presenter fingered his earpiece. The channel switched to adverts.

'I'm going to pack,' Mrs Bakare said, standing and straightening her clothes.

'Mariam, we haven't decided yet.'

'I can't spend another night in this country. Our lives are in danger and even more so because of these people Ahmed has brought here. Do you want us to be killed in our beds? Even if it is Ghana, this time tomorrow I am outside Nigeria.'

Chike rose as she left.

'You should have saluted too. She's the real commanding officer in this house. Sit down. You haven't seen the main news report.'

There was footage of the roadside where the car had been abandoned, a small strip of tarmac crowded on either side by thick bush, a reporter squinting into the sunlight as he gave the summary of events. Then an interview with the hunter who had discovered Sandayọ's severed head, an old man in a brown smock. Around his neck he wore a string of cowries, the shape and colour of teeth. He fingered the charm often as he spoke, a colourful pidgin rendered wooden by the subtitles.

The hunter said: 'I dey find antelope wey dey scarce for market. Nah so I come see human head. I tink say na juju. I come see they never wrap the head, they never bury the

345

head, they just leave am for ground. I come perceive one yamayama odour. As I enter inside bush, I see the rest of 'im body for 'im cloth. I come know say this one no be juju matter. Nah police matter.'

The channel translated: 'I was hunting in the forest. I spotted Chief Sandayọ's head. I also smelled a rotten odour and I followed the smell to the rest of his body. I knew then I had to call the police.'

The car Chief Sandayọ had been abducted in was hired by the Norwegian embassy, which claimed it had done so at the Chief's request. The embassy had chosen a reputable private car hire service. The head of the company, Fleet Cars, was unavailable for comment.

The final analysis of all these bewildering, barbaric facts was brief. Chief Sandayọ had made many enemies over the past few months with his public allegations. Almost anyone could be behind his death.

'Another Nigerian possibility murdered. Ken Saro-Wiwa, Bọla Ige and now Rẹmi Sandayọ. Do you think my son would cry for me if they found me beheaded in the bush tomorrow?'

'I'm sure he would.'

'How well do you know Ahmed? Or more importantly, how well do you know me? I was in government too. No better or worse than anybody. Certainly no Sandayọ.'

'The Chief was not a saint.'

'Yes, but he has become a martyr. It is not for all of us, that transition.'

'I should go and break the news to the others.'

'Yes, of course.'

69

It was Fineboy who brought the news on his radio, rushing into Oma's room and shouting, 'Chief is dead o.'

She had been flicking through a magazine, glossy with the sparkling clothes of Lagos society women. Ahmed's father would not hear of her helping in the kitchen, not knowing that in her brief foray into their cooking space she had been entranced by the metres of marble and steel, rows of gadgets she had no name for, whirring and mixing and blending and pulsing and mashing and slicing and dicing. The Beninese chef in his spotless white uniform had let her watch as he rolled out pasta, winding the crank of the machine, the dough spinning round his arm, stretching thinner and thinner like a band of elastic.

'Are you not hearing me? I said Chief Sandayọ is dead, pafuka. He don pai.'

'Do you have to be so crude?'

There was mud from Fineboy's entrance, tracks that would not leave their carpet without scrubbing. It was not the time for Oma to point out that only slippers were allowed in the women's room. He sat heavily on their cream sheets, switching from station to station, piecing together a story that grew more terrible with each detail. First Chief was dead. Then he was beheaded. Then his body was rotting when they found it.

'Switch that thing off,' Oma said when she heard this last. She imagined Chief Sandayọ's nose starting to cave in, the stump of his neck dripping blood, a globe of flies where his head used to be.

She had an urge for a rosary, for the feel of the smooth plastic, a world of prayer in each bead. She took off her chain from her neck and began passing it, bit by bit, through her fingers.

'Does Chike know?' she asked, when she had finished reciting three Hail Marys, the image of the Virgin rising to comfort her.

'He wasn't in his room and Yẹmi has gone out so I came straight here.'

They knew so little of the Chief. Perhaps they, in this room, were the only ones to mourn him. He had never mentioned a family and he could not have had any true friends to be so easily abandoned. They had never had a real conversation, beyond the jesting compliments he sometimes paid her, but she had known him in the distantly intimate way a doctor knows his patient. Sandayọ had a bowel condition that made pepper like poison to him. She had cooked separately for the Chief, a blander version of the group fare, a small kindness she had kept hidden.

'Come in,' she said in response to the knock on their door. It was Chike.

'We know already,' she said, seeing the news drawn on his face.

'You do?'

'Yes.'

Sandayọ's death would hurt Chike the most. He had refused to admit that the Chief, in coming back to the flat, had redeemed himself and redeemed them all. Now, Chief Sandayọ was dead and it was too late for Chike to visit him. He would forever owe the dead man an apology. It was his age that made him so rigid at times, she thought as she crossed the space between them and took his hand. She began to sing.

'Atulegwu. Nwok'atulegwu.'

Epilogue

I

Chike could pray here. It cleared his mind, to face the sunrise and scatter his prayers over the water. If you looked through the floor planks of their house, you would see the lagoon, much soiled by the waste of their neighbours but still vast, spreading beyond the filth of their settlement. He had looked at a map of Lagos and seen no mention of their new home but they were here nonetheless, their residence defying cartographers.

Fineboy had taken to the place with an ease that showed his riverine origins. The boy went out with the fishermen, bringing a catch that Oma cooked on their kerosene stove, the scales iridescent on the floor, the smell of fried croaker filling the house. There was something wholesome about this fishing, something primordial that stripped Fineboy of his cobbled sophistication. Or so it had seemed to Chike when he asked to go with him.

The spiritual element eluded him. He could not settle in the boat, his slightest movement unsteadied them, his tread too heavy for the hull. He had not wanted to touch the fish thrashing at the bottom of their vessel, slithering from one end to the other as they died. In the end, he had sat quietly in the stern, staring out into the lagoon while the fishermen cast their nets. Fineboy gave him something to take home to Oma, a medium ladyfish he presented as fruit of his day's labour.

Oma slept with him these days. It was not the sleep of consummation but it was something to lie next to her, to have her body pressed against his and his arms clasping her waist, for hers to be the first face he saw when he woke and the last when he slept.

She would get a divorce. It was the lie told to all lovers, to stop them from straying into a protracted future of law courts and alimony. One day she must confront IK and force him to sign away his rights but till then, they would sleep together like a couple grown old, passion withered into two bodies comfortable side by side.

Isoken would go to university. Ahmed's father would see to that. The Bakares had asked her to live with them, to be the daughter they had lost, an offer that excluded Chike and the others. She had turned them down, a gesture touching but impractical. He would convince her to change her mind.

He was not yet thirty but in many ways he felt his life was over, his experiences behind him, even this family he had built needing him less and less. He still read to them at night, the only constant in his day. He wished sometimes he were back in the army, in that regimented life where hours were ordered and accounted for.

Yẹmi most of all had surprised him. His private was a historian, an anthropologist, a sociologist, words his friend would not know to describe his travels in Lagos. Chike had gone with him to Badagry to see the slave forts. He had felt little when confronted with the iron shackles that bound those long-dead people. But for Yẹmi it was like yesterday. His private had wept at the manacles used on a child, heavy for an adult, two hundred years later. Yet the irons had not been able to move Chike or transport him to a time when their pain was fresh. He had commented on their weight and then put them back in the exhibit, leaving Yẹmi alone in his grief.

He woke up most mornings and sat by the door or if he woke and it was still dark, he caught a boat to the middle of the lagoon and paid the owner to wait in silence. *He has set a tabernacle for the sun, which is like a bridegroom coming out of his chamber. Its rising is from one end of heaven and its circuit to the other end. There is nothing hidden from its heat.* If people turned to heaven at their lowest, he should have prayed most fervently in the Delta or under the bridge, not here where they ate fresh fish every day and they lived for free in a house built with their own hands. He rarely went on shore these days. He did not want to step into the stream again, the pull and eddy and swirl of Lagos, pushing him here and there.

They had not been invited to Chief's funeral. Thousands showed up in his hometown to watch the body being lowered into the ground. *Unless a kernel of wheat falls to the ground and dies, it remains only a single seed.* What would be the harvest of Chief Sandayọ's death? What new life would spring forth? Sandayọ Junior stood by the grave, pouring dirt onto the coffin as cameras from all over the world filmed the soil trickling through his hands. Chike wondered if

Sandayọ in his last moments had begged or if he had gone stoically to his cross. *La gloire* at last. Bitterly won.

His prayers were vague, formless and void, but he had lost his self-consciousness in saying them. It was more natural to pray, he felt, when he saw the line of the sun break the edge of the water, more in keeping with the rest of humanity to worship the sun or whatever had made it. Most likely his doubts would return, with activity, with employment, but he would not regret these days of belief, these moments of faith when all seemed plausible and the world was made in seven days.

2

'Hey love, it's me. We got a call today from a Nigerian philanthropist.'

'Yeah?'

'An oil tycoon or something. We're still googling her. She saw the piece on the Chief and wants to get in touch with his team. She called Sandayọ's son but he didn't know anything about it so she called us.'

'What team?'

'You know he said he was working with a team of Nigerians to fix the schools.'

'What does she want?'

'She was a bit cagey. Just put me through to them, she kept saying to my boss, like he was a PA. From what we could gather, she wants to set up an organisation in honour of the Chief but she'll only talk to his team.'

'The Chief Sandayọ Centre for Educational Excellence.

Courses in embezzlement optional.'

'Ahmed! That's a rubbish name. It doesn't acronym well. And leave the poor Chief alone. He's dead.'

'The guy was a crook with good PR. PR from the grave.'

'So are you going to put her in touch or not?'

'I'll give Chike a call. How are the girls?'

'They're doing well. Adla asked yesterday when Ahmed was coming again. Apparently you have a Monopoly rematch.'

'Tell her Ahmed is coming tomorrow.'

'These are Kenyan girls. They shouldn't be calling you by your first name.'

'It's fine. Uncle Ahmed would sound strange.'

'Not in Nigeria.'

'What do you mean?'

'I got the posting. It's not confirmed so I'm not allowed to talk about it but it's almost certain. I don't know how I'm going to tell the girls. Adla won't look back but I'm worried about Afaafa. It took her so long to settle in school. And of course they won't see their dad so often any more. Not that they see him often now.'

'Marry me.'

There was a pause on both ends. It was not too late to say just joking, to brush his proposal aside with a laugh, to hear the crushing relief in her voice as she laughed too.

'Hello, Farida. Are you still there?'

'You're asking me over the phone?'

Acknowledgements

It takes a dossier of interviews to write a second book. Any errors are mine. Many thanks to:

Brigadier-General Amao for sparing a precious hour of his time and Mayọwa Amao for arranging the meeting
   Big Aunty
   My in-law Funṣọ for stories of the Nigerian Military School, Zaria
   My inside men at the BBC, Nkem Ifejika and Tomi Oladipọ
   Dr Oby Ezekwesili and those brief encounters in London
   Aunty Ṣọla Adegbomerin and her stories of the lost in Lagos
   Uncle Karowei Dorgu for my introduction to the Niger Delta
   Emeka Okerulu and his colourful motor park anecdotes
   Wana Udobang and her radio stories
   Tosin Ejike and her team for insights into the Niger Delta

Special thanks to:

My parents for providing me with a room of my own

My mother, Mariam Onuzo, for reading everything I write

My father, Okey Onuzo, for making the Bible come alive

Dilichi for the title

Chinaza for the ending

Dinachi, for providing stellar working conditions

Simeon Agada, the sugar in my tea

Rosie Apponyi, always willing to be a reader

My agent, Georgina Capel, for those early encouraging words

Sola Njoku, who knew what I was trying to say and went through that unsightly draft and produced a page of suggestions

My Igbo consultants, Uncle Obed Onuzo and Ngozi Okerulu

My Yoruba consultants, Risi Lawal, Gbenga Sesan and Kola Tubosun

Liv Digby for pointing out the journalistic tone

Rotimi Babatunde, the most generous of writers, gracious with his time, his praise and his criticism

Fẹla, the bard of Lagos

YouTube, Wikipedia and Google

The *Paris Review* and the countless authors who kept me company in the writing of this book

C. S. Lewis

Kassim Lawal, for being critical with those first few chapters

My early readers, Sharon Lo, Melanie Cheng and Risi Lawal

My second readers, ElNathan John, Ellah Allfrey,

Olusegun Ekundayo and Opeyemi Atawo

My supporters club, for showing up in rain and shine, Chidinma Akin-Ibisagba, Sakina Badamasuiy, Ruki and Foma Brume, Joy Seanehia and Osagie Omokhodion

My Jesus House family, Pastor Agu and Ṣọla Irukwu, Pastor Ṣọla and Funkẹ Adeaga, Pastor Baj and Chizor Akisanya, TOJ and the 'Dequeenesses'

The HTB School of Theology for reintroducing me to the Bible and in particular, the book of John

The girls of Abeokuta Girls' Grammar School, and to Lọla Shoneyin, the Ake Festival team and Ikhide Ikheloa, for making the trip memorable

Victor Ehikhamenor for lending me his column, and for his helpful book, *Excuse Me!*

Will Wiles for his well-timed tweet

Hannah Griffiths, for seeing the book down the last stretch

Sarah Savitt, editor amongst editors

And lastly, to Lagos, city of my birth, my dreams, my frustrations, my imagination.

Also by Chibundu Onuzo

ff

The Spider King's Daughter

Winner of a Betty Trask Award

Shortlisted for the Dylan Thomas Prize and the
Commonwealth Book Prize

Longlisted for the Desmond Elliot Prize

Seventeen-year-old Abike Johnson is the favourite child of
her wealthy father. She lives in a sprawling mansion in Lagos,
protected by armed guards and ferried everywhere in a huge
black jeep. But being her father's favourite comes with uncomfortable duties, and she is often lonely. A world away
from Abike's mansion, in the city's slums, lives a seventeen-
year-old hawker struggling to make sense of the world. His
family lost everything after his father's death and now he runs
after cars on the roadside selling ice cream to support his
mother and sister. When Abike buys ice cream from the
hawker one day, they strike up an unlikely and tentative romance, defying the prejudices of Nigerian society. But as they
grow closer, revelations from the past threaten their relationship and they must both decide where their loyalties lie.

'A dark, tense, gripping first novel, peeling back layers of
Nigerian society.' *The Times*